Somebody

Somebody

Laurie Blauner

Black Heron Press
Post Office Box 95676
Seattle, Washington 98145
www. blackheronpress.com

Somebody is the winner of a 2001 King County Arts
Commission Award for Publication.

Portions of *Somebody* (with slight revision) have appeared in *The
New Orleans Review* and *Phoebe*.

ISBN 0-930773-66-7

Black Heron Press
Post Office Box 95676
Seattle, Washington 98145
www.blackheronpress.com

For Barbara C.

I would like to thank the King County Arts Commission for their generous support. And grateful thanks to my husband, David Dintenfass, for help along the way.

Once I was nobody's somebody
till I met some somebody
nobody loved me somehow

...I'm somebody's somebody now.

from "I'm Somebody's Somebody Now"
by Abner Silver, Al Sherman, and
Howard E. Johnson

PART I

Life with Stan

The Wind, a Flower

Lizzie eats her words, tasting them in her mouth, waiting for a life of their own. Like shadows or ghosts, wanting their say. She wants to let them go but the consequences worry her. They remind her of bees circling around her just waiting for a chance at the pollen. And she wonders what she needs to teach herself about holding something in until she's ready to burst.

Lizzie watches her small bare feet move in front of her one after another (right, left, right, left)... Almost on their own. They remind her of other feet, grown-up feet, only smaller. Leaves are blown by the wind that is her mother's voice arguing with itself. Lizzie's arms lift agitatedly, moving with her mother's breath. Her flannel nightgown with fake roses touches both knees alternately. She feels the roughness against her soft skin. Her feet move through the apartment hallway, through the dining room with wallpaper covered with clematis still climbing silently in the dark.

— I know you can do this. I want him to think I'm younger.

Her voice slips in and out of Lizzie making believe it means nothing. Wind leaves small traces, a leaf turned over or grass patted down. Lizzie feels her dark hair move across her face. This is the first time she asks. Lizzie's toes sink deep into the white plush carpet as into thick grass. She consciously avoids the spot where she sat in front of the television last year peeing quietly. The wash of yellow spread around her like the line policemen draw between where a dead body lay and the rest of the living world. Her father hit her bottom sore with a hairbrush and she still had not said anything, had not confessed.

What does her father think of her mother's men coming and going like conversations, one done, used, and stale, and on to the next one, infinitely more promising? Would he hit her bottom with a hairbrush too?

Lizzie chews on her hair. Its ropy, earthy, tickling familiarity. Like her pillow with the deep, woodsy smell, all her own. She would never sleep on any other pillow or dye her hair the color of tea like her mother.

Her mother is asking for something she doesn't want to give. She wants a conspirator the way a weed basks in the sun, positioning itself above all the other greenery. Was it really that important? She caught Lizzie before she reached the safer confines of the bedroom where her sister is sleeping with the twist of metal that straightens her legs. Where she might meet Dracula or a vampire hiding in the shadows across the other end of the mirror at the worst scenario. Some nights when her mother didn't wake her with her lament, "No one loves me", she dreamt of flying and falling from their chandeliered light with a body as light as a tiny baby. Falling soundlessly. Feeling a part of the wind and thinking the wind also has many names and leaves home to find itself. She wishes she was generously alone again, eyes closed, with just the rough touch of flannel.

— You can do it.

She echoes with need, a long tunnel Lizzie could lose herself in. She looks at her mother's bright red lipstick, at the beautiful face and wonders if the prince ever considered the consequences of waking Sleeping Beauty or did it all end at the crucial moment? She wants to say "no". "Go fuck yourself" as she heard (older) girls at school say. (She knows the meaning is bad.) She doesn't want to do this, doesn't want to have to. But there is just a little of that beautiful face in her and she pinches her night gown thinking of her mother's skin. The words are piling up on her mother's side and threatening to knock her over. Lizzie tries to remember that these are just words. She sighs and breathes:

— Okay.

The beautiful face stained with lipstick moves down the darkened hall of the New York City apartment to the kitchen. Light escapes where it can, around corners, under door cracks, forming a ladder reaching for Lizzie's feet. Lizzie follows like rain after a storm. The smooth floors are cold against her feet. Right, left, the same motion as when she braids her hair for school, half asleep but the fingers are moving. She thinks about sleeping, her head sinking into her pillow. Her heart is a rabbit criss-crossing her chest, following the seams of all seven rooms, following the crinkled flowers of her toes, a part of adult's houses, adult lives.

The air is thick with syllables against Lizzie's face before they enter the stark, bright light of the yellow kitchen. The room opens before her, the grownup body of a lover.

"Come-a-come-a-down-shoo-be-do-down-down..."

Lizzie longingly remembers the sentences in her school books. "Dick pushes Jane in a swing. They are having fun." Against the kitchen table is a large man in a suit with a pool of slicked-back dark hair who smells of a form of perfume. Lizzie thinks of the television game show hosts or a sweet-smelling seal at the zoo. She knows she would be able to smell him before she sees him.

"Hi. You must be Lizzie. I've heard so much about you — from your mother." He turns down the yelps from the radio and stretches a big open palm toward Lizzie. She ignores his hand, concentrating instead on the light shining from his hair in waves, a mesmerizing ocean. He could be a disguised vampire, unlikely, but he could be, she thinks. She feels the cool air rising from the stony, indifferent floor now that she is standing still in one place. She touches the goosebumps on her legs, the hair bristling, her toes squirming, uncomfortable.

He puts his hand behind his back as though removing something offensive.

"How's school?" He seems to be talking to the air. Her mother's lovely dark eyes are on her. Perhaps the ocean waves are just for show. They break in order to catch the light just so. Lizzie looks around the same old kitchen, same refrigerator, same stove, same cabinets. What do they want from her?

Her mostly-gone father unraveling the sudden landscape of trees, grass, houses through his windshield on his way to one of his department stores in Connecticut. She could see his face, squinting, unconcerned and pressed up against the glass. Her sister is sleeping with her small, soft limbs resting on crib sheets and the steel leg brace straightening her crooked legs. Lizzie bit her when she was born as if to say there wasn't room for both of them. Or perhaps it was just a warning. She doesn't care about this big, looming man. She probably won't see him again. He'll be replaced by some other big, looming man. But her mother does care.

— I want you to do this. Tell him.

The whisper in her ear winds around the room like smoke, twisting around cabinet knobs, crawling up room corners, circling the clock, making animal shapes under the bright light. Her feet are cold, heavy stones against the smooth floor. And Lizzie hears the darkness away from the harsh light, in her ears, up her nose, between toes, in her mouth, say,

"But I'm too young for school."

The beautiful red mouth smiles as though that answer is the only one for the question. The man shrugs, his mind on the future when he can unbutton a woman's blouse, pressing tiny buttons through their tiny holes slowly. His hand crawling lightly as an ant up her skirt. He only wants pleasure. Obstacles hold no interest for him. He can get them at home. His suit bends at sharp right angles and his big hands tap Lizzie's back until she is out the kitchen door. She hears "...breaking up is hard to do" on the radio and imagines them dancing. Or more. Although that is vague.

The large man believes her. It is a surprise that he thinks she isn't in school yet with her clothes growing smaller all the time and her feet getting too big for make-shift hopscotch squares on the pavement. So that is some-one else's lie. And one accepted. She has perpetrated her own smaller versions. Words rose in her at school describ-ing her mother's last-minute frozen dinner as a sumptu-ous feast that drew the neighbors by their noses like clouds waiting for a change of weather. Or the time she picked her nose, hiding boogers in a doll's satin hair, and handed it to a playmate. Omissions. Changes. She laughed so hard when her friend admired the doll. Lizzie's toes press the hard floor intermittently like short sentences. One, then another. Her hand turns the knob of the bed-room door slowly and quietly. Darkness and the small knuckle of a night light. Her sister rocked herself to sleep the way a tree knocks at a window, on all fours with her head banging rhythmically against the headboard. Seems painful. Beating yourself into sleep. No visible vampires. Although they can survive in the dark cracks between doors, the pages of books. And when you open the books the words spill out like water, chasing away the vampires. Lights bloom far away in that distant room that she tries to convince herself means nothing. But there is some anger, all the secrets, another lie. Lizzie feels her goosebumps under the bedcovers like tiny birds under her skin. She crosses her arms over her chest to invite sleep.

— You did it.

Lizzie half whispers, half hears. Why does her mother want to be younger? What does it all matter? She won't tell her sister or her father. The lies falling like snow against her skin. Lizzie's beautiful mother begging to be different. Lizzie thinks of rain soaking her skin into sleep, wetting her now deeper shadows. She begins to dream of the glint of the unknown man's hair against the square of her pillow. How you can give so much of yourself until you are a ghost. How Lizzie learns about love given in short paragraphs.

Life with Stan, 1963

First there is fighting and then the darkness. A few years later Lizzie is too big for her father to swing her back and forth in his overnight bag. She is ten and Claire is six. Her dark hair floats slapping her awake, laughing, like an animal kissing her long face. She remembered her small hands gripping the sides of the brown leather carry-on case. The metal rectangles of the open zipper ran beneath her underarms, railroad tracks with a bulge in the center around her tiny body. She felt free, tossed toward the apartment's textured ceiling with her father's hand tethering her from becoming lost in the air, resembling some extinct bird. Her father liked the moments she was suspended, frozen in air at arm's length, a butterfly under glass, interesting, unknowable, untouchable. She could mouth words and not be heard, this mystery in his often used bag.

It is the year President Kennedy is shot and pinned to his car like some specimen. Lizzie is trying to catch goldfish in a pond at the school fair. Her face winks in the corkscrew light from the surface. The other children's and adults' voices recede against the green and brick walls. The tables, games, and shouting seem to be in another world, leaving Lizzie to her own. She opens her mouth to swallow the refracted colors moving down the image of her throat like green and blue clouds. Her fingers resembling grass sway in the shadows of the orange fish. She is less concerned with catching the fish then with holding them. She wonders if they think they are giving themselves to stone gods or are curious enough to breath air, no matter what the result. They affect one another through motion, her movement is the medium, swishing her fingers, they dart the other way. She can feel them brush her fingertips like a new language. And sometimes vocabulary is just beyond her and she feels alone. The goldfish are moving their lips to say something and then a man's face appears in the sequined water, swimming in small waves at first. He is wearing a dark suit and the face of any man. As her hands become still it becomes a familiar face. But it still imitates so many men at the school fair. The loudspeaker tears staccato through her limbs: "President Kennedy has been shot. We are closing the fair immediately. President Kennedy has been shot. Go home." Lizzie touches a fish and doesn't want to release it. It is a muscular part of her that she wants to hold onto but it is struggling separately to be let go. She relinquishes the fish watching the orange curve of its back disappear like a coma fading into a line.

"Hi honey. Let's go."

It is her father with his metal knee cap from the war, his dark hair flying from his scalp in curves, his long Jewish nose resting like a dragonfly on his face and Lizzie's. Now she can smell his clothing stitched with cigarette smoke. He always has a pack tucked in his jacket pocket near his unresolved heart. It is a grainy, pungent odor permeating everything he touches with yellow-tipped fingers. His breath smells of cigarettes as though he inhales a different air. His pants are so tart it is as if he lives and dresses himself in another house entirely.

"Okay" Lizzie says holding his jacket sleeve while colorful crowds of adults and children eddy around them crying. She wants to say good-bye to her classmates but she doesn't see them anymore. Lizzie wonders at so many people weeping for someone they didn't know, someone they never met. But people weeping nonetheless because of what he represented, although she doesn't have the words to say this. Although no one would know what to say if he stood in front of them right now. It is like reading at school. Sharing in someone's life because of who you think they are. It is called history.

Wind combs their hair on the streets. Lizzie's brown leotards make her skin think of static and electricity. She pulls them and they fall comfortably back into the shape of her legs. People on the concrete New York streets are crying or on their way to somewhere they could cry. A footnote of sky is visible between the tall buildings that display their windows like glass doors into other lives. Lizzie thinks of her lost fish, happy in its veils of water and light, glad to no longer feel the spider touch of her treacherous fingers, to no longer think about the lurid end of its life anymore.

***

The elevator leads them loudly past the doormen on the ground floor and to the carpeted hall on the ninth floor. The wallpaper blossoms with fleur-de-lis in the overhead light. Lizzie's father, Stan, short for Stanley, fumbles like an old, harmless bee at the locks on the thick front door. After so many clicks they enter the bright light of the kitchen. Lizzie follows the cigarette smoke, some ghostly presence, like bread crumbs or pebbles to be used to find the way home.

Lizzie hears voices from her parent's bedroom. She thinks longingly for once of Stan's mother's apartment with her living room furniture encased in heavy plastic. Untouchable. Unusable. Quiet. A butterfly collection with fuchsia, chartreuse, magenta and cobalt colors on fire beneath all the wrapping. Holiday presents she wants to quickly tear open. There aren't many other people left in the respective families. Lizzie hears a monologue touching her ears in long waves. She apprehensively follows the smoke trail into the bedroom wondering whose male voice is admonishing her mother. She thinks of a storm rearranging human gestures, upsetting limbs down to the bone.

"He died," Lizzie's mother says calmly, quietly. The television splashing a cold, gray light across her face in the same pattern as fallen leaves.

She is looking at the television screen which is looking back at her as though Stan and Lizzie are interrupting an ongoing conversation.

"Don't you even care?" she says turning part of her classic face toward them, one half dark, one half alive with the flickering moonlight of current events. She is accusing them.

Lizzie's muscles freeze. She shuts her eyes and sees the fish in its wet struggle with her fingers. Its need to escape.

"Yes, yes, of course we care" Stan replies in his New York accent. He is beginning to get agitated. Smoke flies to the corners of the room, crawling past his eyes.

But Lizzie's mother is a long, beautiful vase holding the light and pushing it away. Lizzie is afraid she will overflow and shatter at the same time.

"You have a funny goddamn way of showing it." Her tea hair circles around her head in a beehive. Her deep blue dress rustles as she moves to the dresser. The television moves its leaf motif in a pale blue light up and down her leg and side. Air is inscrutable around her flesh.

Lizzie thinks of the meaning of the President's death running through her fingers like sand from an hourglass. She realizes that is not what her parents are talking about. Light from the television is flicking angrily on her arm.

"Aw, honey, you know I care." Smoke is meandering around his clenched teeth. His fingers are nervous in his pockets. His suit looks deflated as though his body is shrinking. "I'm so sorry." His head is slightly bowed with his nose visible and smoke exhaling, forming a ghostly web around his body.

She turns around undone. Her teeth bared and unbuttoned. The rose of her mouth stretching into a grimace. "Sorry my ass. You stupid goddamn son-of-a-bitch. You don't know a damn thing. You weak, mealy-mouthed asshole, pushed around by his own mother. You really are stupid and pathetic. How could I end up with some stupid asshole like you. I could have done better picking up some jerk on the street..."

Lizzie quietly leaves the shaking and tearing bedroom. She moves out the door backward, heels first until she is outside and then she turns her back to them. She slips like smoke through the foyer, past the living room, into the bedroom she shares with her sister. The whitewashed furniture fastidiously carries the long mirror, the two windows; underneath is a large, round tin ramshackle with toys. It is still and silent except for the faint sound of arguing from her parent's bedroom. She looks at the unmade bed and familiar pillow, companions. She is safe and free for now. She sees her hands take on the shape of birds as they fold and unfold in the mirror as she dances. Her chocolate tights scratch her calves as they move up and down, rubbing her thin legs. She looks at the composition of her face, the large brown eyes, hollowed bones as her body twists in the glass to the invisible music. It is a form of sleeping. The space conforming to her body like a tight-fitting stain of a dress her mother would wear, touching her curving body in arcs. It is the way birds leave the earth to sleep in a tree. Her feet jump into the air. She imitates Isadora Duncan.

In her turning, in her body twisting to say something she knocks her sister's coat rack to the floor. Broken. She bites the skin of her hand between the knuckles, her own taste, her salty fear. A finger of wood is split off and lays on the carpet like a separate path or lost exclamation point. She stares at it with its architecture of judgment and grief, its small abandonment in the history of this household. Broken, and she hears the eloquent punishment but does not know what it is yet.

She scotch-tapes the piece to the rest of the coat rack. The easy sunlight coming through the apartment window dodges the outlines of the other buildings outside. Lizzie thinks of a river with its shadows and light, distracted by stones until they become a part of the flow. She continues dancing by the old birdcage whose canary turned its back on her world and died. By the empty plastic turtle bowl admitting nothing and everything. Turned like a clear shell on its back. She had hamsters who ate one another, mice who escaped and lived behind the walls of the apartment, and even, once, two alligators who squeaked to each other at night. She loves animals. Right now she has a dog, a poodle, called Beauty.

When her sister, Claire, comes home Beauty is behind her feet trailing like a small, loosened shoe, black and curly. Lizzie says "Go put your coat here — on that coat rack."

Thump goes the coat and finger of wood onto the floor. There are vowels of crying.

"I'm going to tell Mom and Dad."

"No...please," sobbing, "Lizzie."

"Oh Mom. Dad," making believe she is shouting,

knowing their parents are too embroiled in their own cruel games and problems to be concerned about Lizzie's and Claire's.

More crying. Beauty is a small sob under her feet. Lizzie hates Claire for letting herself be dressed identically to Lizzie. Matching Doctor Dentons with their thick pebbled feet loose on the floor. Matching sister dresses with frills choking their necks, velvet ones so when they sat together they resembled a blue, pleated ocean. For repeating what Lizzie says as if it is her own thoughts. For following Lizzie and pestering her friends. For changing the channels on the television whenever Lizzie orders her to. She is a mindless robot wanting to be Lizzie. And Lizzie loves her for it too. And for suffering through Lizzie's reading and math lessons. Claire's glamorous sky-blue cats-eye glasses studded with rhinestones concentrating on Lizzie's chalk against the blackboard. The numbers and letters seem small and dangerous. For being in the plays they devised just to charge their parents a quarter. For helping Lizzie sell comic books and lemonade on the cold, gray New York street under the stenciled canopy of their building. For being the one and only witness.

Lizzie had wanted their mother to give Claire away when she was born.

"Couldn't you sell her today?" Lizzie pleaded.

"No, no one wanted her."

"You could give her away. Try the steps of the Metropolitan Museum tomorrow." Knowing everyone would be better off. Knowing there wasn't enough room.

"Okay, I'll try."

"Can't you call her Susan? Claire is such an ugly name."

Claire's first word was "light" with her chubby knob of a finger pointed at the yellow overhead fixture.

Thinking it was something she could bite hard and chew. Hoping it would taste good. She watched with big brown eyes set in her face like dark jewels as Lizzie kicked shoe salesmen, her childish legs resembling scissors at their noses. Or Lizzie stood up and screamed in Temple, "Why do all the people stand up and sit down, stand up and sit down?" Lizzie helped her mother get a garden-sized washing machine by saying to Stan's parents: "Stan and Mother are fighting again over getting a washing machine." A big square, green one arrived the next morning like another child.

***

That night Lizzie, wanting to be held, holds herself in blankets. Sheets become a stranger's soft arms, the pillow, a kiss in another language. She can almost see her lamp stenciled with gray fish holding each other's tails in a line around the circumference with their thick curved lips. The darkness is always a dialogue waiting to begin. And she could hear a murmur of voices like the weight of stars she knows exist beyond the periphery of city lights. The apartment lights would keep her company in her sleeplessness. She would imagine someone eating or reading or thinking or just moving through their apartment restless as a lost mouse or ghost. Her parents grow louder in the mystery of their anger. And her consolation in the stars falls away, a scarf caught in the wind.

"Lillitoes," Lizzie whispers to Claire's bed. Claire had been rocking her head against the headboard until her bones seemed to collapse, falling asleep minutes ago. Perhaps that's why they could not hear the fighting before.

"Lillitoes," she says again and Claire sits bolt up-

right, winces into the darkness tainted with nearby apartment lights. Lizzie knows the words inexplicably make
Claire cry and Claire can't explain what they mean.
They could hear fragments: "Well you did it"; "what
about..."; "shove it." The bodiless voices rising and falling, slipping in and out of names, a long throat of moving
water. Mother locks Stan outside the bedroom door and
they hear the choreography of his screaming through the
thin vertebrae of light under their bedroom door. "Let me
in, you goddamn bitch. Let me in now or I'll break down
this door!" There is pounding and blood runs through
Lizzie beating a vernacular music. She feels his anger
blossoming against the door, on the skin of her small
shoulders as though waves of emotion could lift her up
and take her away. "There" and the thick wood cracks.
Claire's eyes are disassembling the ceiling. Lizzie kneels
at Claire's bed and holds her little sister's weightless
hand. Lizzie thinks of the stars as people in their apartments looking down on them. She tries to think of names
for her goldfish slicing the water like a dream: Goldie;
Hazel; or Mildred. The cracking stops. She feels her heart
speaking to her, saying "forget about it — please."

***

In the morning an eyebrow of light raises itself around the
window shade. Stan has already gone to work at the
clothing stores he owns. Lizzie and Claire tiptoe through
the hall and branches of light to their parent's bedroom
door. It seems unchanged. Lizzie's eyes question the surface and find nothing, no explanations to describe "broken." No trace of the tight, green fruit of their violence to
hold in her hand, to pick apart, to eat and discard.
"Who's that?" Mother mumbles with a black sleep-

ing mask crazy over her eyes. The sheets and blankets stir near the sisters' waists, some landscape changing for the next season.

"If that's you, Lizzie, you know I have a stick under my bed that I'll hit you with if you wake me up again."

Lizzie did actually find a long, thin board tucked into her bed underneath her pillow once. She knows she could outrun her, having done it before. She thinks about bruises with their blue edges budding across her skin. "Anything broken?"

"Nothing but your back if you don't leave right now."

***

Another day. From the big toy tin Claire plays with Barbie and Ken, out on a date in their red plastic car near Barbie's collapsible Dream Home. His hand inches stiffly around her shoulder. She is as cold as winter, eyes unmoving. It is a long afternoon. Ken takes off Barbie's clothes with his stiff, plastic arm. They fall onto the floor, piled like snow. Barbie and Ken roll around in the car rubbing their flesh-colored indentations against one another.

"That was good" Ken says distantly, naked. "When can I see you again?"

"You messed up my hair" Barbie says, walking the steps to her open home with her clothes rolled in her straight-out arms.

"Playing again?" Lizzie says, her utterances drifting past them like songs. She is not expecting an answer. Her feet draped over her flowered bedspread, flying over the carpet. She closes her English book, wedging the lined paper half filled with sentences and a pencil into its thick spine.

Lizzie rewrites her life with poetry, the words "sun" and "moon" crawling across the lined pages. Crayon drawings line the stanzas like colored flowers against the horizon. She thinks, "This is the city," the one where her mother models clothes, floating down a lighted runway. Her red fingernails counting taffeta, chiffon, silk, or crinoline like so much money. It was what Lizzie's grandmother had done in the garment district, meeting her husband there too. Stan says her face called to him, a rose among many flowers (Lizzie wonders what she really called him). She had been born a Jew but had her face chiseled "into a sculpture for God." The rare red kiss of her lips. Lizzie closes her eyes and listens to the eternal traffic, the noise of wings beating against the windows, the occasional headlight searching the walls for rest. There is a whole other world out there, uncoiling beneath Lizzie's fingertips, outside the incandescent glass. She squints. Mother enters with two dresses in her arms.

"Which one should I wear?" Mother asks turning and turning on her subtle S-shaped legs in high heels. She is a carousel, holding up one red cowl-neck dress then a white silk vee-neck one.

"The red one," Lizzie says picking up her homework and poetry and holding them against her chest, no longer interested in this game.

*****

When Mother walks down the runway all eyes are turned toward her and the black linen dress she has on. Lights explode around her. The audience's talk eludes her, sizzling under bright flashes, a murmur that she can't distinguish from the announcer's voice, the shuffling of feet and arms, her own jaunty footsteps to the end and back. She saunters, bounces, loving the ridiculous outfits, the up-turned faces trained on her as though she is an apparition, a prize. She sometimes discovers her photograph on the inside pages of a newspaper or magazine when she occasionally models. She cuts them out, savoring every detail, criticizing her own nose or the frozen arch of an eyebrow. In the back room nearly naked women are being quickly dressed. A tangle of long, thin arms and legs, underwear as second nature as skin, stick pins and bobby pins are scattered over chairs that no one has time to occupy. Lizzie and Claire are behind the movable racks. A red shirt is snapped from its hanger like a bird startled into flight. Mother spies the girls below the horizon of mirrors and fluorescent lights. They are unencumbered by the rush, the deadlines, the drama. They are playing cards. Go Fish. She nudges them onto the burgeoning stage one by one. The children of other models follow them. One rushes on, tottering, surprised by the iridescent light. She falls into the back room again, grateful, glad to be done. Beads of sweat deepen the color of Mother's peach shirt, clear dots gather over her upper lip. A watery necklace is suspended from her neck. Lizzie is hot traipsing down the aisle, sweeping past the eyes at her feet, her aqua organdy dress sticking to her ribcage. She vaguely hears the announcer saying "A night out even for children should be entrancing. Notice the subtle flare beginning at the waist moving down to the hemline." The tone is monotonous, lulling. She pirouettes in the corners, skipping back through the curtains at her own pace, peels off the dress she is allowed to keep. She leaves a damp palm print on a chrome chair, presses her hand on a mirror and writes "Lizzie" with her fingertip in the languorous sweat. Now Mother, Claire, Lizzie and the other models and children have earned a free weekend at this hotel. This fun, large hotel resting in the Catskills where they can play and run up and down the hallways. Lizzie is proud of her mother's beauty.

**

Lizzie picks up the phone receiver in the kitchen and hears a man's disembodied voice say "I want to run my tongue down your long legs, entering every orifice of your body, licking your toes." It's not Stan.

"Yes? And...?" Mother's words.

"Have you ever had anyone suck your toes?" Lizzie puts her hand over the receiver, giggling, fascinated. "Claire, come," she gestures to the far end of the long kitchen. Beauty, the dog, is a lace around Claire's ankles. Claire's hair is a dark tangled cloud at the back of her head. She stopped combing her hair several years ago and wouldn't let anyone touch it. Lizzie holds the phone towards the ceiling and they both press their ears along one side.

"No, tell me more." Mother's words hover in the air.

"I like running my wet tongue along the nails, around the edges, licking between the toes. Taking the whole toe in my mouth." Claire grimaces at Lizzie as though she smells something disgusting.

Lizzie and Claire are laughing so hard soundlessly, that their palms jump off the receiver, the cord is shaking. Their other hands cover their mouths. Their smiles explode over their fingers and it is hard to swallow their laughter.

**

Reruns of "My Three Sons," "My Little Margie," "Andy

Griffith," and "Leave It to Beaver" drift across the television. Household gods describing forms of family life. Highways of light moving up and down Lizzie and Claire's features. Claire is always obedient to Lizzie's directions to change channels. Beauty is a dark spot in the center of the carpet waiting to be loved.

The sound of their parents quarreling wanders from the kitchen, down the hall into their bedroom. It is high-pitched, almost screaming and crumbling like clay into the carpet. Unlike the usual evening arguments where Lizzie wants to hold her breath until it is over. She prays those nights that neither Stan nor Mother will come into their room to dispute their side and reasons. Making believe she is asleep she is slow to answer them. It seems the same blood meanders down all their veins and stops just before the heart. They have stolen the moon and put their faces on it instead. They have buried the stars with all their needs. Some nights Lizzie and Claire sneak up to their parents' bedroom door with drinking glasses to their ears to catch the hiss of their words more clearly, curious and entertained by their struggle. Then they run barefoot back to their beds trying to make sense of the phrases hurled around that room, especially the infidelities thrown like rocks at each other. Then they finally fall into sleep, confetti after a parade.

But this time seems different, more shrill. They follow the sound cautiously, barefoot to the swinging kitchen door exhaling cigarette smoke through the cracks. The smoke and light straying in curlicues around their childish faces. Claire's nose, ears, hair are hidden in the bruise-colored shadows but Lizzie sees the tension, the secrets in her features, the anticipation. They push the kitchen door slightly ajar, their heads are zeroes stacked over one another. Smoke clouds hover in the bright light and their parents don't see them.

"I tell you there's no Lucy at the store," Stan says pacing, his feet ticking in squares on the linoleum floor. Lizzie thinks of adult hopscotch. He is wearing a suit. His cigarette is glowing near his lips, is pacing with him.

There is ice in Mother's eyes, eyebrows arched into blonde bridges, her red mouth tight as an asterisk. Her glassy voice, "You're such a lying son-of-a-bitch. You've taken my father's money for the business and gambled it away. You're never home and you expect me to believe you?"

"I'm always working." Stan stops to hunch his shoulders into the air, the cigarette smoke stops flowing, grows thicker around his dark hair. What do you expect? he is thinking. He is defensive and Lizzie sees he wants to fade into the walls like a shadow. He puts out the cigarette.

"My ass. Then why couldn't I get you yesterday when I called the Connecticut store? Why do you want me to become a redhead — like Lucy?" Her red dress glares in the kitchen light.

Beauty nuzzles the bottom of the door, her black fur brushing their legs tenderly, her eyes a totem below Lizzie's and Claire's.

Stan looks at the floor, moving still. "Aw, fuck it," he says quietly to the cabinets. "Maybe there is something there. Not that I'm admitting..."

Mother becomes a burnt piece of paper flying near the ceiling. She disassembles her limbs, her face is fractured, lacerated. She grasps scissors, her arm glinting high, arching in the air. "You are a stupid asshole. I don't even want you with your small prick," and the scissors comes down toward the landscape of his body. It happens in an instant, so quickly. Lizzie and Claire and Beauty are frozen at the sliver between the door and its frame. They are caught in the drama as though watching a television program. He grabs her arm. "Who would want a poor schmuck like you." He is twisting her hand, their bodies intertwined, until there is a glitter of metal in his other hand.

She is back near the front door, her red lips sneering. "And does Lucy know you are only this big?" She is waving her little pinkie.

***

In the soft geography of her bed Lizzie tries to dream about winter's glance over trees and grass, the weak, fading light. There is gray underneath everything, everywhere. The sidewalks, the sky, even the edges of clouds peeking out from the enormous buildings. Claire and Beauty sleeping in their separate beds.

The grainy, pungent odor opens the door and enters the room. Stan sits on the side of the bed. His clothes exuding smoke, his cigarette pack extending his breast pocket. He sighs deeply.

"Can't you protect me?" Lizzie whispers. Her flannel nightgown twisting with the sheets. She can hear her sleeping sister's refrain: Me too, me too.

"What, Hon?" His mind is elsewhere. He barely knows where he is. He pats his suit breast pocket, instinctively checking his pack.

"Can't you protect us?" Lizzie takes a breathful of Stan.

"What do you mean?" He mumbles, the words falling down a long set of stairs. He is not in this room. Then he wanders outside of it. He only cares for Mother's aching loveliness. The curves of her legs in high heels, the moment of lipstick on her mouth, eyes like deep, dark petals, cascades of wood-colored hair and her flirting way of talking, of drinking liquids, including scotch, first with the flick of her tongue in the glass. It is like having an armful of flowers, a bouquet, without thinking about the future, without thinking about the water they need or how they'll dry out and die. What to do with them. He just likes holding them. Nothing more, nothing less.

Lizzie turns away from Stan, stares momentarily at the corner filled with night, feels a pinch of fear at the possibility of vampires and then pretends she is asleep.

***

Tonight Mother sits on Lizzie's bed with her lament: no one loves me. Her hands crawl through the blankets like shadows, but untouching. She is unsettling Lizzie's limbs, jostling her awake by rearranging the blankets and sheets, by having them tighten and loosen around Lizzie, having them touch her. "I do," Lizzie says, sometimes meaning it. And she often lists other people who might. "Stan and Claire and the man at the grocery store who stares at you with narrow eyes." Lizzie had once entered Stan and Mother's bedroom, forgetting to knock. She discovered Mother's elbows draped on Stan's shoulders and her breast in his mouth. She knew the name, sex.

This night Mother's fingers are stones disheveling the darkness, improvising. Unhappiness is a sleepless horizon she steps into, she knows well, almost the same stars overhead as yesterday. When the world is sleeping, there is little memory — only now or dreams, anything more she cannot remember. The restless problems begin without nouns when most of the apartment lights are gone (with their nostalgic bright stares). She looks at Lizzie and sees a mirror.

"You're just like me," Mother whispers. "Sleepless, restless. Part of the Lowenstein family."

"What about Stan and Claire?"

"They don't count." And she moves off. "Come," she commands.

And Lizzie believes her for a second. Lizzie knows that who she represents is better to Mother than who she is. Some nights she doesn't bother to go to sleep, reading *Grimm's Fairy Tales* or other books, observing the rectangles of apartment lights diminishing one by one, knowing they will return. Small fireflies. This is what she does well. The comfort of her presence like a silent candelabra or pasty moon or the way Lizzie falls onto her own scent on her special pillow in the dark. This is who she is supposed to be: grass pliant to the touch of any little wind. But somewhere inside her she asks: Obedient to whom? Why?

Tonight Mother is drinking and it is harder for her to recognize Lizzie is separate from her. Some nights she drinks, whiskey or vodka crying tears from the glass over her red fingernails. The carpet, a wet trail, traces her steps.

— No one loves me.

And the night begins. Her eye make-up blackens her face in streaks, crimson lipstick smears her lips and the edge of the drink resembles a mouth's insane gestures. When everyone else sleeps she is sadder. Her chin is wet, her hair repeats itself like leaves falling. They are in the living room with Johnny Carson on television. On lucky nights Lizzie goes to sleep to his voice. The shimmering liquid disappears down Mother's throat while Johnny's guests are reflected in the surface of her glass. Beauty is locked in, sleeping on newspaper in the kitchen. And Claire and Stan sleep on, both heavy sleepers, oblivious, quietly tucked into the side pockets of their dreams.

"He's having an affair. That bastard." A knot of television light fills her forehead for a minute. Her glass is on a table in front of beige curtains, squinting against the similar color.

"Who?" Lizzie says almost afraid to remind her that she is in the room, her conscience, her small shadow.

"Who the hell do you think?" Her voice is thick with contempt.

"Stan," Lizzie ventures. The television winks its black and white luminescence over her small body, its pattern dusting the geometric leaves on her nightgown. Her bare feet provisional at the end of the sofa. Mother frightens Lizzie and she moves closer into herself. She thinks: I am afraid she will tell me that I am a dog. One that cannot even bark.

"Hell yes. Schtupping that little bimbo at his store. Like I wouldn't find out." She pauses and pours another drink. Her smudged eyes on Johnny Carson, her mouth twists into a pink splash of water. "I'll fix that stupid son-of-a-bitch bastard." She grows quieter, calmer. "Actually, Lizzie, I'm poisoning the jerk." She's no longer just talking to herself.

Lizzie is startled and believes her. "How?" she says, her heart racing out of her chest, her fingers blur into nothingness in the glaze of the television set.

"Rat poison in his coffee. It's so easy. The stupid dope doesn't even notice the difference. When he's home, that is." Her shadow jumps up and down the sofa from the changing light. "Only it's not killing him. That peasant constitution must be too strong. Shit." She shifts around, making her shadow jump across the length of the coffee table. She looks at Lizzie. "It's embarrassing that he's screwing one of the salesgirls at the Connecticut store. Her

38

name is Lucy. She's a stupid bimbo with dyed red hair."
Lizzie wants to ask more, how she is sure, but knows
better than interrupting her. Mother resembles a vampire
in the pale light, one excited by its prey. "God, I picked
such a weak little twerp, running under his Mother's
skirts. He had that nervous breakdown, too, last year
when he bankrupted some of the stores. Sniveling in his
bed all day and all night. He couldn't do anything. Including having sex." She picks up a drink, water gloving her
fingers. "I could have had anyone — almost anyone at
school. I walked around in my shortie shorts and got asked
out on tons of dates. But no, God, I had to pick your
father." Lizzie reminds herself that it isn't her fault. "We
fooled around a little before we got married. But nothing
much. He was sort of cute and from a good family, I
thought. But he turned out to be such a weak asshole. I
wish he'd just goddamn kick off. It'd give us all a little
peace." Her mouth twists again into a small musical note.
"I wonder if I'm using enough." Lizzie doesn't think she'll
eat or drink anything Mother makes again. "Anyway,
Lizzie, I met this great guy. He's so-o handsome. He's an
Italian ambassador." She gets animated and excited. "You
knew I was having affairs too, right?"
        "Uh huh" Lizzie nods, curious.
        "Well he's got this soft curly dark hair and a great
body. God, he's so much fun. He's married with one
disabled kid — I think she's got a hearing problem or
something. But he gives me the best presents — a pair of
emerald earrings. I'd love to show them to you but they're
in my vault. They are shaped like beautiful insects —
mosquitoes or something. But real emeralds. He's got
these beautiful pointed Italian shoes. He wants to take me
to Europe. How much fun. Not like your stupid father. He
does nothing. Except fool around with salesgirls." She

reaches to pat Lizzie's hand. Lizzie's hand feels like a big carved weight. "Maybe he'll be your next father" she says flicking the hand like a truculent beetle.

Lizzie is wide awake, the scorched television light running over the field of her body. Johnny Carson is laughing. Beauty barks in her sleep from the kitchen. Everyone else in the world is asleep.

"Since you can't sleep I'll give you one of my pills and you can stay home from school in the morning if you want." She hands Lizzie a small red pill. It is as big as a fly and tastes like dust. Lizzie feels the knot move down inside her body. She likes school and wants to go in the morning. She wonders if sleep will come over her like a big black curtain. She faintly hears Mother's complaint: no one really loves me. Fading, Lizzie knows what she is supposed to say.

***

After school, evening, Lizzie is groggy with the tinny taste of metal in her mouth. She is doing dishes in Rubbermaid gloves too big for her hands. She pushes aside the curtains with soapy hands to see the medley of lights outside the dark windows. Not many stars, she reminds herself, in New York City. They look like so many half-eaten vegetables to be scraped off the plate of night. "Me too, me too" Claire says into the sink attempting to help. The kitchen light highlights the white plates, pieces of spaghetti, sauce, beans run into the drain like exhaled breath or the dinners Lizzie wouldn't eat with the German maid they once had. She would store the food she didn't like between her teeth and cheek, ask to go to the bathroom, and spit it all out. Otherwise she would feel the back of the maid's hand, a hard wind, on her face if she refused to eat.

"I want to talk to you about Mother" Lizzie broaches Claire, her child's legs looking pale, vulnerable beneath her pleated school skirt. They are alone, light bright on their backs. The kitchen is yellow with excitement, a detonated chrysanthemum.

"Oh," she says holding a wad of gum between her fingers for a minute. "You mean about her poisoning Stan and having a lover?"

Lizzie is flabbergasted and tries not to show it, the flavor of secrets is tinny and flat, a spoon, a fork, a knife. "Well, yes. How did you know?" Soap covers her gloves, an explosion of white flowers she watches drip down the drain.

Claire looks at Lizzie. "She told me. She also told me that I was the daughter of some Italian ambassador and that's where I got my nose." She chews the gum again. Her dark hair touching the square of her face above her straightened legs.

"She just," chew, "doesn't want," chew, "us to," chew, "like Stan," chew, "so much manymore."

"Do you think she's really poisoning him?"

She takes the gum out again. "I don't know but he seems okay." She goes to the corner to pet the small, dark pillow of a dog, the tiny poodle licking her thumbs, the dewy kisses without obligations. She feels the wiry, curled fur.

Water pours over Lizzie's fingers, a rain, a rope from the faucet painting food in the sink. She picks up a heart-shaped piece of bread as she hears Stan's footsteps. He opens the door, his hair curled with cigarette smoke.

"I think Mother's having an affair," Lizzie says to the basin, afraid to look at his face. Her dark bangs touching her eyebrows like birds hesitating on a tree branch.

"What makes you think that, Lizzie?" he says

calmly, quietly, looking at the linoleum floor with its fading checkerboard pattern in yellow and green.

"Oh, I don't know, the way she acts." She doesn't know what to say, pain knocking at the door, hoping to come in.

He frowns, his features resembling bad weather. He pulls on his jacket, touching the round buttons like rocks. "Well, don't you worry your pretty head about that," he says smiling. His laughter shakes loose, apples from a tree.

Lizzie feels silly for having carried around this secret, adroitly moving it between her head and her heart. See, it wasn't important after all. Sometimes it felt like a huge waxing and waning moon in her chest, heavy and full and then thinner, lighter. Well, she passed it on to Stan who held it up, big as that moon, turned it around and around, and laughed. It was not her concern anymore, this heart hopscotch.

***

Mother's golden hair reverberates in a chignon. It eclipses her head in waves above the long, old-fashioned, high-necked, petticoated dress that Lizzie is releasing herself from by pushing her folded arms against Mother's back. She is hidden underneath the bustle, a cave of fabric rising from Mother's backside. When Mother walks across the stage, Lizzie walks in tiny steps behind her with a newly found faith in Mother's sense of direction. Lizzie's limbs stenciled against her body loosen, her tenebrous view against Mother's back and Mother's humid, sweaty smell are stifling. She hears the audience clapping through the stiff layers of clothing. So she knows it's time to push herself out and into the bright lights. She thinks that she is too big for this. Her thin elbows are embossed against her chest, leaving indentations in the top of her dress. Lights and voices surround her and she is almost completely emerged. She sees the knots of Mother's hair lacquered to the back of her skull. She carves the fresh air around her, taking a large, full breath. It is good, warm under the television lights. This is their first and only time on "To Tell the Truth" where they try to fool people together. The audience tries to decide which one of the four women on-stage has a child tucked underneath her bustle. Lizzie is good at dwindling into nothing, disappearing, keeping pace with Mother's measured steps. And they win, collecting $100, surprising the audience when Lizzie unravels from the complicated clothing.

But Lizzie isn't finished. She sits on-stage under the lights with three other girls her own age. Her face is still creased by the bones in Mother's dress. The audience must guess which girl is eating a potato instead of ice cream under the splayed chocolate sauce. Lizzie can do it without wincing or making any faces. It seems like a long time, eating the starchy potato with the sweet chocolate. It doesn't taste bad. She understands this is pretending, buckled into another face, another person's skin, someone she doesn't know or hasn't met yet. She squanders her honesty, this time there is just a larger audience involved. She smiles prodigiously and swallows. Memories rusting under the lights surface and are warm and tumid on her legs, crawling up her arms like small infants and clasp her head, her features. But she does well enough, again fooling all the people. It is familiar, easy. This time she has more choice, could have said "No" to the lacy lights, the hijacking mouths and hands of the audience. It could feel like kidnapping but Lizzie believes it is borrowing, accumulating the gestures, the speech of someone else for just a little while, at least this time.

She remembers auditioning with Mother. Using imagination instead of history, they alternately answered questions trying to say what the interviewer wanted to hear. Like "Fortunate and alive" to the question "How do you feel under lots of lights?" Mother tilted her head and spoke to him as though he was a god. Her eyelashes twittered, obliterating her eyes for whole minutes. Lizzie tap danced and sang slightly out of tune, imitating the child stars she had seen in the movies who won stranger's hearts. Her voice tentative against the notes. The air around them vibrated with shuffling papers, colors, the propitious, glaring light. "Happiness waits in the palm of my hands." Lizzie held out an upturned hand to the man. Mother nudged her and she said, "Television," nodding, "A television, of course" to the question "What do you want most of all?" She pulled her frilly, ruffled party dress over the plates of her knees while Mother signed papers filled with insect-sized writing.

***

A different lover convinces Mother to divorce Stan, promising her unforgettable nights, travel, riches, and marriage. It is the inclination of snow to fall where it may. Its whiteness covers knuckles of earth, the mistakes and imperfections, so succinctly. Her belief in its butterfly touch is all it takes. Stan moves to a nearby hotel and then a glass and chrome apartment where his thoughts ricochet against the walls, where he sleeps like a guest on a new sofa covered in a borrowed blanket, and he sees the children occasionally. He gives them a little money and elaborate presents he has seen advertised on television. He asks them "How are your bowel movements?" as he has ques-

tioned them for years, concerned, chagrined by their careless, embarrassed, muffled answers. "Fine," they say, turning their heads away. He wants details. He smokes more,
breathing hard against the cement streets, wanting to
forget the past with its many faces. He presses his own face
against his new mirror and forgets who the children are,
using them instead as messengers, birds carrying notes to
Mother who doesn't respond. He describes women he sees
on the street. His anger is unfathomable, like a song in his
head that keeps repeating, a catchy song that tells him
what a fool he has been. And at night he closes his eyes and
sees Mother with her eyes deep in a flirtation, her hair
brushing her neck, her lovely, dizzy legs and her red "o"
of a mouth calling to someone else, buried within his skull.
He grows lost in this big, new world.

Mother flits about the apartment like a moth, alighting in rooms and leaving, looking anxiously, apprehensively for a better place. She is impatient for the future,
leaving dust from her wings behind. It is the choreography of flight. How to leave your old life behind while still
living it. She wants to fall out of herself and into the first
open arms she sees. Even if they are made of smoke and
mirrors. Even if they are a dream she turns to in the middle
of the night. They are better than the nothingness you can
drift into one day at a time until your life is used up and
gone. To where? To the washing machine, the meals cooked,
house cleaned, dishes done. For what? The stale breath of
a husband at your neck. Or how about a heart quickening
to the size of an insect or bird at the touch of a new man,
the blood humming. She dreams of a chorus in which she
is always the lead singer. She dreams of growing younger
in the arms of a complicated, wealthy stranger. She doesn't
think about the children at all, yet she is left with them and
the child-support they should receive.

Lizzie and Claire can take care of themselves. They make Pop-Tarts before school as usual. They are given frozen TV dinners or spaghetti for dinner. The girls, as they are called, as if they are one person, are allowed to fall like leaves. The girls are tense beneath the melodies they hum to themselves. They don't know who wants them or what for. Lizzie thinks that if she had talked to Stan more her parents would still be together. Perhaps time would have been a backbone they could both lean against and it could have held both of them up. She sees the meaningless smile her father now gives her over meals at restaurants. She sees the air is restless around her mother, that she spends hours applying cosmetics and perfume to all the recesses of her body, including the skin behind her knees and her clavicle near her throat. Like her mother, Lizzie too wanders the unchanged yet startled apartment, beginning to realize how easy it is to make someone disappear. If you don't care for someone, how simple it is to cut them out of your life the way Mother cuts Stan out of all her photographs, as if he were never there to begin with. Lizzie wonders if this can happen to her.

Claire takes a pair of scissors and cuts off her hair in pieces. It is slightly wavy since she has been combing and washing it. She barely looks in the mirror. She says she is tired of it in her eyes, reminding her of the child she used to be, the knots that used to tie her small face when she didn't brush. She knows now she will be different, that she will change. The strands of hair fall slowly like secret love notes to the floor. She sweeps them up in her hand, throws them in the garbage, tired beyond her years. She sighs at Mother always inventing herself — different age, income, ethnicity (sometimes she's Jewish, sometimes not), or marital status (sometimes married or widowed). It is as if you cannot really grasp who Mother is because she has not

46

yet decided today, so that she can create desire through fabrication. One day she is an older, married, wealthy woman and the next she is a young, poor, divorced one needing help. For the children, of course. She claims she has to do everything for the sake of the children. Sometimes Claire thinks Mother surprises herself, delights herself with the stories of her lies. But the lies can be difficult to remember. Sometimes she gets caught, a spider turning and turning in its own web along with the dying insects. Claire believes lies are complications, cluttering a life like hair haunting our features, hair ceaselessly arranged around a face to transform us into something else, something close to desire or beauty. She is weary of being a collaborator in Mother's lies, of being poked by Mother's elbow or kicked by Mother's foot under a table as Mother beatifically looks at a man and lies. The dog is unaware of the cascading hair lying at Claire's feet, an offering, Claire's first comfort in this new life.

Lizzie slowly turns the pages of her new school books waiting to see what will happen. She stays away from the activity, the excitement, an observer. She disbands the large toy box, watching the Salvation Army cart the painted tin away. She brings their old toys to school or the grocery stores as presents for needy children. She thinks about poetry, folk music, boys. She assumes she can wait anything out.

***

Mother's lover, a boisterous gourmet cook, big as scenery or sky, goes back to his wife and new daughter after holding their newborn with her reddened parts, her little wrinkled feet, her indecipherable expressions. Lizzie, Claire, and Mother are left with illusions. The parties Stan

and Mother used to have would overfill the hall with silk
and linen, jewelry-laden arms and throats, the noise of
talking soon forgotten, the smell of hors d'oeuvres set
symmetrically on table cloths. Lizzie and Claire would be
trotted out self-consciously in sister outfits, wishing they
could stay in their separate expanses of bed. The clamor
winding through their small skulls. When everyone left
there was nothing remaining except stains, crumpled paper, uneaten food, headaches, and empty promises. But
Mother always liked the possibilities, the prayer of something glinting from the shadows.

   Mother is the kind of woman who doesn't want to
be seen without make-up, vermilion lips, blackness around
the pockets of her eyes, powder and foundation recon-
structing her skin, a breath of blush on her cheeks. She
becomes another woman. It is as if she says to herself:
Don't show me your real countenance but show me who
you would like to be. A movie star or a wealthy woman?
Take your pick.

   More men come and go in the apartment. Different
hats, suits, different expressions on their faces. She dates
a lot. She tells one man she has "children, small children,
babies really." Late afternoon light slices into the pale
living room carpet, bouncing off the fireplace with its
angry marble, touching the comic books tucked underneath a stuffed paisley chair.

   "Come here," Mother says to Claire as though she
is a tourist wanting to take a picture of an interesting
native. A drink full of ice cubes licking her hand.

   "I just got out of school." Claire's boots tentatively
take the three steps down to the living room. Books
stumble and bump in her arms.

   "This is my oldest girl, Lizzie. Claire, the youngest,
is visiting some friends," she says to the man drenched in

48

a fading light, his fingers holding a drink in the air until it ascends to his open mouth.

"Hello, Lizzie" he says. There are gold rings on several of his fingers. He nods with the drink in his hand, this stranger who means nothing.

Claire breathes glass. She feels a small wound at her stomach spreading. The scar that is left is who she is. "Hello," she says softly. She doesn't want her mother to be combustible. She wants peace. She doesn't think about what she gives up.

"Lizzie is such a good girl at school. Aren't you? Getting lots of A's," Mother says, the ice cubes applauding at the sides of the glass.

Claire thinks: All right already. Don't push your luck. Lizzie does get A's and I don't. She sees the shine from the man's gold ring fly against the wall like tinfoil. It crawls up the painted wall, an insect or a message Claire wants to take and hurl at him.

"Here's some lollipops I brought for you." He leans down and puts the scramble of color and sticks into her small palm.

"Thank you," she says, thinking: Oh brother. Wondering where he got them (a doctor's office?).

"You can go now." Mother is dismissing her. "You can go back and do your homework."

Claire pivots into her bedroom. Beauty runs to her feet like evidence or pain. Her small shoulders glide apart and she throws the colored O's of candy resembling tiny edible balloons into the garbage can. She wonders if flesh is interchangeable. That if she wishes hard enough she will become Lizzie. She holds up Lizzie's bigger clothes from her drawers and questions what it would be like to be someone else. To eat food differently, changing her ladder of bones, to live in another house. She vows not to say "Me too" again. She elevates Lizzie's shirt in the mirror until dreams of another life cover her and her reflection looks smaller and smaller in the inconsequential glass. She wrongly believes there are some essential things no one can take away from you.

***

One afternoon Mother's breasts come to Lizzie and Claire's bedroom door to say good-bye. Mother wears a black dress that barely fits her, squeezing her hips, tossed over her legs, sticking tightly to her backbone, flinging her breasts into the air and piling one next to the another. She is a sophisticated dresser (as many people in New York are), covering herself in the short, sequined, cut-out, fishnet, tight, leather fashions of the time.

She says: When I come home with Him later you lock yourselves in the bedroom, girls. No lights, no noise, nothing. I don't want to hear or see anything. I told Him I don't have children. Many men don't like children, you see. So you two don't exist. Get it?

She doesn't expect an answer.

Lizzie feels her heart, a wing beating against stone. Claire feels the hollows of her bones, tributaries running through her body. Mother said what they had suspected all along: I wish you didn't exist. Disappear like a magic trick when I don't want to see you. I can tell the world that you were not born and no one will know the difference. No one cares.

Lizzie and Claire play, watch television, new shows, game shows drift by them vacantly with their neon, music, clapping and shouting. They try to read but discover they don't remember what the last sentence said. They are frightened deer in Mother's oncoming headlights. Distracted, Claire asks, "Lizzie, do you think it will be okay to open our clothes closets with the little lights in them?" Angrily Lizzie answers, "I don't care." When they hear the front door close they enclose themselves in darkness. It is a sudden, expected, and never-ending darkness. It seems imposed forever. And darkness is always there, in the periphery of objects and people. Everyone has a relationship to darkness, which is eventually discovered. Lizzie sees it when Mother wakes her in the middle of the night and there are thin slices of light around the adjoining bathroom door and window curtains like threads. Or just before she goes to sleep and the dinosaur shapes of overhead lights are fading. Claire sees darkness in the folds of soft clothes and the dead sound her head makes against the headboard when she demands answers from the wood just before she goes to sleep. She knows darkness as a bandage covering up any wounds until morning or light.

Lizzie doesn't know what to do with herself in the darkness even though she knew it was coming. Its immediacy leaves her hungry and angry. She closes her eyes and hears Mother and her date go into her bedroom, shutting the door. She imagines Mother's body lying in a ravine, trampled fervently by a passing wind. She thinks of Mother's mouth open with a button of saliva resting on the surface and only the whistle of vanishing air. She decides that she and Claire will make an expedition into the kitchen for food very quietly. Claire goes along, having no other ideas. They make believe they are in a spy movie, turning corners quickly, scoping out the dining room, making it on tiptoe into the kitchen, watching for any signs of life. The remnants of their mother's bedroom lights and lights from other apartments help them find their direction. Their socks polish the floors that resemble boarded up, mysterious windows. They give each other hand signals to stop or continue. As the kitchen unfolds in the refrigerator light they see Beauty sleeping with her paws in the air, slightly snoring. She whimpers in her ongoing dreams. They grab some cookies and bread and glide imperceptibly back to their bedroom, checking for any ambushes along the way. Safely, back in their room they cross their legs on the carpet and eat. Lizzie thinks of her mother's stain of red lipstick smeared over sheets and the man's arms. She wonders if sex is worth it, giving yourself away like some birthday present someone might have already received. How men make Mother blind to anything except sex and money. Claire thinks men are adjectives making their way into sentences. She thinks about sleep and the undiminished ache of being closed out like ice against a window. She wonders what her own life will be. Lizzie wants to scream so loudly she could be heard two buildings away.

So you two don't exist. Get it?

What would it matter? Since she doesn't really exist. It could be the crazy child next door. The scream piercing everyone's mind for just one moment. Lizzie is a bird silently screeching within the walls of her self-imposed cage. Her mouth quietly opens and closes, opens and closes in the indifferent darkness. She thinks: I never asked to be born.

The Face of the Moon, 1969

The year men walk on the moon Lizzie's nose changes its shape. Her hair falls smooth and thick as rain to her waist. A dark cascade falls across her new breasts and across her back. She parts the weight of her hair down the middle of her head. Everyone wears rings, bellbottoms, bare breasts without bras and no make-up. Lizzie likes that, the natural look, although everyone looks the same, sort of. She talks to her best friend from high school for hours on her private Princess phone, watching movies on television together, gossip zigzagging across the lines. Sometimes they fall asleep in their own separate bedrooms with the receiver against their ears like bulky jewelry, listening to each other sleep as though they could trade lives. It is comforting to Lizzie to be at her best friend's house without moving from her bedroom the way a leaf falling to the earth forgets the tree branch. To share. All her friends try sex and multi-colored drugs. They want Lizzie to share. The horizon looks interesting with its blue water, striped and dotted towels positioned against warm sand, sunlit bathing suits, repeating murmur of waves.

"We were on the bed, smoking a joint, and every-thing just kept going," her best friend describes losing her virginity. It is peeling a flower until you get to the center, the removal of petals one by one, a sequence just not stopped until the end.

"Now you have to do it too." Lizzie senses the fresh collapse of water from the vast ocean against her temples. It is a pounding that pushes rocks, smoothes glass, mixes with the beat of her heart in this thought of a seaside.

Yet Lizzie feels clumsy, the fence of metal on her

teeth, the braces, just removed. Her mouth finally free of the barbed wire, the blood, the gnarled texture of each tooth against her tongue. The food she could barely eat. Her limbs are overgrown, knobby branches reaching around the trunk of her body. Her fingernails bitten to ragged edges by habit. Her breasts are happy on their own. Even her elbows form unlikely sharp, awkward angles.

She doesn't invite anyone to her house except occasionally her best friend. She lets girlfriends bring their boyfriends briefly to a room in the apartment, saying to Mother, "They are doing the same thing as you. Don't be hypocritical." She remembers the time she brought a date home and Mother, with her hair done, her small pleasure of lipstick, fresh make-up and going-out-soon dress came into the blue living room. Lizzie and her date, a boy her own age with wheat-colored hair, dressed neatly, sat on the velveteen sofa deciding where to go.

"A dance at St. Augustine's?"

"Or a walk."

Mother sat down next to Lizzie's date, her body sinking into the cushions, her dress spreading itself over the edges.

"Where did you say you go to school?" She asked, placing her hand on his knee.

"Bernard's." He looked at her, her beautiful face.

"Do you like it there?" Her hand ran appraisingly along his leg, unconscious, having a mind of its own, as though she didn't realize what she was doing.

"Yes, ma'am, it's a good school." Their conversation didn't miss a beat.

No one looked at Mother's fingers and they eventually crawled back to her body. "I have to go meet my date." And she left.

Lizzie was embarrassed, grateful she was gone. They didn't talk about it and she never saw him again.

Once Mother left Lizzie sitting over a pot of boiling water with herbs and a towel on her head. This was an expensive hair and beauty salon in New York. She tried to get rid of Lizzie's pimples by opening up the pores in her skin. She also takes her to skin doctors in this year that men listen to the voice of the moon, touching its craters with enormous moon shoes.

The apartment hasn't changed much with the fashions since Stan. Lizzie misses the few books that were stacked haphazardly like errant dishes or towels on the hall table. The dining room has been changed into a television sitting room with the appropriate glass and chrome furniture. Lucite sculpture lets the weather into the room and bends it into birds of light and color against the deep blue walls. Lizzie walks by the blue velour sofa and television with its shows about spies, romance, police squads and double agents. The sound of this television follows the tap of her feet on the wood and linoleum floors. She can still hear it when she drifts off to sleep.

No one loves me. No one cares.

There is still Mother's lament, a wake-up call, a story without an end in the middle of the night. A star that calls Lizzie to its history as if this is what she was intended for. It is telling. She learns to immerse herself in the tale of this other. She is sometimes angry or tired, sometimes entrenched in this other life. Some nights she is a moth to a flame, forgetting herself so thoroughly when she accidentally brushes her leg she is startled by its paleness. Johnny Carson is still on but now her mother gives her dalmaine, a non-barbiturate that leaves no taste in her mouth. Some nights she fights sleep after swallowing the pill with letters and numbers etched on its red and yellow side. For fun. To see her hand move differently through air, to see what hieroglyphics the impossible moonlight leaves on her windowsill, her eyes growing darker and deeper into her skull. Her long brown hair sweeps her waist, burying her shoulders. It has the weight of an extra body pressing across her chest, back and shoulders, hugging her as she moves, a companion. Several mornings she feels like a corpse at school. But she still does well. She is at the age she wishes all parents were invisible.

Pills, pieces of paper and bags full of dried green leaves are passed around at school, precious commodities. Her friends' faces light up at the sight of particular drugs they believe disassemble them. Only to be reassembled differently, better. It is a religious belief, this transformation from being human to being one with the air, the wind. Lizzie could see patterns in snow, the chemistry of objects such as tables or chairs. She could also be paranoid and sensitive to light like some vampire. Lizzie wants to see what is offered by the world.

***

"Don't come home tonight," Mother says. "Stay at a friend's house because I'm going to have a party and I don't want you there."

Okay, Lizzie thinks, how strange.

Claire and Lizzie stay with friends. Claire says good-bye to Beauty kissing her fur, smelling each sweet and sour patch of the dog on her head, back, the impossible small paws. Claire is taller, thinner, half-finished. Her legs are perfectly straight and there are no more cats-eye glasses. Lizzie watches her put a few clothes into a shoulder bag. She is angular with dark, wavy hair swinging near her neck. Her blue jumpsuit with pleats, a uniform from school, silhouettes the beige walls and angry marble rimming the doors and windows. Lizzie's own overnight bag is full of books and one change of clothes. She has a pink diary with a lock and key that has dried flowers and a scarab pasted on the pages. Mother once thought the brittle leaves were drugs and tried to pry the book open like an oyster holding its luminous pearl tightly. She finally cut the clasp sending the stiff leaves scattering as though she was a whirlwind that could not be stopped by the mere resistance of words or gestures. She blew right through.

"Why does she want us out of the house?" Lizzie's eyes are suspicious, darting from one object to another.

"I don't know. I didn't ask but I don't mind going." Claire is dreamy, other-worldly. She is thinking of her friend Barbara's house. She is already there with her friend's easy dialogue, kind considerations and a telescope that catalogues the hidden stars, constellations buried like the blaze of treasure concealed under New York lights.

"We could hide and pop out and scare the shit out of them." Lizzie knows she is going but doesn't want to make it easy. Like Stan who just disappeared from the fabric of their everyday lives, who wasn't there much to begin with. But who seemed to slip away like grass on their ankles, appearing now and again, distracted, thinner, a smoking shadow, taking the "girls" out for dinner. His child support payments have become as intermittent as signals on a faulty radio.

Lizzie goes to her friend's house humming a Beatle's tune, the chorus repeating as she sits on a bus facing backward. The people and buildings become a smaller blur, less specific with more interesting possibilities. Like time. She is hungry to be an adult with a life fashioned that is all her own. She thinks: this is a rehearsal for later. She wants to manipulate the tiny tableaux the bus window frames. She combs her hair with her hands, feeling the sheer impenetrable weight of it.

"You look troubled," an older man sitting near her says to the sheen of her hair. He's bald, wears a tweed jacket, has narrow eyes. "I'm a psychiatrist and you can tell me anything you want to." He is using his hands to describe some unseen object. "Let me tell you how one can distill events from their life and analyze them until they have lost their power. Or misinterpret a philosophy that governs everything you do like mismatched clothes."

She is interested and polite but suspicious. "No, no. But thanks." She sees his bald head gathering the steely light within the bus and shining, roundly, out of the corner of her eyes.

"Let me tell you about the tennis shoes, canoes, thin, black dresses, cigars people have piled in my office to rid themselves of unflagging reminders or obsessions. These objects of people's problems finally cast away as though a faith healer had come and released them in the form of objects. I can see that furrow in your forehead holding in your thousand skirmishes — that is what I call problems..."

She could listen to him a long time but decides this is an elaborate pick-up. "Thanks, but no." She gets up and sits next to an elderly, hopefully quiet woman. She stretches her arms around the familiar bulge of her bag. When she reaches her friend's house she slides off the bus giving the older man a last look. The windows of the stores are so clear Lizzie is walking with a version of herself, one with light highlighting her hair.

At her friend's apartment with its wide, fearless windows and long parquet floors she decides to haunt her mother's party, a fly on the wall, curious. She wants the glass cup against the door, the telescope or binoculars trained against the partygoers until she can visualize each sip from a drink, the blotted lipstick on a white napkin, who is kissing whom, every last detail. She doesn't understand what is so compelling about men and women and small talk and the desire for something new. She wants to understand it. Talking about the casual touch of a man's arm against a neck for days. Not like the friend's parties Lizzie swims through and out of where teenagers pass out for days or leave and reappear in strange outfits. Interpretations. She wonders what it is about this lake of arms and legs, food, and drink, the gestures, conversations set to memory, perhaps dancing that attracts her mother so. The mystery of bad music that someday she will grow up and enjoy.

So she returns. She slips back into her apartment, a fish navigating subterranean water where darkness and light are gradients giving her direction. It is very crowded and no one notices her, an observer, a detective, a spy. She doesn't recognize this group of party-goers, a few wearing colorful bellbottoms but mostly halter dresses, big earrings, men with jackets whose collars hide their necks. She doesn't stand out in the mini skirt, boots she borrowed from her girlfriend. Outside her mother's bedroom, in the hallway, is a long table with a white tablecloth and there are bottles of liquor and glasses stacked and half used. The noise is lyrical, loud, blending into a murmur above the music. She hears her mother on the phone inside the bedroom. "And that Lizzie is so difficult. I don't know what to do with her — no boyfriend, acne, her hair covering her face like some little animal. Those girls are such a burden. And the little one, Claire, is hard and crusty, nothing comes in or goes out. I don't know what to do with them. Teenagers. And the little one is just starting up with the cold shoulder and the fights..." It is the drone and long complaint of her life. The way she purchases memory, adapts it to her use, and shapes it into her own creation like a painting with its collection of reds and blacks muscling the canvas into constantly changing shapes. One day it is a picture of a ball and the next day a tree. Never predictable. Streaked with random colors. She shudders to think of her mother's mind. She has heard her before, yet it hurts to see herself through that mind. Is she a still life or a caricature? Which is right? Which one serves her purpose?

Lizzie drinks a half glass of colorless liquid abandoned by a chair. She gulps it in two big sips so she doesn't have to taste it, only feel it warm and falling down the length of her stomach. She winds through the discussions sentence by sentence, climbing toward the door, until a man jumps through the crowd and opens up his cigarette pack, offering her a smoke. With a start she realizes it is Stan with a grin on his face. She notices the cigarettes are joints stacked neatly together like fish in their shining rows at the store, patinaed, orderly, and ready to be used. She realizes her mother is having a pot party and laughs.

***

Claire returns to the apartment and unloads more out of her overnight bag than what was in it originally. She likes it when the building doormen greet her with mirrors and marble widening in mazes behind them. She enjoys the rattle of the elevator as it reaches the ninth floor. Alone, in the elevator, there are a few moments of enforced peace, a time after pushing the buttons to think and wait quietly, standing in the moving rectangle, listening attentively to

all the gears, anticipating. A little like praying. In the
apartment there is the tapping of traffic against the window glass. Claire sees the twist of white, the back of the
spiraling Guggenheim Museum, out their bedroom window. Claire's eyes are shining with possession, exploding
with the joy of ownership. She is wearing a patterned shirt
swirling with red and green horses that Lizzie has not seen
before.

"That shirt hurts my eyes."

"It's nice, isn't it?"

"I have to ask," Lizzie is almost talking to herself,
"where did you get it?"

"Around." Claire is cagey.

"Around your friend's house or around a department store?"

"What does it matter? It's nice, and look at this."
Claire pulls out a black pair of pants and holds them up
over her legs.

"Well it's just that someone I know was caught
stealing at a department store and they called her parents,
talked about the police and she's not allowed near that
store for years."

"Oh, Lizzie, I know what I'm doing." As though
she is talking to a child.

"Well, in that case can I put in a request?" Lizzie
says.

***

"How's your sex life?" Mother asks as though Lizzie
would be silly enough to tell her.

"Fine," Lizzie mumbles towards Beauty's sleeping
form in the kitchen.

"Let me tell you about the new man I met. He has

these distinguished gray sideburns and the best smile. He seems really nice and seems to have lots of money to spend. Maybe you'll get to meet him. I get so excited thinking about him." She dips her spoon into the milky cereal in the bowl with its "O" of exclamation. She watches the milk drip from the spoon back into the curls of cereal. "But cousin George is going to call you about someone he wants you to meet. He's older and RICH. I think he even drives a Ferrari. If you don't take him, I will." She looks fatigued with no lipstick and the shiny utensil held in the split of her mouth like a breath she could not quite take. As an afterthought she says "I bet you had sex with that friend of yours, Bill. Well? Did he get into your tight, little pants?" as though no one could get through Lizzie's clenched legs, as though she was the only one left pleasuring herself with her own long, slow fingers.

Lizzie thinks of Bill undoing her clothes and dropping them on the floor like a sigh. But there was nothing more than his hand methodically describing the curves of her body. Nothing "just kept going" as her best friend said. It always stopped. But Lizzie's mother wants details, facts that she can refract through her mind, a prism, until the knowledge is made into something else. The way a shadow of leaves can describe the leaves, branch or tree or some imaginative bird fabricated by the storyteller that can become romantic or a killer.

"Maybe." Lizzie is talking to Beauty, petting her graying fur, feeling it lengthen under her fingertips. She hopes to have dreams about fur tonight.

"Maybe?" Her Mother's face gathers air, she is becoming interested. "Exactly what did he do?"

"I have to go to school," Lizzie says, pressing against the kitchen door with relief. The pleats of her jumper describe the varieties of darkness, air straining through her nose. The books jutting from her chest and covered by her hair are excuses, a form of protection.

***

The net of streets in New York, interwoven, patterned, catches Lizzie by surprise with cold air and dirt-tinged snow pushed into gutters by rotating tires. The city is vacant, abandoned, frustrated by the sudden snow storm. Traffic flows slowly, leisurely sculpting the snow into long scarves lost to the wind, elevated and then dropped again. The alchemy. Some honking. But mostly there is a wet sound, pavement assessing the weight, the toppling of fistfuls of snow from ledges and sills. The inhalation, sucking noise of water. The smell of damp flesh in the icy, clear air. Lizzie's blue, wool jumper tucked around her under her coat, her school uniform, as she walks empty side streets home from school. She feels cold seeping through her clothes, feels it down to her bones. Her books are held close to her chest. Windows are steamed with heat, breath, and colorful light. In the distance she sees a speck growing larger. It is the size of a pencil eraser, the brown color of stone. Snow sticks to her boots. Its whiteness dripping to a recognizable puddle. A block away Lizzie welcomes the figure, a man gesticulating under his dark coat, his hair unshaped by the knit cap. Less than a block away he is shaking something under his coat. Lizzie sees his pants are unzipped, he is aiming himself at her, furiously pumping with his forearm. She looks at him, frozen for a moment at this strange gesture, laughs at its insignificance and futility and walks on.

***

It is time to get this over with, Lizzie thinks, time to let this virginity go. Please give it away. Who will take it? It is the dark print of a dress she has outgrown. There is a club, a part of the rustle of the world, she wants to belong to where the touch of a collarbone, a rib means something she doesn't yet understand. The smell of a flower will be different. The stars will be different in their invisible vigilance over her closed eyes at night. She will know things. Her skin will be peeled to reveal her essence like a balloon holding the impermanence of water. She wants to release that part of her held inside since childhood, to move into herself as though she is a languorous gown waiting for the outlines of a body to be filled. To be complete. She wants to let it go and get it over with as casually as dropping a glove so she can move into another way of life as though she was there already. Sophisticated, easy.

Lizzie goes out with her cousin George's acquaintance, a man in his mid-forties with a deep blue Ferrari. She is a sleepwalker, dressing matter-of-factly as though she is listening to an otherworldly conversation at the same time. Mother walks down to the trompe l'oeil lobby with Lizzie, the murals, the doorman all observers. The mirrors doubling her so there are two Lizzies walking out the front door under the canopy. Mother presses her nose against the side of glass between the outside and inside. Her breath fogs it in concentric circles, little round exhalations going nowhere, circling themselves rhythmically without thought. She is staring at the Ferrari as Lizzie steps into it. Mother's face is a blur by the door.

At Henry's apartment there is a painting of mermaids in various poses and dress on his wall. The faces, though, are detailed, populated with distinctive features.

"Those are all the important women in my life."

There were about fifteen of them. "I want to be one of them," Lizzie says, thinking about joining this group of women looking at her, waiting, their faces trying to say something. She doesn't care about this man, too old, too strange. Why would he want to go out with a teenager anyway? He is just the means to an end. Hopefully kind, gentle, slow. She leans her head against his shoulder.

He says, "Let's go into the bedroom." Soft rock music drifts through his living room and into his bedroom.

She slopes her body horizontally against the contour of the big bed. She is dreamy, a stone. She wants to be tossed against the waves, skipping over them at a slant. She thinks of the men walking on the moon: how they felt afterward, how their vision of earth and the universe must have been transformed. A new perspective. She feels the man's hands acknowledging her clothes, discarding them, running his hand up her thigh. He turns on a nearby light. She shuts her eyes to the gray hair on his chest and shoulders, his flesh creased over itself on his neck like messy sheets.

"I want to see your face as I make love to you."

No, you don't, she thinks. I am the moon, cold, hard, disinterested. Go ahead, release me. See what you can find that I have not already closed off from you. I won't hide my face, in pain or distorted into a grimace. This is about me.

Afterwards she rests her cheek against his newly found arms. That's it? she thinks. It didn't take long. It is "everything just kept going." There isn't much to this, this fucking. Finally. Not much grace. It is all logistics and details, somewhat uncomfortable. She wonders when she will feel different, more womanly. Perhaps it happens slowly the way spilt water makes a path across a table, dripping onto the floor, claiming its space. Or perhaps the astronauts didn't think about the way they changed until they neared the earth's orbit or even later in a casual comment to their wives or children. It seems like one more need like eating. Not knowing what you want until you've tasted it and then giving it a name and a focus.

She still doesn't understand all the emphasis on beauty. She looks at her leg stretched out, the long clouds of her hair against an unfamiliar pillow. Beauty is what men want, what men seek, a prize. A delightful face added to the collection, always looking at the movements in this room. But empty. Lizzie thinks of the lovely ache of her mother. How much men will do just to fuck her like this. How with beauty you can be a leaf left to the desire of the wind, moved this way and that. You would have to learn to say no a lot. The weight of it like pebbles running through your blood, so heavy. Until you grow old and anonymous, resembling everyone else. She wonders what the point is: to not be taken seriously, to be a bauble passed from hand to hand just for show.

"How was it?"

"Fine," she says and means just that, hoping not to see him again.

***

Mother, Claire and Lizzie are downtown in one of the enormous department stores that take up several city blocks. Perfume rambles unseen around them. Lipstick stains the glass counters in rows like multi-colored scars or the accidental strokes from an artist's brush. There is fuschia, pumpkin, tangerine, apricot, carnation, peach. Mostly flowers or fruits. High heels click on the expanse of faux marble floors echoing against leather handbags and ties and belts. The sheen of hair that is curled, sprayed, dyed and shaped is reflected in the mirrors surrounding all the merchandise available for the asking and the right amount of change. Now there is also a contingency of people devoid of make-up, with commas of bright beads around their necks and wrists, clothes from foreign countries and long, unruly hair as expressive as words. Mother says they are "inconsequential." Lizzie likes them and Claire is indifferent.

"Oh, no. Get something in leather and shorter," Mother says to Lizzie.

"Gross. Never." Clothes fly between them across the racks, the hangers screeching their discontent, until one of them gives in.

"Here, try this on," Mother says to Claire.

"Try what on?" Claire holds the few inches of cut-out material up to her growing chest. It barely covers her thighs.

Claire's hands are smoothing the short dress, her forehead frowning. She doesn't like it but avoids the lightning and thunder of Mother's determined opinions by agreeing with her. Mother lifts a sequined black dress to her shoulders, looks in the mirror, turning her legs to the sides. "This is really cute," she murmurs to herself, stains of lipstick and mascara widening against her reflection. Claire thinks: You don't know me and don't want to. It takes time. (I am not you. I am another.)

When they thread their way home through cars, taxis, streets littered with people, their eyes turn toward the white sky riding the cold between the tops of the tall buildings, an angel playing hide and seek. The corridors of apartment houses bitten by the breeze, looking unfazed, gripping their stone and cement tighter. The fists of buildings holding onto their glass and brick like precious commodities, a last light fading out of reach. It is a cold, hard landscape translated into the voice of traffic, horns, pieces of speech, garbage, broken glass.

Claire tosses the short dress onto a chair covered with her other clothes (some illicit), hoping to lose the dress. Lizzie leaves the clothes she picked out hanging empty in her closets, touched only by her transitory breath or other dresses or shirts.

"You girls are ungrateful. My mother never bought me any clothes. Pick them up. I don't know why I kept you girls. Now get them off the floor."

"No," Lizzie says, pressing her face against Mother's eyes, standing her ground, overhead light freckling her arms.

Lizzie feels Mother's hand against her cheek. The bones make sense, make room. She thinks hands come in all sizes. The ringing as in "please answer" or "come in", the knock along the shell of her. It's not just theory. It's practice. And the body is dangerous. Lizzie is tall enough, impersonating a woman. Lizzie's hand flattens itself against Mother's cheek, a puddle as tenuous as water, the flesh soft and yielding beneath her palm. She feels a layer of make-up, powder, between her fingers. Mother's cheek is surprisingly real, solid. Their hands resembled birds thrashing, beginning flight. It happens quickly. There we have both told our stories, she thinks, each with its own version, each ricocheting off the skull of the other.

***

"You need to have it fixed."

"Fixed as in it's not right now? Fixed as in broken?"

"You'll look so much better." Mother assesses Lizzie's sixteen-year-old nose as though it could be money.

"Just say yes to everything the doctor says. And please, Lizzie, act enthusiastic. It's for your own good." The white walls of the doctor's waiting room hum with a music that wants to drown out everything else.

It is odd the way Mother can dislike a part of Lizzie's body as though it is a part of Mother's own body. Lizzie thinks: Okay, a change. And perhaps I will be beautiful. Perhaps not. Lizzie says yes to everything the doctor says but she can't fake enthusiasm.

She puts herself into the hands of this expert on perfection. He rotates her head, an unsettling basketball, a blemished sun rolling on the horizon.

"We'll have to break it and then put it back together."

"Fine," Mother says, folding her gloves on her lap. "It'll look great," she says to Lizzie.

Lizzie realizes there is a fiction of the self that can be rewritten. Sometimes it happens accidentally and sometimes it is planned. She understands that people are always changing, but often it is imperceptible.

The doctor describes the operation with diagrams and a plastic nose. Lizzie sees the ease with which the body is disassembled as in love. Here, take my arm that you are so serenely sleeping on, my lover. It is yours. I give it to you. She hopes she isn't tossing away the one endearing part, the scar in the shape of a cat for example, that her future husband would rub, loving it vehemently, until he could feel it on his own skin. How do the parts make up a whole?

When she goes to the large, white hospital she misses the beginning of school. The rumor has spread among the girl's school like a song drifting among open windows. It will be obvious how she changes her body, her compromise apparent to the world. She is embarrassed. But she won't do any more than this, she vows. No make-up like a wound. No lipstick, a red incision. She won't dye her hair the color of tea for a husband or children, the latter she wouldn't even know what to do with. There is too much reconciliation with the world and she sees how much Mother hates it, the compromising, the children.

The night before surgery Lizzie lingers on her face in the small square of the hospital mirror. Her room darkens to the measure of rain, a rhythm at the window pane. Light falls on her neck, on her nose, an ant, a butterfly ready to ascend. The last part of Stan in her. Not that she misses him. He was a component of her past and she rarely sees him. When she does it is a surprise and she realizes she doesn't know him or what he is thinking. He is just passing through. But he made her nose as though he gave her a small version of his own as a gift. She can't visualize the new one. Perhaps it is one borrowed from another family's history or the replica of a statue the doctor once saw in an art museum. Or as her best friend said "Model number 329."

She hears moaning in a nearby hospital room and the young woman out of surgery a few hours ago lies in a bed with her wrists against a pillow. A bandage is across her nose and Lizzie stares at the terrace of her eyes with the dark bruises circling her cheeks. Lizzie touches the edge of her bed as gently as an insect alighting on a careful petal.

"Does it hurt?"

"Yes. A lot," says the woman's voice from the ocean of white sheets.

"They said it wouldn't be bad."

"Well, they lied."

Lizzie leaves the room and the woman's pain plasters itself against the clean, white walls. Perhaps she can get out of having the operation. Perhaps there is a woman who wants the surgery and will slip under the anesthesia as across a border, into a new life. One who will take her place. She takes the familiar sleeping pill and sleeps.

In the morning her arms are tied to the sides of the surgery table after she is given just enough anesthesia so she will be awake.

"You will hear breaking," the doctor says as he breaks Lizzie's nose, the music of it reverberating in her head. So many changes to her body. A hammer echoes in her skull, then sawing. It is the silence she is most fearful of. She imagines long, sharp instruments inching toward her brain. She is slightly relieved by a deep grinding sound, a file seesawing against rock. He is intent with instruments on her damaged face. He seems to take a long time, perhaps several hours. Finally he holds up a mirror to show Lizzie her profile hours before the bruising begins, "What do you think?"

"It looks like a ski jump" is all she can manage to say.

"Take her out." And she is wheeled out still attached to the sides of her hospital bed.

The experienced woman was right. It does hurt. She feels birds in the cage of her bones whistling to leave. She loses herself in the question of what she will look like without bandages, wounds or contusions the color of night lining her eyes like theories on sleeplessness. She isn't allowed to answer the phone or do much because she might hit her new nose by mistake. Then it would metamorphosize into an unplanned nose. She must be careful. Mother comes to visit and looks pleased. Claire brings flowers with diamond-shaped petals grown in another state with different weather. Her best friend tells her about all the schoolwork she is missing.

She dreams she is painting a self-portrait with effusive flowers explaining the space around her. There is a hole in the center of her face and it is spreading. She can't recognize herself any longer. She can't tell whether she's becoming someone else or nothing, emptiness, a mouth taking over skin. When she screams she wakes herself up. The nurses can't tell what expression is on her bandaged face.

Nobody, Claire, 1971

Claire suspects she has become a statue. The war in Vietnam is raging and older boys are disappearing in its midst or to Canada. Lizzie has gone to college, leaving her alone with Mother. Stan has left the country to avoid paying child support. Mother has taken in a boarder at the apartment to pay the bills. His name is Victor and he sleeps in the old maid's room next to the kitchen. Claire touches her fingernails, her elbow, her neck, her ears progressively to see if she feels anything. She doesn't. It's as if her body is a ball positioned in all the right places. Thrown palm to palm, it doesn't matter just as long as she's finally where she's supposed to be. She knows the body is a utensil, part of who she is and part mystery in the process of eating. She just wishes she could feel Beauty's ashes running through her fingers from the porcelain jar. (She will take the container with her wherever she goes.) Or feel the rhomboid of sun below her dark eyelashes. She could be smoke that can be seen in the shape of a body. Her arms may be moving right through. It is almost a spiritual insistence. She has seen the statues of saints in Little Italy and thought: Now that's what they have finally become. But first they had the chance to talk to God.

Victor is standing in the kitchen, his wavy gray hair undulating under the sharp light, a landscape of the mind. Claire visually traces his wrinkles, mapping his features, holding up his glittering eyes. A handful of thin branches thrown against his cheeks. A pinch of white hair in his ears. A woven plaid shirt, brown corduroy pants. He has just finished eating cereal for dinner. Art and prison have swept him into this apartment. Not much money and paintings that imitate other painters too well.

"You look like a Modigliani," says the rasping voice. He thinks she looks like a flower to be plucked and pinned against a black tuxedo.

Her long pale head and neck resting against a wall. The light is an umbrella. "Okay," she says. The museums she's been to make her uncomfortable. The silence, the walls whispering askance, the cold statues, paintings abandoned in rooms like book covers you cannot read. A form of prison. The air is dry, old, used up. She might do something wrong in all the dust and age with its attending courtesies.

"How old are you?" He remembers color photographs with children and wives peeping at him from rows in various cells, almost interchangeable, in the gentleman's prison. He posted "The Blue House" by Chagall with its blue wooden beams, one person inside, the landscape with a monastery, the door of the house always open.

"Fifteen."

"Umm." He is opening the refrigerator door. The extra light falls in a stripe onto the corner where Beauty slept on her nest of paper. Her fur head and wet nose used to lift toward Claire's hand. Now she is ashes, an accompaniment to memory.

Victor sees himself at fifteen. Thirty years ago, before the war. White vee-neck undershirt, where he could hide a cigarette tucked into his shoulder. He would sweat in the summer under the lamp, leaving wet fingerprints, his head tilted, following his hand as he drew muscle, bone, curves, angles, clothes, whatever he could see from the Bronx window or whatever he could find in the kitchen. The cigarette would nudge him, tap him on the shoulder, a proverbial finger, reminding him of the time. He would forget everything, love, school, the hour, his parents calling him. All that mattered was his drawing.

That was before he had spent his life. When everything he liked to do was a dream he didn't want to wake from. Before his ex-wife, Gloria, and prison. He used to daydream about the possibilities: artist; teacher; art restorer. Now what is left?

Claire sits on a vinyl, stainless steel chair that bends the kitchen light. She feels its coolness, the unyielding, stiff yellow plastic pushing against her legs through her clothes. "Can I ask you a question?"

"That depends what it is."

"Why did you go to prison?"

"Have you ever heard of Rousseau?"

"Well, sort of."

"In 1907 he went to prison. He was taken in by a swindler called Louis Sauvaget who said he was deceived by bankers. Well Rousseau felt bad for him and helped him forge documents to get some money back but Rousseau only got a small portion of the money. Then he ended up spending his share on lottery tickets that helped tubercular children."

"What about you?"

Victor stood with his back against the counters. Painted shelves decorate his torso and drawers and knobs push against his legs. He's not sure how much she'll understand. Although fifteen-year-olds are different now. "I was naive like Rousseau. It was my ex-wife, Gloria. She'd been my great love. She was my whole world. We met in high school. I was crazy about her. Well, she told me we needed money right away because she was pregnant. That I could do a painting and sign someone else's name to it and get lots of money from this rich friend a friend of hers knew. She used to come into my studio and rub my hands when it got too cold, just to encourage me. Anyway, to make a long story short, she ended up giving me to the FBI after the whole deal went through. For the money, the reward money. But I found out I was incriminated for several other forgeries Gloria's friend had done. It was a pattern. And that the baby was really her friend's child. I haven't heard from her in years and hope they are both happy together." His arms move quietly across the counters.

His partial shadow fractures her cheeks into various quadrangles and triangles. Her dark hair washing her neck. Her eyes scurry through the cupboards, mice. "I wouldn't want them to be."

"Tell me about you. Tell me about school."

No one has asked her for a long time. She closes her eyes and thinks of the brief responses to Lizzie, the receiver held to the flesh of her ear. She imagines carrier pigeons. She wants to say so much more. She thinks of the time she wanted a gun against her heart, the shot would ring out like the call of a solitary bird. But she couldn't stand all the blood. Or the time she rubbed a razor against the thin blue veins of her wrists, slightly scratching them. She doesn't know how to say those things, only their detailed descriptions in her hidden diary. She tells him instead about the man Mother wants to marry. "Mother wants to marry a man that is old with some kind of a health problem. He just made some money and he's generous. Thank God."

There is the click of Mother's heels at the kitchen door, the ticking like a bomb. Mother is finished and ready to go out: the moist, red lipstick; stockings, a clear sheath, another skin; blonde hair trembling down toward her back; and black chiffon. "Here, honey." She is digging through her purse. "Here's two dollars for dinner. I probably won't be home again tonight."

"Okay." Claire is watching Mother like a full moon making its way to the edge of the horizon and then out of sight. The door closes behind her but Claire can still see the ghostly shape of her. "She's pretty," Claire says softly. Almost to herself. She knows Mother isn't interested in Victor because he's so poor. He barely exists.

"Yes," Victor says. "And trouble."

***

Have you ever thought of painting or drawing?

Me?

No, I'm talking to the wall.

Not me. I couldn't.

Why not?

I just can't.

I wish we could meet Chagall. Then you would want to paint.

What's it like?

Painting?

Yes.

Like sex or food, only better. But you wouldn't understand.

What's it like, painting in your studio?

Sometimes, when it's going really well, I redefine time. It becomes an object with shape. At the same time I'm only thinking about the future. And what that would look like. About what I'm doing at that moment and what I will be doing. But that's when it's going well. Do you understand?

No, not really.

Chagall called his windows "the transparent division between my heart and the world's heart."

Okay.

***

Claire tiptoes silently through the hall from her bedroom. Her hair is crushed from sleep. She wears socks that have dropped to her ankles underneath her nightgown. She misses Lizzie with their nightly food raids. Now she does these things alone. Her skin slips through the darkness like an unlit candle. Her new breasts are comforted by the gauzy nightdress. She pushes open the kitchen door and then carefully turns the knob on the door of the rectangular old maid's room. He is sleeping there. Moonlight paints the room, a bony hand is flung out over the side of his bed as though he wants to be free of this sleep soon and climb out. She wants to touch a finger of this artist lightly like a good luck charm without waking him. She watches Victor sleep with a slight frown, his lips open, his breath a slight exhaling noise joining the space between them. She wants to stretch her lips over his and let his breath enter her. She looks at him for a long while and touches his inconsolable hair as tenuously as a breeze. Then she leaves.

***

Waking up, Victor greets the turned photograph of Gloria like a wayward star in the early morning. It's been years. But he remembers her lips pursing with displeasure, the thin wire of her red hair, her version of a sunset where they had to hold hands for the sun to finally sink. Romance. The dream that frames a life. He would paint her portrait with the intense bright light trying to focus her. Define her for him. Yet he knew that if he ever could predict her the knowledge would choke him as surely as an arm wrapped around his neck in his sleep. A noose. Prison, no matter how comparatively nice it was, cured him of all that, the ideals , the romance, even the betrayals.

He picks up the one book he found in this new apartment, Wallace Steven's *The Palm at the End of the Mind*, poetry left by Lizzie. Is abstraction romantic? he wonders. Chagall said "If one speaks of literature in art, he does not understand either painting or literature." He reads "Notes from a Supreme Fiction." He reads:

You must become an ignorant man again
And see the sun again with an ignorant eye
And see it clearly in the idea of it.

Claire had wanted to be Lizzie, singing the tunes from musicals from the last seven years, fascinated by the hysterical patterns of stars, scratching her way out of the square rooms of this apartment. Victor has never met her, only seen the shy resemblance to Claire in a photograph once. And Claire is Claire. Her intent eyes watching him, her reluctance for conversation, the teenage years making her limbs fall over each other. He knows he can reach her sometimes. He can see the slight red color crawl up her body and shade her face. She is listening and being heard. And her mother is never here.

***

"Don't you think she looks great, Victor?" Mother is turning Claire around in circles. Claire is wearing make-up, her hair is pulled like a stream into a clip, and she is modeling a red dress smothered with lace, white cobwebs pinned to her neckbone and wrists. Mother's drink swirls around the inside of her hand. Her lipstick rims the glass, leaving red streaks on her skin as though she has been kissing the inside of her fingers.

"Yes, she looks great."

Claire makes a funny face at Victor when Mother

can't see her. She sticks out her tongue.

"My new husband-to-be, Carl, is coming over and she has to look good." Mother takes another gulp.

Or what? Claire thinks. He won't marry you?

"Now you have to be on your best behavior." Mother has forgotten Victor already and is looking at Claire.

When the doorbell rings it is the new father-to-be. A jacket barely wraps around his middle, his white hair is steamed over his face, he is laughing already, his face and nose reddening to almost a plum color. Claire thinks: Three more years till I'm gone. What can their relationship be? If Mother is so worried about Claire it must be like chalk on a blackboard. Easily erased. It is too much for her to ponder.

He says, "I'll describe where we'll live in another few years..."

I will be gone, Claire realizes without listening. Although he doesn't know how old I really am. I will be a scribble, remembered before vanishing. Mother is nodding her head in agreement, a kewpie doll. Claire is very polite. She is contained, a flower uncurling in its own pot, holding her blossom, feeling it unfold only against her own stem.

Claire excuses herself. They are enfolded in a conversation. When she opens the maid's room door Victor is listening to the radio with his eyes closed. Music glides around them. He opens his eyelids briefly, sees her, and closes them again. As if to say: I'm not surprised.

Let me do this.

Claire unzips his pants and, as her friends instructed, thinks of a fish in her mouth, the sparkling, winnowing wetness, the slipping in and out. The moving and sliding until she succumbs to the rhythm. Victor's gasp of air. The muscle flat, done. He doesn't touch her. It is illegal. It has been a long time. He closes his eyes again and feels the length and width of the room with his mind. He understands its limitations and thinks it is elongating.

Claire returns to the living room, mirrors are reeling in the light, the curtains static in their refined etiquette. The two figures are inventing their marriage with Claire as an accompaniment. She negotiates the carpeted steps, the obstacle course of furniture. She stuffs her red dress daintily under her knees as she sits down, arranges the lace near her throat. "May I have some soda, please?"

The father-to-be says, "And there will be all the soda you'd like when we move to the new place. There will be brand new furniture, new appliances, new carpet. You'll see. Everything will be great. Just great."

Claire smiles, straightening out her dress.

***

"We have to talk about this." Victor's arms are limp against his side, his pants are crushed around his ankles. Claire's hair is pulled tight and shining to the back of her neck. Her head moves around him like music. Perhaps this is a form of conversation. His body is defused, a shadow.

Claire comes to him at his bidding. Sometimes she enters his room in the middle of the night on her own. He hears a rustling, he'll turn suddenly and she will be covering him like a sleepwalker, as though she was claiming her territory. Victor will look into her eyes and see: Mine. He will never touch her. He won't go back to prison or to jail. He doesn't have anything else except this unacknowledged contact. What they haven't talked about. Gloria's breath flutters in his ears for a moment. He feels his voice percolating through his limbs. He swallows the sound. He pulls up his pants and zips them. He sits Claire down on the bed. Out of all the buildings visible from his one window he thinks, I picked this apartment. "We need to talk."

"About what?"

"About what we do together."

"I like being with you and talking to you."

"I know. I mean about what we just did. The sex."

"Oh. I don't think of that as sex."

"What do you think of it as?"

"Something fun. Something to do with you." She doesn't have the words yet to describe it.

"You don't understand sex yet. Someday you will and it will be different. It will move you in ways that reach deep down into you. It opens you up and makes you feel vulnerable." She is looking at him with her big, brown eyes. She can't argue with him. "Some day you will leave this apartment and become yourself fully and find someone your own age." He is thinking of her unhappiness surrounding them, cocooning them like clothes.

"I hate it when people tell me what I will or won't do."

He reaches for a ribbon of her hair, holding it a minute, forgetting himself.

***

Dear Claire,

Italy is wonderful. Men swarm on a woman alone here. The weather is lovely. Stan is back in town and I've given him keys to the apartment so he can see you. Carl and I will see you soon.

***

Love, Mom

Victor painted a window on the limited walls in his studio when he first rented it. Now he can look out into a blooming garden when he wants to. He wasn't allowed to paint on anything in his cell in prison and that nearly killed him more than the food, the fighting, the limited freedom, his life reduced to its most basic activities. But he liked the solitude, moving into its flow like a water current sweeping him along. Here he mostly has that too. Closing his eyes and then opening them onto effusive flowers, the paroxysm of color, the green leaves and stems, an angle of sky, the perfect light. The scene always the same, always out his window, just waiting for him. Looking at Claire, he disassembles her. He follows the curving lines, paths. Considering her dark hair, her sharp eyes, a cheek, a throat. He gathers her together differently, rearranging her portrait, the colors to fit his concept, his idea of her. Like Picasso, later. What is it to be human? So different from a tree? Painting is about seeing. Just as Wallace Stevens said. It is about what is contained within the mind. And Claire still is unformed. She will be glad to leave home. He doesn't want to harm her in any way. He knew Gloria at fifteen, the hug of long gold earrings around her neck, the black circling her eyes like an adventure, the hair shivering across her arms was as soft as fur.

"Are you done yet?" Claire is holding her head still but her feet are shuffling around the chair.

"No, not quite yet. Can you hold still for a little while longer?" His paint brush is poised against the canvas. The window stares at him from behind her head. Flowers halo her hair. Turpentine, acrid, sharp, and the thick, wet, earthy smell of oil paint fills their inconsolable nostrils, rummages through their bodies and clothes.

"I don't know. No. Probably not. I need to get up and walk around." Her elbow cracks as her shirt sleeve reaches for the ceiling. She is already rising, stretching, and walking toward him.

"I tried to have sex two days ago," she tells him, coming around the canvas to see the little work he has completed. To see his reaction.

"What do you mean tried?"

"I mean we tried." She's slightly annoyed.

"Usually you either do or you don't."

"Well, David...", she's aware of having his full attention, "...that's the guy's name. He tried to put it in but I closed up. It was like a clam. We couldn't do anything. Have you ever heard of that?"

"Yes, it means you aren't ready." He has become her confidante. He is more comfortable with this role rather than possible jail material.

She goes to her chair and sits down. She positions herself just so in the embrace of the still, damp air. The flowers lining her face give her cheeks color. Victor sees her eyelashes rise like two butterflies toward him. The crease of her lips. He wonders what she is thinking. "I'm ready," she says to the hand of the artist.

***

Dear Claire,

London is wonderful. Carl and I are having a great time. And guess what, honey? We got married. We'll get married again in the U.S. See you soon, sweetheart.

Love, Mom

***

Mother is back and pulling textures and colors from her luggage in fistfuls. Dresses and shirts fall across her bed, some onto the floor. Her movements are reflected many times in the prism of the overhead chandelier as if there is a movie of Mother unpacking on many screens. There is a large diamond near her left knuckle, sparkling and sending unintentional light across her headboard like an inscription.

"What do you think of Carl?" she asks Claire, who is sitting in a chair watching her with her legs crossed.

"He's okay." She can't say what she really thinks.

"They all seem great and then once you marry them it all seems to go downhill." She pulls out some mosaic earrings with pink and green designs and hands them to Claire. "Here, these are for you." She is in her stockinged feet with her high heels laying on their sides, forlorn on the carpet.

"Thanks. These are nice." Claire holds the earrings up above her chin.

"Carl will be moving into this apartment in a few weeks." She stops and looks at Claire, descending pink and green birds at her ears.

"What will happen to Victor?" Claire feels her heart fluttering but she tries not to show her concern.

"Oh, he can stay here for a while. But we'll be moving soon to a great big new apartment." She hesitates. "At least we better be."

Claire knows Mother likes getting exactly what she wants. Claire wouldn't cross her. Claire is glad Victor can stay. At least for a while.

"Has Stan called you or come by?"

"No. Do you think he will?"

"I don't know." Mother has completed unpacking, her embroidered bedspread is slightly furrowed. She sits on the bed and turns to Claire. "So how's your sex life?" She is seeking a dialogue, a chance to discuss her own. As though Claire would tell her anything.

***

Claire pulls out the worn gray diary.

Dear Diary,

Will somebody ever love me? I am on the borderline of depression today. I want to invent a father: Stan's patience (before he erupts but not his creepiness), Victor's knowledge and kindness. I don't know Carl. Sigh. We'll have to see how he is. I wish I could dissolve some of the men and make a father soup.

School is okay but has no relevance to my life. One of the teachers called me "Lizzie" last week. I'm so anti-social. I have only a few friends. While watching TV last night I started to cry at absolutely nothing. I'm tired of not being seen for myself. But who am I?

I'm not one of the snots at school. Or a painter. Or a poet like Lizzie. I know I'm not Mother with her handbook of what to do and who to do it with, screeching at me about how I ruined all her other relationships and don't do nice things for her. She is crazy. Some days she doesn't even pretend to like me. I don't like her too much either. At least Mother's men aren't coming in and out of our house anymore. They would all hang their coats on the same chair and give me an embarrassed smile. Then quickly disappear into her bedroom. That is, if she had children that day. Even Carl has started asking me about my sex life. What sex life? I want to ask them. Nothing works.

The air chokes me today. I'm lonely. Lizzie is gone and I feel very little hope. And then I think nothing will ever change. I can't imagine feeling differently. I used to dream about dying: the nothingness. Now there is David. At least he is my own age. I can look at him at school and wave and think that there are parts of him that are all mine right now. I hope he's not a season, here and then gone. Like everything else.

Some days I believe I'm a building. Where it doesn't matter who goes in or comes out, I still feel cold, hard, and untouchable. Victor says I'll grow out of it. That I have a lot of love to give and get.

He says I'll grow out of everything. That it's all a phase. And then what's left? Is what's left me? I guess I'm whatever falls to the granite floor and stays.

***

Mother calls Lizzie at college, "I want you to tell your father to leave me alone." Her bedroom is paralyzed by light, nothing moves except sunlight and Mother. Her furniture and papers are quiet and still.

"He said to tell you that there isn't anyone moaning in the apartment next door to him anymore. And anyway you both live in the same city now. Can't you talk to each other? I'm not your relay messenger." But Lizzie knows that is exactly what she is right now. Even many miles away and by long distance.

Mother ignores her anyway. "Carl and I were married in London. We're going to make it legal here also. You don't need to come. He'll be moving into this apartment in a few weeks. I'll send you the new keys for the door."

"How's marriage?" (A new variation on the sex life question). Lizzie watches the moon rise over new cement dorm buildings in the small, sleepy Ohio town. Room after room identical to her own. The tranquillity of familiarity, of sameness and belonging to a group. She could see her shadow move like a curtain in moonlight against the plasterboard wall. She rests her elbow against the cheap, normal, particle board, built-in study desk. Lizzie likes the concept of not taking up a lot of space, living with the minimal, not overextending herself in the world. Her torn blue jeans fray along the sharp angles of the wooden chair.

"I'm hoping for the best. After all, Carl said 'money is made to be enjoyed and given away.'" Mother is looking at the smooth edges of her fingernails.

"Your kind of man." Lights are beginning to go on in the dorm rooms, reminding Lizzie of an unfinished sentence. She is lulled by their distance, their safe, immutable distance.

"Don't say anything, Lizzie, but I met this really interesting man yesterday. He's Italian with long, curly hair. Probably the Mafia." She's watching her diamond swim through the partial darkness of the room.

"Ma, you just got married. Lay off just a little bit. Give it a rest." Lizzie decides the stars she can see out her single window look like graceful winnows, indistinguishable from one another at this distance. All shining. "You really are incredible."

"Yeah, I'm one feisty lady." The diamond turns on its side.

"How old am I supposed to be for Carl?" She can imagine the stars with visages and small, talking mouths.

"Seventeen."

"How can that be? Where am I now?"

"You're at boarding school."

"Which one?"

"The one named after a saint."

"Which one?" Lizzie doesn't like making it easy for her.

"Oh, we'll worry about that when you get here." She is bored with Lizzie. "Let me see if Claire's here. Claire!" she calls.

Claire comes into Mother's bedroom in her blue jeans. "Yes."

"It's Lizzie on the phone." Mother gets up and leaves, giving Claire her seat on the wrinkled bed with abundant flower petals unfurling over one another. She leaves a large, round, warm indentation.

"Hi." Mother is looking at some papers covering

her desk.

"Hi. It's great to hear your voice. Is she still there?"

"Yes."

"I'll ask you yes or no questions. How are things there, Okay?"

"Sort of yes, sort of no."

"I heard she got married. How is he?"

"Okay." Mother exits the room and Claire exhales, waits until she hears the television speaking to anyone who will listen in the living room. "Oh, Lizzie, it's lonely here. Mother's either gone or busy. Or even worse, still around. You know how she is. At least Victor will get to stay until Carl comes to live here."

"Hang in there. I know it's hard but you don't have much longer." Lizzie is assessing the chair that has collected her clothes for days. Its shadow could be a mountain lion ready to pounce or an unending human back.

"I love you."

"I love you too. Call me collect anytime." The pattern of leaves from trees sinking into the darkness rolls down her legs. The musical chair game played by their ever-changing fathers. Who will sit down and stay and who will be left out? She feels bad for Claire, left at home. Lizzie turns on the light as she leaves the dorm room, as if the space was occupied. Some ghostly figure. A shadow's shadow. The light from under the door follows the aimless direction of her feet.

***

Claire listens to her breath rising and falling. This is a winter when things are jumbled up and slip away. The astronomers lose sight of a star in their powerful telescopes. It is there one minute and gone the next, they declare. Some of the fish off Long Island are swimming backwards without explanation. Claire is unsure: bored or sick or both? No one can tell her. No one knows. In the large mirror is a knot of light, colors and shapes defining the morning. She watches it change slowly for a while. Claire's hair reaches for the edges of the pillow. Victor and Carl, Stan and David are all mixed up. She can't distinguish between them. As if they represent aspects of one person. Men. Women are not necessarily better. Different disguises. The zigzagging around what they want. The landscape is so full of lies that it is hard to tell what is real and what isn't. Was there really a star there to disappear into the night to begin with? Can fish swim backwards? Claire's toes curl like starfish at the bottom of this ocean of a bed. That way she knows they are still there. She can actually see them wiggling.

She hears yelling in the apartment hallway. The noise of men's voices reverberates inside her apartment where she is alone. Claire pulls on yesterday's disheveled pants and shirt and socks from the floor, she scurries to Victor's room but he isn't there and Mother is out. She heard her leave at least an hour ago. A shred of panic tears in her like a page ripping down the middle. It is still a page but it is in two pieces. Separated. She recognizes one of the voices: Victor's deep lilt. He is screaming just outside the front door. She puts her ear and tangled hair against the thick wood.

"What the hell are you doing?" He is shouting.

Another man, "Fuck you."

"Ow. Goddam you."

What is going on? Is Victor having a fight with some painter, or some ex-prisoner? Claire timidly opens the peephole. She puts one frightened eye to the glass. She sees Stan in a rage pulling Victor by the hair across the carpet. The fleur-de-lis from the wallpaper covering them in their struggle. The peephole limits her range of sight into a small circle and she attempts to move her head around. She locks the door very quietly. The dim hallway light pooling in the indentations of an arm, the crook of a neck, a shock of hair. Victor's hair.

"Fucking my wife, are you?" Stan yells and Claire notices a rain of spit from his mouth watering the carpet.

"No, you stupid idiot. I'm not."

Claire views vignettes of Victor with his pants down in the maid's room, in his studio. His face resembles a discarded towel. His hair flipping forward. He was not fucking Mother. They rarely even talked to one another. Besides she is no longer Stan's wife. Stan doesn't seem to hear a word Victor is saying. He begins to shake, his eyes are glaring down the hallway. He seems full of an energy Claire has not seen before, can't identify, his muscles pulling him apart. He lets go of Victor's graying hair. Victor is shoeless, sweating, panting. Claire can only watch parts of them through the tiny peephole. They float into her vision and fade down the long corridor.

"You cowardly faggots on this hall. Watch this, why don't you." Stan wraps Victor's bolo tie around his neck, choking him. He is talking to the neighbors at their peepholes, animals curiously watching a fight to see who will win. Claire is frightened by Stan's eyes, by his hard breath, wondering if he could really kill Victor for no reason at all. She is uncertain what her father has become. Victor had to know what to do because of prison. Claire didn't. Should she call the police? Probably not. Their faces surface. Victor has Stan's raging arms in his hands. He is bending them.

"Fuck you too." Claire hears Victor say. The elevator door rolls open on this floor and shuts again under the starless, New York sky. Claire can't see whether anyone tried to get off or not. She just knows it's gone. Her father lies alone on the floor like some lost doll dropped by a careless child. Just as she wishes he would go away he stands up, scours the hallway, stares straight at Claire's eye concealed by the tiny hole. He dusts himself off and goes down the elevator. He is shaking his head.

Claire thinks about a self-portrait Victor completed at the studio. Crazy with shape and color. No comfort in the texture of the skin. Nose rearranged and light blue. An emptiness near the white hair, an expanse of forehead. The ubiquitous eyes were full of pity. A sadness among the landlocked ears. The sea was in the background.

Victor knocks on the door softly, breathing hard. He enters the apartment, gathers his few possessions to take to the studio, some photographs from his pre-prison life, a lamp made from a wine bottle, clothes, the few books he recently acquired. "He was waiting for me when I took my garbage to the incinerator. So I'm going." And he remembers prison. The sudden attacks on other prisoners or attempts on guards. But, he thinks, they did something to provoke it. They knew it would probably be coming.

Claire wants to tie him to the bed so he can't leave. Instead she proclaims, "You are lucky." Not about Stan. Sorry, she wants to say, apologizing for her father.

"Here," he says, giving her a pencil drawing of a graceful model with long, curvaceous lines. He holds his pillowcase full of his possessions between his legs, ready to leave near the kitchen door.

"Thanks." She smoothes the corners with her fingernails. "Who is it?" She glances at his ruffled hair, disheveled features, a few pronounced lacerations.

Victor looks at her, finally smiling with his scratched

cheeks. His hand on the doorknob. "You," he says walking out the door.

**

Mother comes home to the glass and marble apartment, the phone ringing, Claire's tears dropping into the chipped enamel bowl saved for terrible stomach illnesses. She puts down the paper shopping bags with women's names etched along their sides.

"Hello," her lipstick smears the tip of the receiver. "They hung up on me." She places the receiver back into the corner of the phone. "What's going on?"

Claire tells her in the almost dark blue living room. She gives Mother fragments of Stan and Victor, leaving out the drawing he gave her. "The struggle," she keeps on saying. She speaks about the nervous peepholes opening aligned in a row along the hallway. The neighbors' eyes watching. No one said anything, no one came. The enamel bowl is awash with dampness. Claire is still crying. Victor is gone.

Mother clears her nose. "We'll see."

Just then they hear a loud thudding sound like a slight earthquake or a truck nudging the building. The floor vibrates as if to the steady beat of music under their feet. Claire's eyes widen. She stops crying. They follow the sound, noise detectives. They hear the noise in every room they enter and leave. Claire believes the whole building is moving to another spot. The constant clanging climbs into her skull as though someone keeps ringing the doorbell, trying to get in. She can feel the skin on her arms jump in unison. She has goosebumps and the hair near her elbows stands straight up in alarm, bristling. Right now she misses the silence, the loneliness, the boredom. Gossamer birds plummet into her stomach. Mother is irritated, a swimmer shifting her weight around to find the best path to go through a current.

It is from the kitchen. They weave their way there and Claire hesitates at the threshold. The back door is pounding. They can see it shaking from several feet away. Claire begins to hate the kitchen door. After everything she has seen there she hopes the entire room will disappear. Mother spreads out her fingers and presses them against the loud door. She opens the peephole. "Stan," she whispers.

Claire should have known.

They hear him now. "This is my house. My home. Let me in. You can't change the locks on the goddamn door. Let me in, you whore."

Mother backs away from the door as if it is on fire. Her arms and legs are shaking. "He has a crowbar," she whispers. Claire hears what Mother says without listening to her. Stan is hammering at the door even more vigorously now that he knows someone is on the other side. He noticed the slide of the peephole cover and the small magnifier shifting the light almost imperceptibly. Then it closed again, right above his head. He has a renewed energy. Mother's face drips down to her feet. She loses all her color. Claire holds a chair as though it could anchor her. But the chair is dancing too. Why can't I fly away, she thinks, and let them kill each other. She is frightened, her clothes separate from her body and flutter in fear. Mother's hands are agitated, flying around the kitchen cabinets, looking for a tool to send Stan away. Mother wishes she had a gun. Time is moving so slowly for them that Claire knows Stan will break down the door soon. She can taste the metal and wood falling apart in between her teeth. It is the dust in the air. And there is the constant pounding, a headache that doesn't go away.

"Should we call the police?" Claire whispers to the curved shell of Mother's ear. Her blonde hair is wispy over the opening like an overgrown plant. Or will he really kill us? she wonders. She doesn't know what to do.

"Yes." Mother dials the number and speaks. When she is done she says loudly to Stan, "I dialed the police and they should be here any minute. So scram."

"You whore. It's my house," he mumbles, hitting the door harder and faster with the crowbar as if it was Mother's skull.

The door creaks. Mother and Claire look at each other. They are frozen. They stand close to one another, not touching. Claire is too scared to cry. She wants to hold Mother's hand but is too afraid of that too. She holds her own trembling leg instead. Their fear rises up, evaporating into the ceiling, leaving their bodies motionless in the kitchen. They can see the top of Stan's head, his slick, dark hair through a piece of the door. He is working furiously. Wood splinters and dust fall onto the linoleum floor. He is breaking down the thick wood door and they are running out of time. They don't know what more to do. The sound isn't as terrifying anymore. They are getting used to the rhythm of it. But to see through a hole and into the hall and to actually see Stan breaking in is startling. Claire silently clenches and opens her fists. The hole is getting bigger.

Finally. It seems like forever. The police come. Claire and Mother hear the elevator doors and men's voices. They can see a flash of metal and blue uniforms through the broken door. The banging and ripping stops. Stan goes away fairly quietly with them. They hear him say, "Okay, okay," his hands in the air. Mother collapses into a kitchen chair. Claire resumes her crying.

Sticks and Stones, Stan, 1972

A domestic squabble, the police call it. Their useless lights in Stan's eyes. His dark hair wild, tearing into space, crawling toward the fleur-de-lis. His arm with the crowbar grows slack, forgetting. His wet face becomes as quiet as a stone. He will not remember this, this dance in the growing night. He already can't remember where he got the crowbar. Was it his car? Or the drugstore tucked in the bottom of the apartment building? Who would lend a man a crowbar and let him walk out their business door? He won't remember what he doesn't want to. His shame touches him on the shoulder twenty years later in the middle of a mall and he cries and cannot stop.

He wishes life were simpler, easier. Married for nineteen years and she locks him out of the apartment he paid for. She discards him like some map for a place she will never travel to.

He does remember meeting her and her family and taking her to the Philadelphia aquarium to kiss while red and blue fish navigated past their embraces. Water full of bubbles and fins and scales swaying by their intertwined bodies. He remembers the wet touch of her lips and how much he wanted to marry her.

But he can't go back there. Their lists of bruises. The inhalation of her he can't have. And he knows her so well: her tea hair covers her eyes in the morning; the long baths with water uncovering the undulant parts of her body like an island landscape; her rages dismantling furniture, scratching the flesh from his hands. Flowers, cards, nothing appeased her except expensive presents.

He tells his dates he hates her. Her inaccessibility,

her unnaturalness. The pain. He doesn't even know how to reach her. And yet he chose her. For nineteen years. His dates nod. They have heard it before, the hate grown from love. The pain.

He doesn't mean to scare away his dates, these women he meets, waitresses, salesgirls, cashiers. Accessible. The only people he talks to outside of work. Their red fingernails clink on formica tables, against drinking glasses when he gets going. They turn their tired, iridescent blue lidded eyes toward the ceiling when he's not looking. They don't share his little life ringed by the familiar pain. In their own lives he is a pebble dropped in water, a concentric ripple a woman brushes away with her hand. He is insignificant compared to the problems of her own husband, money or children. He has not adjusted to his own shrinking importance, to his lack of a family life.

Yet every woman is a possibility. A matter of sustaining his interest. Mother didn't sleep with him before they were married. But they came close one night on her parent's couch, tossing around the pillows like extra limbs. Until her parent's headlights came through the Philadelphia window, over their heads, staring from the wall, two large eyes. He wants those promises fulfilled.

Stan is deep in the cocoon of his own thoughts in a beanbag chair at his new apartment. He believes he can feel each individual muscle in his body if he closes his eyes and concentrates enough. He can move them at will.

The only time he ever hurt anyone was the bridal salesgirl whose mother died. He had to slap her to stop her screams and sobs when she hung up the phone. It was a grisly auto accident and the other salesgirls told him to stop her because she kept seeing her mother's head rolling along a highway ditch. He hit her reluctantly.

He drives his car a lot when he isn't at work or on

a date. The lights mesmerize him at night, the passing landscape seems to blur by day. He finds himself on long highways with no idea how to get home. His children are becoming women, more complicated mysteries he can't comprehend. He is closer to Claire because she tells him more, calls him "Father" or "Dad" sometimes on the telephone. He needs to be reminded. Lizzie is further away, physically but also emotionally at college in Ohio. She gives Mother messages.

He cuts his hair shorter and visits a therapist who discusses "relationships." On the phone with Claire he says he's trying to "maintain their relationship" as though it is a living creature that has to be fed periodically. One that he would never understand. He worries about his "relationship" to Mother. Claire thinks: what "relationship"? He starts to imagine relationships where none exist. With operators exchanging numbers across telephone lines, with men innocently walking their dogs on the city streets, with the author of a mystery novel he has just finished reading. He decides a "relationship" is the basis for all communication.

He willingly allows his apartment to confine him, a caged bird able to peer out the enormous windows overlooking several New York streets. He watches people, trying to determine what they are doing or are supposed to be doing. A young couple stop an elderly man on the corner. Asking for change or directions or just plain crazy? Who can tell. He shuffles from window to window on long, thin legs. At night he watches other apartment buildings shellacked to the dark sky like a Chinese screen unfolding its landscapes. He sees tidbits of other people's activities. He lives through their windows. This anonymous apartment, all glass and chrome, modern, with an exercise room on another floor, is where a lot of singles also live. He has very little furniture, a few angular chairs, a table, a bed, a bean bag chair in front of a television. All replaceable. There is nothing of him that resides here, nothing left of anyone's history to put on a fireplace mantle, if there was one.

And Stan is afraid of Mother. He dreams she is a bird, a small colorful type that plucks out his eyes slowly and carefully while he cannot move. The bird ignores his cluttered heart below. He knows now that he cannot be in the same room with her. She knows him well enough to dismantle him, step on the remaining pieces and throw him away. He smokes and drinks more until he can no longer see her face. It fades into an alcoholic blur, tinged with nicotine, a sepia photograph from long ago.

***

Summer light from Stan's black lace shoes darts across his jawbone. He is standing behind the glass entrance of his clothing store in Brooklyn. His name is etched on the other side. He is surrounded by various clothes on hangers, whispering across the space of the room, the silver racks reach all over the floor, spreading up into the second floor and blossoming into frilly white bridal gowns in the back. Fitting rooms and mirrors are tucked into the corners. The ceilings are large and the rooms echo slightly so sounds grow larger and seem to multiply into similar noises. The fluorescent lights are on and the store has been open for several hours. There are not many customers. Perhaps two or three women browsing, admonishing the chiffon or silk, running their fingers over the clothing surfaces in large parabolas. Lizzie is working at the store in "Dresses" in the back. It is her first job besides baby-sitting and she's working along with several women recently out of prison.

One woman has a white jagged scar like a river zigzagging down the side of her cheek with flesh tufting out around its hard polish, its tight seam. Lizzie has worked there a few days selling and rearranging clothes, having asked Stan months ago for the job. She doesn't talk much to anyone. Her feet scatter back and forth across the solid floor and ache at night. Stan is tapping his pants leg with his fingers as he is looking onto the street. He thinks of cigarette smoke curling through his fingers and into the Brooklyn air. He can almost taste it. Lizzie is watching some dust dancing around the legs of a dress rack near the tips of her shoes. The phone rings. Lizzie can hear it ringing after a woman picks it up and shouts down the stairs, "Stan, it's the ex for you."

He runs upstairs past Lizzie and the dust around her shoes swirls frenetically. He goes into his private office upstairs where Lizzie and anyone else can see him pacing, gesturing, his neck turning redder. Lizzie thinks about never getting married, about all the white ornamentation and decoration upstairs to use when you do. She doesn't think he will explode like he did months ago with Claire and Mother in the apartment. Mother said he would probably be fine, quieter, subdued, ashamed. "Cooled off." Claire said, "But you can't be sure. Perhaps he's like a time bomb. Boom." And her hands flew into the air. Lizzie feels a sheen of sweat from her neck to her underarms. She realizes she doesn't really know him.

She closes her eyes and remembers how she bit Claire after she was born, her blood was a red streak against Lizzie's new teeth. She feels the dust settle onto her skin from oversized, polyester women's dresses in bright patterns. She tries to hear the words contained within the thickly walled office but only thinks she can discern the start or end of words reverberating within the closed room. She opens her eyes to the clothes' demanding colors and sorts through them. She's in college and feels too old. He is her father and she will refuse to be afraid of him.

Stan's ears are ringing when he slams the phone down with its stinging, disembodied voice. He felt her presence in the store, his remaining territory, when she accused him of taking the savings bonds her parents gave to Claire and Lizzie. He did. But he is angry she discovered him, the true self of him even he doesn't want to meet. He denied it. Uselessly. It is as if he invents another person he can slip into by denying it. He is also this other person, better in many ways, someone he can create and perhaps become. The money is gone like a rabbit disappearing into a hat. So she took the opportunity to tell him who she believes he is: a dirty, rotten, little thief. He had much to tell her too. "I don't give a shit what you think."

"You are the lowest, most disgusting scum, taking the girls' savings bonds that their grandparents left for them. I wish they weren't dead, my father would show you. What did you do, sign their names?"

"And what about you, you took my money and the apartment I paid for."

"Are we going to start that shit all over again?"

And here. Where he works and she's not allowed. He feels his forehead burn, his cheeks redden, the veins in his neck pulsing with his heartbeat, an animal in rhythm with its own savage music, its instinctual timing. He doesn't think about her words but their aftermath agitates him. As if he was set over a roasting grill and taken down so even if his flesh is burned now at least he can no longer feel the fire. He wants a cigarette badly. To have the tart smoke running through him, a calming bitter tasting part of him. His legs are moving and nothing will stop him.

His hand is on the cigarette pack in his suit pants pocket. Down the stairs he sees Lizzie and in the edges of her he notices the resemblance to his ex. She is sorting through dresses as if in slow motion. As he passes her he says, "You are fired." He is on his way out the glass door, a cigarette between his fingers. "Because of your mother" as he is out the door.

Lizzie swallows her words. They become thoughts that pass through her mind so quickly she cannot acknowledge them. And yet they are a part of her. Lizzie is not shaking with fear but with anger. She drops the too large dresses on the floor and puts a dusty footprint against the crumpled, empty material. It is a branding, a logo. To remind her never to come back. She cannot accept anything from her parents. The summer sun bounces from the corners of buildings outside and sticks to the wall inside the store, beckoning her. As she moves through the glass door into the sunlit street she wants to bury this job in her memory on her way home. She no longer needs her parents. And she won't speak to Stan for twenty more years.

***

Stan glares at Claire sitting primly and uncomfortably in the witness seat at court. Lizzie is at college. But Mother is there in a Chanel pink buttoned suit, her blond hair pulled back into the shape of a doorknob whose shine reflects the whole room, distorting the scene, making everything appear wider, fatter. She stares at Claire and won't take her eyes off of her. Claire is in a dress, tights, and shoes, a growing child. Claire is speaking. At least her lips are moving and sentences are coming out like a cluster of balloons evaporating as they reach the tall ceiling of this official room. Stan cannot hear her. He feels his blood pulsing in spurts against the inside of his jacket pockets. The redness creeps up his neck clawing at his face. His own body holds him in its angry grip. How can Claire do this to him? His favorite. He remembers her baby face crawling toward him with the pads of her Doctor Dentons trailing her feet. They want the child support money he cannot give. It seems that they always want money from him. Something he doesn't have enough of himself. He feels everyone reaching into the air of that room as though he is a magician that could make money appear or as though a miracle would occur. Instead everyone closes their fists around nothing. The judge and the attorneys drone on and on. The court room is ornate. The murals of some ancient gods seem involved with the proceedings and consult one another. Their curly white hair blends with clouds. The trees and hills are a place he would rather be. He imagines himself there, leaping after a bird, his feet thundering with the gods against the earth. He jumps into the sky so high he is almost flying, leaves brush past his nose, clouds open their snowy arms. He is far away. The other figures are as small as strewn ants scattered against meadows. He waves but they cannot see him any longer. He can feel the warmth of the sun pressing through his clothes. Then there is silence. A man, his attorney, turns to him and says, "I'm sorry we lost. You owe all the back support and expenses. You aren't allowed in New York state until it's all paid."

Synchronously wooden chairs scrape the floor and the roomful of people start to leave. "Wait," Stan says, "I didn't do it. Whatever it is. I didn't do it." He says to the backs of people already out the door.

***

Claire waits to visit Stan at his apartment as they arranged
weeks ago. She sits in her blue jeans and a tie-dyed shirt
outside his metal door, smooth except for the peephole, a
tiny, round ridge. He's never late. He's usually at least ten
minutes early. She has rung the doorbell several times in
the last three hours. She anticipates the opening, electronic doors of the elevator as dirt from strangers' footsteps coats her pants legs, the heels of her palms. The
elevator stopped briefly once on this floor, rang its fretful
bell, shuffling open, empty, making an electronic error,
closing, shifting downward again. She can hear it sweeping up and down, whirring, searching, carrying passen-
gers the length of this modern building. She brushes his
"welcome" straw doormat with her wrist as she rises,
agitated, to call Mother. On the street outside articulated
with cars rolling past her, their engines greeting her, she
drops a coin into the pay phone and Mother says "I'll be
right there."

When Mother arrives with two policemen Claire is
sobbing plaintively. Worried. A cog in the mechanism of
adult communication, relationships. Mother hugs her,
feigns her own granular, crocodile tears, dabs her eyes
with an embroidered handkerchief, foliage on linen hiding her careless, thick eyelashes. "I think he might be
dead" she declares to the officers. The apartment manager
opens Stan's metal door and the bachelor apartment is
bare, devoid of furniture, no trace of food, deserted, stuffy
and hot as though no one has lived there for months.

The War, Stan, 1945

The Philadelphia apartment seems as if it has always been ensconced in plastic. At least the very first room anyone walks into, the living room, has several chairs and two sofas covered in thick, clear, tight fitting plastic. It is cheap, modern furniture, not old, valuable antiques. Plastic enhances the carpet like see-through frosting on a new cake. The two wooden tables, an end table and a coffee table, are suffused with shine like a pomade because no one is allowed there, no one is allowed to touch anything. Everything is exceptionally neat and perfectly preserved. Pillows are extremely clean, upright. Not a particle of dirt in the beige rug covered with plastic. Curtains are perfectly pleated, pure white. All the table tops are tidy, unblemished. A landscape of clear, crinkly hills, the untouchable valleys. Colors beckon from beneath the surface. It always looks as though no one lives there.

Stan is just back from the war and all he can think about is sex and its expediency. The provocative peach buttons on a woman's dress down the street as she stopped a moment for her dog to sniff a fire hydrant. He had noticed how the seams on her stockings disappeared up her legs.

His mother is in the small backyard clamoring with insects. He hears the wincing water underneath her continual "harumph"s. A word she grinds between her teeth every few minutes either because of an ingrained habit or to show how displeased she is with everything around her. As she waters and harumphs he can hear plants scraping their pots, asking when they can leave.

After being abroad in the Navy on a ship going

from port to port, paying for the willing girls unable to speak much English, Philadelphia feels provincial. His grandparents were Austrian Jews who learned English by reading the newspaper and then using it as toilet paper. When they came to America they began retail and bridal clothing stores with the family name, Lowenstein, years ago. It is his inheritance. His younger brother is interested only in opera with its dignified arias, its escape into glamour and music, betrayal and longing with dramatic and final resolutions. His younger sister, lovely and smart and refined in soft sweaters, seems to be following the clouds ahead of her, nose in the air, breathing deeply. She giggles to her girlfriends when Stan is behind her.

He removes a picture frame from a conclave near the meticulously scrubbed and disinfected kitchen. It is the photograph of a five-year-old child in a dress, with long, beautiful dark hair sweeping past her shoulders filled with ribbons. No smile, slightly chubby arms and legs. It is a picture of Stan who was dressed as a girl until he was six years old. Perhaps his mother missed the girl that died before he was ever born. He doesn't really know. Every time he asks his mother she sprouts a headache. All his needs or questions conclude with one of her headaches. His poor father.

He scratches the seam of skin, puckered in an irregular circle, around his kneecap. He thinks of the metal, a big coin, lodged at the bend in his leg like some lozenge that doesn't dissolve. It itches daily, docilely. He hates being back home except for his father with a bird twittering around his heart and his angina pills, his blue eyes scampering with the energy and light of his personality.

His mother sees him and clutches at the wind as though in its disobedience it could steady her. She puts the watering can next to the fence, pats her hair with her palm and walks inside the apartment.

"You're back," she exclaims, touching her still perfectly coiffed hair, filled with curls and hairspray, with both hands. She leans over the space between them pecking him on both cheeks with fractional kisses. "Harumph," the interruptive comment. "So how was the Navy?"

"Fine, Mother." He looks around the apartment, is unsure if he is allowed to sit anywhere. He imagines the thick plastic stuck to the back of his pants legs like another skin. "I'll have to show you my scar. It itches like anything. You know they had to give me a blood transfusion and they gave me a Negro's blood."

"Harumph" she says loudly. She turns away. "I don't want to hear about it. Harumph." She is in a beige dress with silk stockings. Her face powder and make-up are flawless even after being in the yard. She hasn't touched her children in years unless she absolutely had to.

"Mother?" The sky is the color of pearls behind her head. He wants a cigarette. Badly. He sees the mask of her face, the cold, indifferent eyes.

"Harumph."

"Where's my trumpet? The one I love." He had scoured his old bedroom for his companion, the hours they spent together with music flooding the arguments with his mother, her disapproval, the growing up they enacted together song by song. It was his own voice, sweet, melancholy, unheard. And he could hear traces of his own sound on the ship in the swing music of Harry James and Bunny Berrigan. He swallowed during the silence, wishing he could rub the pencil sized cigarette between his fingers, hold it close to a match, feel the slow burn, the ignition.

"There." She points to a corner of the room where

on a waxed table is a shiver of brassy light, a lamp with a
stiff, white hat of a lampshade. Polished, smooth, buttons
in rows as on a coat, the curved metal lines, the string to
turn it on and off. It takes him a minute to realize what the
ridiculous lamp is. Assimilated. Varnished. Cleaned and
silly. He is furious. What right did she have? Did she hope
he wouldn't come back?

"Mother, how could you?" he manages. Redness
glazes his neck, tiptoes up his chin. His new metal kneecap
shakes. His hands are implacable, forming fists. He is
weary of the injustices. He unravels in the very tidy house.

"Harumph," she utters and walks into another
room. He wishes the bone-white sky would choke her, this
woman who will live to be almost one hundred years old.

***

Stan is up early, before anyone. He is eating Mallomars,
marshmallow and cracker cookies covered with chocolate,
and milk straight out of the carton before anyone comes
into the spotless kitchen. Little dark crumbs fall like freckles onto the clean, orange floor. He is thinking about
wiping them up. He is thinking about a woman with blond
hair and large breasts in the Pacific. She was learning
English and said to Stan, "Would you like subscription
now or later?" He was never sure what she meant even
when he screwed her and her eyes turned up into her head
like lidded nipples. Pornographic magazines are fraying
from his bed here, tucked into the brightly patterned
sheets. What is he doing here? He'll work in his father's
store. A nice place to visit but he wouldn't want to live
here.

His father shuffles in wearing a stained terrycloth
robe. His father and mother have slept in separate rooms

as long as he can remember and have very different hygiene. He always seems to be smiling, his bright blue eyes dancing. He is good natured. "I always promised you we'd go to a ballgame. So I'll get ready and we'll go. How does that sound?"

"Great, just the two of us?" Stan feels like a small child again, anticipating, the excitement of a fulfilled promise. Yet he has recently seen too much of the world.

"Yes," and he smiles at his son. "I'll tell Mother."

Harumph, Stan thinks. And his father wobbles toward the bedrooms holding his robe tightly, in a ball, at his open chest.

Stan cleans his crumbs, carefully brushing them into a pan and into the garbage. He closes the milk container, wiping it, placing it gently in the refrigerator. He combs his dark hair, raking it into furrows, strands going their own individual ways, yet all towards one apparently invisible goal. He uses the stainless steel toaster to see his reflection, a restless snapshot. He stands there a few minutes and says to himself under his breath, "Not bad." It has been at least half an hour since his father went upstairs. Oh, well. He's impatient for the flowering of his father's laughter, the baseball thrown in the ballpark from hand to hand, just the two of them, close, raucous, mentioning women obliquely like a river brushing its hard pebbles and yet so transparently you can see the autumn colors of the stones underneath.

It is his mother that steps into the kitchen. Retrospectively he'll think that she walks leisurely, casually, lingering at the threshold. She is fully made-up, her hair in place, but she is in a fresh, blue robe the color of his father's eyes and wrapped tightly around her body. She frowns.

"Harumph. Henry's heart seems to have exploded.

I just called an ambulance."

"No baseball today," he says, but it isn't what he means. She looks at him as he falls into the pellucid, thick, celluloid arms of a chair.

The World and its Gold, Mother, 1972

Watergate and President Nixon. Even Mother knows there is so much a person needs to keep to herself. The names are a sky dense with birds that never seem to land: age, men, places. She remembers a vacation she took with another model to Rome, Italy last year. The fashionable clothes piled into three rooms like a jungle. The colors, the heat, buyers, sellers, and models congregating around hangers and racks in shifting formations like fish surfacing for food or religious supplicants exhorting a prayer. The mix of flowery perfumes and deep fruits and spices and, underneath it all, a tinge of sweat. Summer. She could feel the temperature pressing its steady fingers against her wet throat. And a man in a pinstriped suit emerged and touched the dampness at the back of her neck, under her hair. She felt her attention gravitate there. His fingertips were flies buzzing around their meaningless exchange, their constant patter, diverting her wandering concentration. She unwittingly flirted with him. "What big, strong hands you have." Unthinkingly. Unconsciously. As though it were a fairy tale. Not too hot, not too cold. Your hands are just right for this moment. Their eyes were locked together. A fin steadied in the surface of his iris. "How smart of you," Mother said and their bodies said something else. She gave him her hotel room phone number. She was relieved when he moved away into the din, the heat resembled a person he walked right through, banishing the heavy air into the corners. His fingertips gone. The back of his jacket with its thin, pinstripes swaying, lasciviously wavering, a shoal of reflective water in a heat wave. She wiped the perspiration from the jagged necklace of small bones at the nape of her neck.

She decided not to see him that night, her last night in Rome. She'd be in London soon. She didn't answer the hotel phone at six p.m. when he rang. Or at seven p.m. or eight p.m. when he also rang. Then at nine p.m. when he began calling every fifteen minutes. The other model told her to stop this or she would throw her out of the hotel room and lock her out. "Don't bother," Mother said and left. She perused the downstairs bar for any familiar acquaintances, other models or buyers, and, there being none, she went in. It was an older bar, carved wood that circled the bartender ornately. A marbled mirror made the bottles of liquor look doubled and aged with wrinkles threading the glass.

"Something stiff," she said to the bartender who smiled. She drank shots until she could feel the warmth like a small bonfire snaking lazily from her stomach to her ears. Her hair fell lifeless across her cheeks. The glass was clear and cool between her fingers. She thought of her parents, two Polish Jews who met in the retail district, stars attempting to shimmer over their heads by the time they went out for coffee. A model and a salesman. What would they think of her now? They traveled all over the country from Philadelphia, where she was born and named Isabelle after a theatrical star, leaving her with her older sister, crazy, who heard voices whispering from the walls, settling like sparrows against her receptive ear. Later, lithium helped. Her father compensated her with a car (she crashed it the first week); a fur coat (she left it folded over a restaurant chair); a trip to Europe (she almost lost her virginity); and a nose job (she bumped it kissing in the front seat of a car). All she really wanted was her handsome, exciting, dapper father for herself.

She liked the wet, translucent colors of whiskey

resting against her hands. She thought of an amber river she could swim in, shaking off droplets into her mouth. She said to herself: This is like love, the obsession and then the forgetting. She wanted the stars to crawl to her on their hands and knees. She deserved it. She searched through her handbag for the gold pin in the shape of an ethereal feather her father gave her. Probably at home. She's been through a lot. She didn't understand why the same person reoccurred in her life. Always a man. He has different faces but the same bad personality. Stan. Carl. What does it matter? Lizzie exclaimed, "If you don't love yourself you will destroy everything around you." How would she know? They are okay sometimes, Lizzie and Claire, not much trouble.

She lifted the slick, short glass to her lips again and again. Her tongue was furred, flickering inside the glass. Leaves crackled inside her forehead. Her side bangs loosened over her eyebrows like wayward bandages. And sex was wonderful. How she enjoyed screaming. Once she found Claire asleep with her hands covering her ears. Probably when she was dating a lot. It was probably the Latin lover who liked putting fruit across her naked stomach and eating his way on top of her. A kaleidoscope of sex. And to travel. That is what life is about. Not your head in books like Lizzie or afraid of everything like Claire. She focused again on her drink, the way she concentrated on what she wanted next until she would get it, a bird feeling the wind and then jumping into it. Then another hand around another drink appeared. A man's hand. A cornucopia of drinks.

"Can I offer you another one?"

"Sure. As long as your intentions are good."

"How do you define good?"

"Now don't do anything I wouldn't do."

***

Light throbbed on the metal sink pipes underneath the porcelain basin so they looked alive, winking with an energy Isabelle didn't have. The bedsheets were pale, rumpled Kleenex, all used up. The room wasn't familiar, not her hotel room. She tried to focus, narrowing her eyes. The pugnacious, long, gauzy chintz curtains enter and exit the window looking for a fight. She breathed the stale air, tasted the insipid dirt gritting her teeth. She has misplaced her head. It ached. And who was the man sleeping peacefully next to her with his wrist near a red, plastic bucket on the floor? She dressed quietly, stealthily. Careful not to make any noise, hearing the circus continuing in her thoughts, loudly. She toppled into her scratched pantyhose, entered and zipped her crumpled dress. She held her shoes in one hand. Her joints cracked, her muscles stiff and stretching and luckily he still slept. She pocketed his gold wrist watch abandoned on a chair and walked quietly out the door.

That afternoon Carl called long distance. "Honey, I'm on my way for our vacation in London. How have you been?"

"Bored without you, sweetheart." She pulled the wrist watch between her thumb and forefinger watching the metal band flex, adapting to the distances, then cringing back to its original shape. The shape of a hollow moon or uneaten donut. There were initials carved into its back, "J.D.," whoever that was. She hadn't recognized him, even with the prismatic vision of a drunk in the morning.

"Don't worry, I'll be there soon."

And she hoped no one was spying on her. With her tightly kept secrets. The boldfaced lies she tried to remember.

***

And Carl. Carl saved her from selling palates. Although she would never tell him that. "I was a career girl, independent." Like Watergate, like a presidency, nothing is as it appears to be. There is much roiling and planning underneath. No money and Stan vanished, she had gone door to door asking for any job. "I have three mouths to feed," she gasped to the jeweler. "I'm sorry you don't have any experience," he stated to her crestfallen features. "I'm sorry I don't have any jobs," said the stationer. She shuffled through the New York streets, unsure where to go, where to try. Taxicabs, cars, buses leaving her behind, baffled. Her clothes and make-up wilting, her hair color fading to nothing. She marched into another business, the next one on the street, walked past chagrined secretaries, pencils poised in the air and mouths blooming into emphatic statements, past men pacing around desks, telephones attached to their ears, dirt under their fingernails, their shirts becoming unmoored from their pants, clutching their stomachs and backs as they fretted. She could see her determined features enlarged in their shiny belt buckles. Into the biggest office. An older man stands up behind his large desk, gestures her to sit in one of the chairs surrounding the desk, puts the telephone down.

"What can I do for you?" as though he's accustomed to desperate women barging into his office.

And then she started crying, not crocodile tears, but creases in her eyeliner and mascara, water slicing her remaining flesh colored powder and base.

"It can't be that bad," and he handed her a tissue, this lovely, rumpled woman from the street. Unknown. Welling with sorrow and need, a distraught moment, a present, something wrapped up with paper and bows, coming undone.

"I need a job" she blurted out.

He looked at her Italian shoes with stiletto heels, the geometric gold jewelry, the scent of expensive perfume between them and knew she wasn't a secretary. "Do you have any experience?"

"No." She sobbed more plaintively. "I have to feed two very young children." She found her handbag and began to place the used tissue inside.

He reached out and held her warm hand in his. She looked straight into his pale eyes, a stranger's, interested. A brightness clustering there like stars beginning to reveal their light when night first arrives. "I'll tell you what I can do. You can be a palate salesman with a salary."

"What's a palate?" And she placed her other hand gently over his, sandwiching it between both of hers.

"You can work at home and use your own telephone and I'll come and show you the ropes when I'm free. How does that sound?"

A slight smile began to move her eyes and nose upward, mascara tangled in her hair, her face shifted into pleasure. "Thank you."

And she hadn't done much since then except call a few steady customers from her apartment, still not absolutely sure what a palate was. But she maintained the previous orders. And she liked this generous man who visited her periodically when his wife was out of town. He would bring her gifts of scarves, and artificial jewelry, martini glasses with dolphins swimming along the sides, and sheets with paisley green motifs. Until she quit to marry Carl.

How she had wanted Carl. His consideration made him appear larger. She could feel the hush, then a whisper between her legs, a flutter like wings at the tips of her breasts when he walked by. A passing shiver. And now she has him. After the pomp and ritual at their small London wedding, where they invited any other hotel guests who wanted to celebrate. After enduring his profanity in bed that was intended to excite her. She wants to give him away. It's too much. He wants more than she can give, fetched drinks, an arranged social life, business dinners, his false teeth bubbling in a glass while he wants attention lavished on his bare gums. She thinks about the money. And the terrible husbands she's destined to feign pleasing, Stan, Carl. She saw a film about pirates when she was a child and can remember their hearty laughs, their joviality, the sheer joy in stealing because that was all they had — what they had gallantly taken from someone else. Survival and bold improvisation. Gold leaking from their hands and off the screen over and over again. But she's discontent again, missing the romance, the chase, the assignations, a man loving her enough to tap her phone lines and hurl her own words against her. A man who upon saying he's not jealous discovers he spends his afternoons following her, forgetting who he is. She misses the subtle gestures between new lovers, the excitement, the exchanges like wishbones that they can only share. The promises. She no longer trusts those.

***

"I want to adopt the girls," Carl says before the marriage drains away, something liquid and fluid and oozing into oblivion. He watches his breath against the ravaged indigo sky of Manhattan just beyond a plate of window glass that changes color according to the slight variation in weather — gray, deep gray, china white or light blue. He feels inexplicably alone. A chauffeur, a cook, a house-keeper, a young, glittering wife who doesn't seem to care for him. And doesn't knock herself out trying.

Isabelle saunters by the army of intractable glass animals, ships, and nature scenes twisting the afternoon light, resting on an antique table. Wonderful, she thinks, calculating the size of an inheritance. Perfect timing. Just when she's so bored she could almost taste the handyman's kiss like a hammer resonating right through her bones. Good for the girls and so good for her. Cement and security. She sits in a wooden chair with needlework decorating her outline, complimenting her black and white suit, her nylon encased legs floating underneath the seat like dreams of a better life or graceful birds considering their freedom. "How nice of you," she says, forcing a smile. "I'll ask them. But I'm sure they'll be thrilled." She would be.

***

"Sure," Lizzie says across the long distance wires, liking Carl better than Stan; almost any other father would be an improvement. Carl is kind enough to ask. She has the hope of being heard or seen or even possibly understood, a honeymoon just beginning when the newlyweds' limbs are learning to casually rest against one another. She would easily relinquish Stan.

"Good girl," Mother says. That kind of money makes her feel sexual, makes her think of long afternoons disheveling someone's bed.

"No." Claire is emphatic. "I already have a father." She is loyal to a past she wants like a television program she watches continuously until it becomes her own private history. She is certain of this one fact and clings to it. She holds the door frame in Mother's bedroom, a last stop on

118

a bus she wants to exit. She can hear her own breathing in the angry silence.

"But Lizzie already said yes." She is pleading, seeing her good fortune cartwheeling out the door. Claire determines that her hands are parachutes rescuing her from an oncoming plane wreck. She waves them in the bedroom air, testing their viability, their purpose in ejecting her and allowing her to fall free form gently into another room, another conversation. "I'm not Lizzie and I won't."

"You're going to ruin my marriage."

***

And she's not responsible for these men, these stupid men like Stan who don't know whether they are coming or going. The tangle of their ridiculous emotions smothering them. Stan had given her a pin with LOVE written in diamonds. She kept it tucked in a red velvet pouch in her jewelry drawer, the top drawer of her dresser. One day after she had given Stan the keys to the apartment she realized that the pin was gone. That son-of-a bitch came and took her diamond pin. LOVE was gone. He probably gave it to some new girlfriend. The velvet pouch sat there creased and empty. She was mad, naturally. Proportionally. God knows what else he could steal. The sabotage. She changed the locks on the apartment doors.

And these men make too much of everything, their small semi-precious gifts, their foreign attention, the landscape of the good New York restaurants. She knows these men. The compliments she emanates, heaping them around their ears, the dinners she buys at restaurants and declares she made just for them, especially before marriage, the right clothes. It is all about power. Needing them but not wanting them — the same way she needs food but hates how it changes her body. So many of them like it when she's mean. She can tell, how they come back for more. She doesn't know what she'll do about Carl. Put him in a raft and let him drift out to sea. It would be different to be a widow rather than divorced again. She'll figure it out. God help anyone that stands in her way. Men are insect bites, itching, painful, continually reoccurring, that are absorbed eventually into the body.

***

"Who do you think you are, Mother?" Lizzie asks, curious. A tincture of ecru staining the infringing sky at her dorm window. College life, students entering and exiting buildings with books and papers, is giddily continuing within her view. She is far enough away to be able to ask.

"I'm a drama queen deserving of everyone's attention. Is that what you want to hear?" She's impatient. Such silliness. So limiting, definitive and irrelevant. She pulls a thread jutting from the bottom of her flowered sheets. She twists it like nonsense, letting it rest on the unyielding bedside table top. Her nails click their own messages on the wooden surface. "Listen to this letter to Carl's boss:

"Dear Mr. Marlitch,

"I've heard that Carl Peterson is having an affair with his secretary there. I have been a loyal buyer of your typewriters for my various businesses for years. I think this is disgraceful and not appropriate for the kind of workplace I like to buy my merchandise from. I heard that is what ruined his marriage and initiated his divorce a few months ago. I think you should look into this situation. I have spoken to several other business people that agree with me.

"Signed,

"Anonymous."

120

"Are you really going to send it?"

"Probably."

"What do you hope will happen?"

"That Carl and his bimbo secretary will be fired."

"You were divorced months ago. Let it go."

"Not after the way he's embarrassing me by carrying on with his secretary."

"But he's been doing that since the divorce, right?"

"Who knows. That little bastard was probably cheating on me."

"They say revenge is a dish best served cold." They both find it easier to communicate in sayings or clichés. To convey meanings that someone else has already interpreted.

"What does that mean?"

"Not to get so worked up."

"After what he did to me? The divorce and not enough money. Claire destroyed the marriage because she wouldn't let Carl adopt her. You bet he'll feel the cold."

"Claire had nothing to do with it." She has told her this several times. "Do you think they'll do anything to Carl?"

"I hope so. I want to change his whole life."

PART II

Fairy Tales

Skyscraper Blues

New asphalt and cement buildings drown the warm sunset resembling the interior of a pink flower. The bobbing sky seems to ask for help surfacing in between the hard square shapes as if floating on water. College. Night and the stars are festooned with additional lights like garlands hanging from a perfectly symmetrical ceiling. It is quieter, invariable.

With Lizzie's new nose she has had several boyfriends. One gave her a bicycle she left outside her dorm to rust, each week she watched orange bubbling incrementally up the metal frame, resembling a row of ants. She would not be paid directly or indirectly for her choices. Like her mother. She would try to make men insignificant to her life, her life of writing. She would dislodge the careless disease gnarled at the edge of her skin. Unable to control a crush on a student, she sat outside his dorm room watching his lit window half the night. A land with its own self-contained horizon. She sat in the darkness of an Ohio hill with her head tilted toward the square light of his window, watching the gradations of light from white to various grays to a nearly pure black. She occasionally saw him move back and forth well into the night while dorm rooms lit up in other buildings at intervals. She imagined him rearranging objects on his desk, writing, or reading, or perhaps listening to music near the window, wondering if the weather will change. It felt like the New York skyline of her childhood as dark came on, always contemplating what could be happening behind another window. She felt lulled, eased into this difficulty between men and women. She longed for the mundane, the normal. What her mother would call "boring." She wished she could shut her eyelids and fall backwards and be caught gently by the waiting arms of society. But she wouldn't sacrifice her writing for anything or anyone because that was the true core of her, the seed within the apple. With one of her favorite boyfriends they would communicate as though to tame animals or pets, making baby sounds to one another. There was lots of kissing and oohing and aahing. It was their own language and Lizzie felt safe, hidden, secure and remembered. Then she moved on. One made his bowtie into a phenomenon, bouncing it up and down his neck with his Adam's apple. He would talk and the bowtie would jump toward his chin at intervals, catching more of Lizzie's attention than his words. There was one who didn't believe in monogamy and one who worked for a political advertiser, falling asleep at concerts under the loudspeaker. She doesn't know how much her new nose has to do with her boyfriends. It is becoming a part of her. She can barely remember the angles of the old one, the curves like handwriting, the shadows across her eyes. Her old face is a memory, the new one is a flood that permanently changed the landscape it touched. Her boyfriends drift in and out of the cresting and sinking water.

She thinks of Claire at home, about to leave. Mother is divorced again. A houseful of women becoming smaller. Men coming and going. She is reminded of a bee's hive where the queen grows fatter and fatter until she can no longer move. It is the drones with their excitable activity that bring her the food, do the work. But she alone guarantees their existence into the unknowable future, their genetic continuity. "Just wait until you have children of your own" Mother said.

"I won't," Lizzie said.

Once Lizzie asked Mother, "Answer honestly. Why

did you have children?"
"Because we were supposed to in the 'fifties."

***

Lizzie is finished with school in Ohio with its rolling green
hills, occasional trees, meadows like indentations from
large, faltering clouds, cows with snoring eyes and the
black and white recurring landscape of their bodies. She
likes the country more than the city where everything is
unnatural — the sidewalks, large cement buildings, the
way windows stare at her without blinking. In late spring-
time she would recline in an Ohio field and allow the long
grass and wheat to hug her, leave her enough space to see
the blue sky with its fan of trees. She enjoys the dance of
the natural world with her or without her, knowing her
presence makes no difference whatsoever. She tries Boston, a smaller version of New York, and decides to go west.
Somewhere the cold, like heat, bumps its icy body against
hers. That's when every hair stands straight up from her
skin, at attention, and she can see her fingers clearly,
sharply in the frost-tinged air. Somewhere ice finds the
weakness in objects, making patterns on glass, crawling
into the cracks of wood or cement. Somewhere bare skin is
a foreigner that needs to be protected from any touch,
from the cold boiling through the trees. Where snow is
jewelry amassed, collected and gleaming in sunlight.
Where important events can occur outside. Lizzie loves
expectations. She loves the dream of her new life-to-be.

***

Lizzie's hair swings across her shoulders, brown strands
careless in the regulated oxygen on the airplane. She

supposes she seems older without the wrap of hair down her back. The hair she sometimes sat on accidentally, tugging at her scalp. It would tingle. But those youthful days are over. The plane is circling over Missoula, Montana, where the university's writing program awaits her. The metal holds everything she owns: clothes in one bag; a small, portable, black and white television one of the stepfathers gave her; her one and only pillow; and a sheaf of poems. She looks down at this new place and there are mountains tumbling over one another in the distance like women at an especially good sale. They ring the town with nervous lights starting to appear with evening. She rubs the veins in her pale arm and flips her new hair back. She believes her hair now has a mind of its own, running free of her head when it can, so light and lively. The town looks beautiful. She didn't know much about it before arriving here. She'd heard a poet in Boston and liked him and his work. After his reading he said to the audience, "If you are ever in Missoula come look me up." She thought she would. She could view the fading green swarm of the treetops. Then the individual branches and then the trunks. It is lusher, thicker than she imagined. She thinks that among all the lights beginning to illuminate the dark there is some place there for her. Among the houses, the streets, the forest, the rivers. She is far enough away from her remaining family.

***

Mother phones Lizzie: "How do you give a blow job?"

"Why? Is this something you need to learn right now?" Mother is dating again, divorced. Lizzie is envisioning body strategies, angles of New York sky voyeuristic through the windows.

"No. I just wanted to know how you do it." There is a pause. "You do it, don't you?"

"Yes."

"Well, describe it." A child's lilt is sewn into her voice.

Lizzie closes her eyes and visualizes the details of a man's anatomy like a familiar place she travels to again and again. She thinks she is taking a trip elsewhere and somehow ends up in this well-known territory. She can't. She can't give her these instructions, these words. "I can't. I have to go. I'm meeting someone."

"Well let me tell you how I do it...."

And Lizzie stops listening. Mother repeats herself constantly and Lizzie will probably hear it all over again.

Flies, Perfume, Claire, 1975

At three in the afternoon Claire is thinking about the perfume wafting through the apartment, a pungent floral scent that coats every surface, alive to any movement in the rooms and following it, going to the pit of her stomach. She judges its viscosity by rubbing her forefinger and thumb together. Mother is dressing and it can take her hours. A bath, make-up applied with an enlarging mirror surrounded by Lucite, all near the window light. The usual questions emerging from the clothes closet. It is the equivalent of finishing a painting that is animated, walks across spaces, talks, and eats. The last brushstrokes are often the most important.

Claire finished packing to go to college in upstate New York days ago. She is bringing clothes with their difficulties of color, pattern, zippers, snaps and buttons, and Beauty's ashes piled in their porcelain container with its cold, moth odor. The jar has an unending pastoral scene painted in blues and greens around its circumference. Beauty's death is so silent and enduring, she thinks, the dog's quick cancer that had already spread. She will carry Beauty with her wherever she goes, a sleepy moon, a reminder of that pure animal trust where she can unfold and relax. She is ready to go. Even the apartment seems indifferent to her, ignoring the creak of her step on the slick linoleum floors, keeping her music tucked into the walls of her room, all traces of her gone from chairs and table tops. She no longer hears the woman upstairs, who sounded as if she was vacuuming in her high heels.

She has a terrible thought: that we become what we try to escape the most. She is lying across her chintz bedspread like a bandage, her arms are cradling her head. The traffic is serenading her. She is content to walk away with so little and begin again the same way her father and stepfathers have done, although they didn't necessarily do so voluntarily. The same way Lizzie did, but now there is less money and no stepfather.

She notices a fly like an idea flitting from object to object caught in her bedroom. She hears the slight buzzing now underneath the constant hum of traffic. She wonders: the more I try and run away from her will I become less or more like her? Either way I am reacting to her and not listening to myself. It is a black speck moving from lamp to wall, wall to ceiling, ceiling to headboard and into her cupped hands. She feels it knocking frantically against her enclosing palms. It is buzzing with undisguised anger and intensity, with the weight of a single letter from the alphabet. She opens the latch to the window with her elbow and releases her hands over the slit between glass and sky. The fly takes off for the famous New York skyline rising above the backs of buildings, the geometrical edges grown into the air.

The door opens and Mother comes into the bedroom followed by her perfume. Her rhinestone jewelry mingles with her taffeta dress. She looks lovely. She hands Claire a creased map of New York state with its intertwining red and blue lines across the green spaces interlaced with black dots resembling frozen bluebottle flies. These are all the cities and towns spread over New York. There are so many of them. She hugs Claire, enfolding her in the crispness of her dress, the material makes scraping sounds around her. Mother starts crying. "My baby is leaving." Her mascara disobeys, running streaks, dark arteries down the side of her face. Claire hasn't seen her cry like this, noise in waves, the pull of sadness to an empty desert with no escape, the heart smashed into its small, separate fragments. Finally she is sobbing. Her perfume rests and surrounds them both with its sharp, false, floral tinge stinging Claire's nostrils. Claire is holding her as if she is a delicate bird whose breath is labored from fear, shaking her whole body. She stops, wiping her eyes with their black soot. Mother is calmed thinking of how waves wash along the shore rhythmically, soothing in their mechanical continuity. She laughs a little in her discomfort, making light of it. Claire has discovered that she likes being held even if her shoulders look as though they have been splashed with mud.

Mother clenches Claire's arms and gives her advice. "You can love a rich man just as easily as a poor man. That's all I have to say to you."

Claire realizes that Mother loves her own inventions, the sad mother, the wild, glamorous woman, the party girl who could start thunder and lightning at will just by raising her wine glass. She likes being the center of her own rich world where gossip belongs to everyone in the midst of silver forks, white linen, the bent necks of tulips. She leans over and says: now let's talk about me. And me can be so many different people.

Mother believes she has done so much for the girls, ignoring their teenage tantrums when they tossed themselves on top of the furniture, screaming, shouting, crying. And now her last girl is leaving. The house will seem so empty, skeletal. No one else is left. She loves Claire to the best of her ability which doesn't seem enough of a relationship to either one of them.

Snow, 1982

Lizzie meets Jay at a poker game. It is at a friend's house in Missoula where the stars come out but don't feel like themselves. A river runs past the house, announcing its presence in tiny splashes. The moon circles the A-frame, clear, and looking as if it had forgotten some small errand. Perhaps it involves the stuffed elk head with glass eyes on the wall, or the poker table carved from logs topped with glass, or the guns lined up by size in a cabinet like thin organ pipes in a row. It was culture shock, the animals she could meet walking outside — snakes, coyote, eagles, even bear — the isolation (although people help each other when they can), the lack of arts, an assumption of poverty, the outdoor sports, the self-sufficiency, the bars. She gradually likes Montana still clinging sometimes to its myths about cowboys and ranchers, its wonderful live-and-let-live attitude, the slow pace of life, the mountains surrounding her, tucking her in at night and first thing up in the morning. It is clean, self-contained, fun. Every person is important because there are so few people. Mother calls Montana "a great place to hide."

Claire calls, "Are you lost out there? Are the mountains mesmerizing you?"

Lizzie spends an inordinate amount of time in bars. First with the writing program students and teachers sitting around seance-sized tables, pounding them with a stray fist, spilling drinks, expounding and analyzing, gazing at their favorite velvet paintings. The teachers were the worst, falling off their chairs and getting up to demand a to-go cup so they could drink all the way home. Lizzie could tell who was there by whose car was parked perpen-

132

dicularly to the lot. An added source of amusement was guessing who was in a parked car with whom (if anyone could tell). Then she went by herself or she would meet friends at bars, proud that she could drink big, strong men under the table with shots of liquor. Their eyes were teary, unfocused, before they dropped to the floor, their mutable hands grasping at emptiness. She enjoyed overhearing the tales of the old-timers, some concocted and some merely exaggerated. Photographs of men and some women in their seventies and eighties framed the bottles behind the wood carved bar, around the mirror that reflected the embarrassing antics of the patrons. The black and white pictures displayed crusty, wrinkled faces with names pinned beneath. A few among the customers were close to attaining "photograph status." Some patrons brought dogs or children or sometimes wives or girlfriends. Every once in a while someone invited a mother or grandmother. There were bars that served the best hamburgers in town or breakfast twenty four hours a day; some wouldn't serve a fancy drink like a manhattan or a martini (one of Lizzie's favorites). People would find the bar that matched their personality the way Mother would sort through her dresses to find the right one, the perfect one, disdainful of all the others.

In the back rooms of some bars are the poker tables where playing cards are arranged in handfuls of bouquets like spring flowers. Green felt covers the tables. The dealers shuffle and distribute cards at a flying speed, resembling the good bartenders with their drinks. The cards are suspended under the dealer's breath a moment before they hit ground and their true value is determined. The players at these tables are serious or frowning while they stare, shifting their fan of cards as though they could always do better. No one ever jumps up to say, "What a

great hand!" For all the players are anonymous around
these professional tables, often using phony names to
protect their private lives, their identities, hoping these
fake names will bring them the luck they ultimately de-
serve. It is quiet in these back rooms, unlike around the
bar. Except for an occasional exhalation or the deep breath
of a cigarette or the calling of games or numbers. In the
silence there is an anxiety and a reverence for the cards,
the way they are handled can predict the future, can leave
a wife hungry for a week or a child abandoned at a
relative's home. The silence is for fortune changing, not
always for the better.

And there are fights in the bars and card rooms. A
fist flies towards someone's jaw like a bird gone crazy. A
head is thrown back as in sex or love. Every once in a while
men will pummel each other with empty bottles or drinks
and bystanders will jump out of the way. Violence distorts
the images reflected in the half-filled drinks, tables shake
against the drum of a thrown body. Liquor spills and
voices rise, nuzzling the pressed tin ceiling. Lizzie is
comfortable here, part of this unsteady audience, searching for something larger than herself. And the fights lead
to something. They are the stuff of the Native American
legends from this area: arguments and fist fights between
the sun and the moon formed stars many, many years ago.
The stories explain the disagreements or misunderstand-
ings between men: Two men were out in a canoe with a bag
full of heavy stones and when they began pushing each
other over the alleged infidelity of one of their wives the
stones rolled about, creating a loud noise, thunder. Then it
rained and in this manner the men became rain-makers.
The explanations are lovelier than some drunk being
thrown out into the alley garbage, waking up with bits of
old food plastered in his ears and hair. Some arguments go

back many years and are long standing between tribes, others are over someone who just stole a drink, swallowing it quickly in a gulp. Stealing a lover or a spouse is also an issue in these rooms, as people seem to lose their loved ones in Montana. In the musical chairs of love.

Lizzie is watching the cards, the black and red rectangles upside down, misspelling themselves. She is concentrating on the numbers, the suites of colors. She likes the whistling noise of shuffling, the banter between friends, the new games they try. Chicago High where the highest, unseen spade splits the pot with the best hand. Baseball with its wild cards. Her friend's house is warm with large windows squinting at starlight. She presses her finger into the table top just to watch her fingernail blush maroon and when she lifts it up the nail returns to its usual, whitish flesh color. She does this several times, meandering in and out of the conversation.

"I can't believe you really had that straight." A well-paid office worker says sulking. "I can't go home yet. Now I can't buy any beer for tonight."

"What do you think of Jimmy marrying Elaine?" someone else asks.

"Dreamers."

"I say it can't be done."

"Imitative of Rudy and Ann."

"Undying. Like a commercial or the living dead."

Everyone comments. This poker room of mostly men. The moon passing over the elk head is winking, the light intermittently stopped by the house walls. Nobody lies to Lizzie except when it comes to cards. It's called bluffing.

"I'd like to see a really big wedding. Full of white and blue. With flowers, lots of flowers." Lizzie insists on a woman's point of view just for the hell of it. She'd like to see an explosion of flowers in the middle of another unending winter. It would be a stubborn, lovely magic trick.

There is a knock at the thick wood door and Lizzie is thinking of another couple, thinking that they have survived their marriage by holding their breath. They pretend that nothing has changed and it seems to be working so far for them. A man with dark hair and dark eyes comes in with Michael, another friend. They greet the room and begin playing poker intensely, intent on the cards, the reverie of color and numbers, the sequence of marine life slipping in and out of the sea water nonchalantly. The stuffed elk's glass eyes seem to follow them wherever they go. The talk continues but Michael and his friend are enraptured by the playing cards, a beach constantly rearranged by the shifting waves.

"And Dennis used to be a good person."

"Used to be?"

"Didn't you hear?" The cards are distributed into piles resembling nocturnal debris collecting on sand.

"About what?"

"When did divorce become equivalent with death?"

"No."

"Yes."

"Let's talk about movies." Lizzie again. She is merely a cog in a wheel. And she likes it.

The chips rustle and clink accompanied by their patter. Lizzie once watched a one-armed man argue with a fish he caught in a lake. He had lost himself in the fish's struggle, the thumping and twisting, its appointment with air, destiny. When he thought he had made his point and won he returned the fish to the glassy water. Piles of chips come and go. That is the nature of money. To change sides often. Fickle. But Michael's friend's stack is large, an accumulation, several small skyscrapers.

Michael stands up. "We have to leave and meet someone." The warm air eddies, the piles of chips are gone. Time runs through them like water. They are distracted by the world, by unfinished business, by the translucent moonlight. Michael's friend scrapes his chair as he stands in his blue jeans, plaid flannel shirt. A light scar trails behind the chair leg, a pale shadow. His nose is a fish, long and sinuous, swimming toward his thin mouth. The elk eyes move with them as they walk out the door with most of the money.

There is silence, empty space where the money had rested. With its monologue about value, blame, attainability they are sorry to see it go. With its traces of an old, revered language understood by almost everyone. It had resided in their pockets, traversed the table and left for a new life. Cards, beer, snacks sit quietly on the glass table top, looking abandoned, their reflection resembles bass scattered by a rock, waiting to return to their positions underneath the light-filled water.

"What did Michael's friend say his name was?" George, disabled with multiple sclerosis, questions, sitting uncharacteristically subdued against the canvas back of his wheelchair.

"Jay."

"I saw him working at the pizza place in town as a waiter," someone else adds.

"Do you think we could apply some of the money we lost toward free pizzas?" George has a sly smile.

"I think he's cute," Lizzie says to further silence, to the eyes in the room. It is more of a request than a statement. The wind scratching its name on leaves outside. Lizzie notices the guns in the periphery of the room and is soothed by their quiet anatomy which belies their usefulness, fragmenting a body into parts until it is down to nothing. She admires their predictable sleekness, the preparation, the ritual of change, reminding her of a human heart. The elk follows her with its eyes, aware of the consequences.

***

Lizzie is landlocked, debating the finer points of nearby lakes with friends. The splatter of fresh water in the white-capped mountains and the valleys as compared to the ocean confiscating half the horizon, expanding far into the sky, submerging the land. They laugh about the geography of choice or luck and about extending their weekly poker meetings into the future indefinitely.

"Like seeing *The Wizard of Oz* every year."

"More like *It's a Wonderful Life* over and over again. We're sure to see it more than once a year and at least it explains what life would have been like without you."

Trees whine around George's house because of the wind. It has been a week since Jay and Michael were there. Lizzie looks up "surreptitious" in the thick dictionary between hands of cards. The weather seems to be gearing up for a storm. Ribbons of lightning see themselves in the rivers and leave. Lizzie wants to be challenged, alive with the possibilities, transformed. She can view the rows of mountains nodding their heads to dark clouds and disappearing. She wonders where they go, what they can become against the gray sky. The phone rings. George wheels to the black telephone and picks up the receiver awkwardly in his unsteady hands.

He holds it up. "Lizzie, it's for you."

Lizzie takes the slightly warm handle, perplexed. She looks outside as she is speaking, wondering at the mysterious weather. She stares at the road to Missoula curving among the blind trees like letters of the alphabet. She cannot fathom their meaning. She realizes she is waiting. Waiting for the voice at the other end. Waiting for the dramatic roar of a tremendous storm, something she can acquiesce to, a premonition.

"Hello." "Yes, great." "I'll see you there."

"Jay's not coming here, is he?" George inquires with a slight dread in his voice. He looks at Lizzie but his glasses are so thick they distort his eyes, which resemble small fish moving under the blur of water.

"No, don't worry. I'm the only one who'll take all your money."

***

Lizzie loses herself at a lake. Mountains with white foreheads encroach on the metallic water. They leave fragments of a winsome smile refracted on the still surface. Coldness informs Lizzie and her writing teacher and two friends that they are elevated into a different atmosphere. They want to fish. Under the sherbet-colored apron of water draped out in front of them fish subside, oblivious, happily, offhandedly swimming, living their short, rectilinear lives. Fishing paraphernalia sprawls before them, rods and reels, bobbers with their red and white dichotomy, hooks and bait with their shimmering curves, worms turning in on themselves, curling over and over. The lake is clairvoyant with light, understanding what spirals below the visible, the half shadows circling, darting, content under the wet skin, consoled by a damp nudge or by breathing water. The writing teacher wants the first fish. But Lizzie throws her line and bait, plumbing the unknown, the mysterious shore. It's inevitable and she's excited, listening to birds bickering, the skein of tree branches overhead, the way the earth cups the mischievous water in its hands. Air rubs her cheeks meticulously, slowly, as her bobber attempts to disappear, waving goodbye, then running. She catches the first fish drizzling with water, crazy between lake and sky, angry at this unexpected perspective, irreconcilable. She throws it back in, disturbing the patinaed surface again.

***

Jay is sitting in a pool of light, his face with its sharp right angles, the green foliage of indoor plants fan him at the restaurant where they meet. "Look at our waiter serving us on the wrong side. He should be serving on our left, not our right." He is in the restaurant business.

A mountain rises steeply behind his head. Lizzie searches for the peaks, the cliffs cut by snow into long geometrical shapes. She imagines people holding hands, climbing to the top or bobsledding down to their mutual happiness with the greatest of ease. Snow sticks to the creases in their clothes, to the lines in their temples, in their wide, open grins. Lizzie wants that kind of uncomplicated, artless contentment. The kind that warms you from the inside and guides you thoughtlessly like a lighthouse beacon. No one can take it away.

Lizzie is distracted from her daydreams by waiters carrying silver trays aloft like clouds tinged by a dubious moonlight. They bring full glasses and warm, white plates. These are endearments. They place wine in front of her, an offering she can't decline. Songs tap her on the back, asking her to dance and refused, excuse themselves, misunderstood, then move on to touch the shoulders of another diner. She thinks about dancing but is suddenly weary watching the waiters leave footprints of shadows in the deep carpet under the soft light. The low noise of silverware on plates and discreet conversations permeates the background. "I don't want you to think I'll just be a waiter all my life. I have ambitions. I'd like to have my own restaurant one day." Candles flicker in their enthusiasm about fire underneath his chin. This is a place that venerates food. "I'm sure that would be nice." Lizzie doesn't really care what his ambitions are. She is intent on waves of light making patterns against his face. She notices in between there is a moment of darkness. Then the sentimental lapping candlelight shaping the side of his cheek again. "Tell me about your family."

"My father recently switched sales jobs and my mother's an alcoholic." Succinct. He is looking at his spoon. Lizzie is aware of people's intricate disguises, the way they clothe their needs. But this is direct, pure evidence, plain and simple. It is the plates apologizing for their whiteness.

"Oh, I'm sorry," Lizzie says. "How does that make you feel?"

He leans over and kisses Lizzie slowly. His lips are as light as wind at first. A monotone of touch. Then harder with flesh the color of wood or bricks, wet, a river unruly against stones. She wants an arm around her, to hold her to him, a fish turning, caught in a space that is too small. She feels the limitations, the border of his body and yet she loses herself in it like a family heirloom purposefully dropped into the water of a well. No more obvious attachments. The symptoms of place, time, meaning are fading, disappearing. She is happily lost. And yet she knows she needs to remind herself of where she is and swim out and shake herself off from this pleasure. It is a new language.

***

Mother's profile is a coin against the front car window when she makes a short visit to Montana. Jay is driving toward a mountain, scrimshaw against the sky, a lake capriciously close to their tires. From the back seat it appears that Mother has a mouthful of mountain, the curving lines impulsively enter her lips. She is speaking in vowels and consonants that Lizzie is barely able to hear and is making into arbitrary fiction.

"My last husband...", "toppled..." and "through the heart..." And Lizzie imagines a wedding cake squashed in the center. Calm hides in the sweet, white, oozing frosting.

"Lizzie had this pillow ...", "and smell it..." And Mother becomes a cigarette end crushed in an astray. These are Lizzie's secrets, her own fragile bones, the creation of her own spidery skeleton.

Lizzie nibbles on her fingernails as Mother finds what she is looking for before going back to New York tomorrow. "She says sex with you is great..." Lizzie watches Mother's feathery hands like birds against the mountains. They had better not land. Jay is stony, unhinged. Lizzie sees the scythe in her hand, the full swing, the continuous movement of flight, clean, sure. Mother's head would drop quickly to the seat, the odd combination of muscle, bone, blood and skin remaining upright, the body forgotten like a vase broken and without flowers. A last word spills from the severed head, "Sorry," then unadulterated silence.

"Flathead Lake." Jay points to the lake with his finger horizontal to a tree against the windshield, trying desperately to change the subject.

***

Jay moves in with Lizzie in the sparse, brown-splashed, rented house ten miles away from town. Cold air enters through the pipes, through the wooden spine that wraps around Jay and Lizzie, a ghost coming closer, inspecting their fingers, the diagrams of their entangled bodies. "Jay," she sighs at night when the conspicuous birds feign sleep in the evergreens and are empty of their music. "Jay," the surrounding hills return in the morning when Lizzie discovers skeletons of animals, a snake, a cat, once a coyote. Mother calls often. And Jay barks as insistently as a hungry dog when he thinks she's been on the telephone too long.

"You need to get married" Mother demands. "You are over thirty and living with a man just doesn't cut it anymore. Besides if you don't get married soon people might think that you are a lesbian."

"Maybe I am." Lizzie doesn't want to make any final decisions or rule out any possibilities. "And, besides, what people?" She gazes at the few possessions Jay brought with him, clothes and four books.

Jay is barking at the window. Lizzie remembers a recurring dream, walking up stairs to the back of a throne. When the chair swivels around it is Mother, and she is a vampire. The dream always concludes then.

"Bark" Jay is whining. Rain begins with its numerous things to say, the perpetual pleasure of ground, choosing its companions from so many, the vividly realized musical notes, the laws it creates following its true nature. Jay's barks become brown leaves crackling under the voice of rain until Mother asks, "Is that stupid dog barking again?"

"Yes, it's the neighbor's dog and I have to go out

and return it to the owners or it'll keep on barking."

"All right." And they hang up their respective phones.

There is the maze of the mind, Lizzie thinks as lightning shakes the house, lighting the furniture and the no-man's-land of the partially empty rooms. Jay pulls Lizzie onto the couch as she is mumbling something about the mind. One kiss and he can feel her small mouse bones in his hands. He holds her, feeling her breath condensing against his chest. She is drowning and opens her eyes. Her body is gripped in the undertow of his arms as lightning highlights a chair and releases it. A kiss, the glare of a table, then darkness. Daffodils in a blue vase light up with details. It is one long moment from a string of time, memory illuminated to recognition. Jay's face appears, unraveling into the night as if counting minutes. He brushes her collarbone with his dark hair, breathing her skin and its shadows. Lizzie's hand is caught reaching for a pillow, the stone of sleep. She is weightless and grabs handfuls of him. She is annoyed by this mystery of sex yet throws herself into it.

***

Lizzie is brushing her hair in Jay's car mirror as houses, yards, trees fly by on the way to Jay's friend in Oregon. The car drives into a crow's call and then it fades. The sun cuts her hair into a shiny helmet. She feels like a child who could open her mouth and swallow all the passing people, backyards, bushes. Jay is hunched over the wheel concentrating on the white lines stitching the black road. His eyeglasses have white stripes down the lenses.

"Do you want to get married?" he asks, staring out the windshield as though the landscape would answer him.

It takes Lizzie a few minutes to realize what he is asking. She thinks she hears the hammer of a woodpecker against a pole or a house. Then it's gone. The car is losing everything, going by too quickly, accelerating and abandoning at the same time. Lizzie smoothes the side of her warm hair, pushing back a strand that fell across her forehead. She is a cat: When in doubt, groom. She wonders if this is her mother's voodoo. If Mother keeps any funny little dolls and pins hidden in the apartment. She wants to stop the car. To be on one street, to be at one house instead of traveling by. Instead of having everything around her vanish so swiftly. She wants to hold onto something real. Not just see it pass in the window.

"Yes," she says. "I'd love to. Yes, but can you pull over for a minute?"

"Sure. Are you okay?"

"Yes. I just feel a little dizzy."

The car stops by a row of bushes starting to turn green. When they step through them they are on a golf course the shape of a hairpin. There is no one in sight. Just flags marking the golf holes waving along with a little grass in the sad wind. The beige pools of sand traps.

"My favorite place to make love." And he pulls Lizzie down into his unfolding jacket spread adjacent to a sand trap. "This always makes me feel better."

***

Lizzie calls George, her closest friend, from Oregon. Afterwards she will call Mother. "I've always thought you'd make a great best man."

"I refuse to play poker with you guys if both of you are in the same room. Too much money." George sounds far away as his voice crackles in low tones across the wires. His wheelchair is making whirring noises as he moves the wheels back and forth. "Congratulations."

***

The courthouse in Missoula takes up a whole block. Charles Russell paintings of cowboys and Indians from the beginning of the twentieth century line the walls. The ceilings and high walls are painted intricately in pastel colors. Thick wood and etched glass doors separate the offices and bathrooms from the unending corridors and hallways. Tributaries of marble vein the floors and door frames and banisters. Lizzie wonders how many years of feet have shuffled up and down this twist of solid, dusty stairs. The courthouse has long serenely accepted the weather, snow or hail or sun, knocking at its doors. The fresco ceilings have adjusted to the lives of others, considered their transitory dreams. Jay and Lizzie are pronounced man and wife by the Justice of the Peace after a man before them is convicted of a crime and sent to prison. At the judge's pronouncement, the man had turned his eyes away, towards a painting of woodlands with intertwined branches and leaves against the wall. Lizzie keeps her own last name, Lowenstein, not out of sentimentality but because it seems easier than changing her identification or checks. Outside George pelts Jay and Lizzie with rice and a few poker chips, bouncing in a small round fury against his dark suit and her short, pale dress. Lizzie catches a few in her fingers and throws them back at George. There is a clank against his metal wheelchair and they fall to the ground, reminding them of the dangers in the world, of the tinny sound of money.

***

In their first year of marriage Lizzie and Jay go to Astoria, a small beach town on the Oregon coast. Wind tufts the water into spiky, white wings. All the driftwood and large rocks jutting onto the shore are polished into large, round curves like eggs in various shapes and sizes, small, medium, more circular, more elliptical, giant. The wood and stone begin to resemble one another. Jagged rocks leap from the nearby surface of the ocean. Bushes and trees are scrubby, half-grown, never burgeon. But Lizzie and Jay enjoy the sand, granular, shifting, always ready to adapt to shoes, bare toes, bird legs or stones. Seagulls spread their wings looking like clouds at a distance and, moving closer too fast, they complain about the air to the air. They are white mustaches against the face of sky. Jay can name all the birds they see. And Lizzie and Jay tell each other stories. They walk along the beach together and describe old girlfriends and boyfriends.

"My first girlfriend was a masseuse."

"How did you meet her?"

"Guess."

"Was she really your girlfriend? Or everyone's girlfriend?"

"She said she was mine. The rest didn't matter."

"I had a boyfriend that made his bowtie dance up and down his neck with his Adam's Apple." It didn't seem nearly as exciting now to Lizzie.

"My second girlfriend grew up to be a bank robber."

"Was it something she took at college like 'What to Do in the Current Economy 101'? Or like Patty Hearst?"

"A little grittier. I heard she's in prison for a long time. She got caught somewhere in Florida after a string of fifteen robberies."

"Wow. You win." She just couldn't tell him about the forty-year-olds. Not yet.

That night they envelope each other. Lizzie kisses the sheets once, mistaking them for his skin in her passion. Sand leaks from the creases in their flesh, crumbling and hard onto the soft cotton. Little piles form at the foot of the bed. They brush it from their skin with their fingertips over and over again. Jay's face is baffled with desire against the pillow. Then they roll over to sleep. They vow in serious voices to always tell each other the truth. Whatever that is, Lizzie thinks.

***

Lizzie doesn't miss the bars she stopped frequenting. She had blacked out twice, unable to remember anything about the night before. Time seemed incongruous. It frightened her too much, to completely lose so much time. Instead she takes walks, reads, embellishes her own stories, plays poker with her friends under the glacial mountain's suspicious stare. Jay goes into the woods to smoke dope, his hands skittering like hurt birds. Light worries his back into the shapes of small, unpredictable hills.

***

"I'm ready to start a restaurant and make money for myself instead of for other people," Jay claims after the first year of marriage. Trees shred light into commas on the floors around the mostly empty house. There is so little furniture Lizzie and Jay bump into walls in the middle of the night when they go to the bathroom.

"What will you use for money?" Lizzie is waking

up from sleep, suddenly awake to her house like a bright firefly.

"You have some money saved, and we are married. That's the concept of marriage — to share and share alike." He is staring at his hands as though they are foreign objects that could leap up and bite him. He holds a soda with them because he never drinks any liquor. "I'll also ask my family."

"Okay," Lizzie says. "I can work my full-time job and help you out evenings and weekends." She is pleased to pursue a dream. It's so American. Especially Jay's dream with its implication of the happy-ever-after. And money. And freedom. "It's wonderful to have a dream." She thinks of her low-paying social service job where the staff often resemble the clients. All she wants to do is write. She looks into his deep, unfathomable, liquid eyes. She tries to read his face but all she can see is the sparrow brushing off sky in the tree branches outside. Nothing else.

Jay chooses the location for the restaurant, an oriental style restaurant called The Fuschia Express. He paints it purple. It is a former gas station seating only about twenty-five people and he hopes for a lot of take-out business. The large windows in front overlook the black tarred parking lot rimmed by wooden houses across the surrounding streets. A solitary tree stands in a planting box in the parking lot. It is run over by a customer's car within the first week.

Lizzie wears a purple tee-shirt advertising "The Fuschia Express" and slides between chairs and tables carrying colorful food on thick white plates stacked up and down her arms. She reels in the empty oval plates. It is fall when little things fade away. Trees are flicking off brown-edged leaves and Lizzie wonders if she is asleep but her feet are shuffling on their own. She believes she could curl up under the warm dishwasher and sleep with its constant hum on her back.

A woman and her family come into the restaurant. She has waist-length dark hair, her face is exhausted with make-up and she wraps long pink fingernails around a cigarette.

"No smoking here," Lizzie says, tapping the sign.

"I came here to see Steve." She nods at Jay as she inhales, burning the length of the cigarette and exhaling in a sigh at the purple wall. Smoke passes between them like a signal or a dare.

"Who the hell is that?" Lizzie tiredly asks Jay. She is bone-weary, drying, losing life like those leaves.

"A dealer from the King Bar and Card Room."

"Why did she call you Steve?"

"Because I play there under the name of Steve Glaze." He is quickly angry, a sudden fire consuming his gestures and his voice. He grabs at a water pitcher on the counter behind the cash register. He knocks it onto the floor spilling water in furious puddles around their feet. He yells, "Now look what you did, putting the pitcher in the wrong place."

"You're the one who knocked it down." Lizzie screams back at him. She feels customers' heads swivel in their direction. She feels the dazzle of their eyes against her cheeks. "When do you find the time and the money to play professional poker?" she says more quietly. They are both bent over the wet floor with towels. His knuckles are moving so fast they appear to be dissolving. She sees her wrist making slow, subsiding circles in the water.

He grasps a soaking ball of towel and walks away as though he didn't hear her, as though her questions aren't worth answering. He thinks that if he keeps moving he will never be caught. He doesn't feel fully in this world or he feels about to leave for someplace better. If he can't be pinned down then he's not responsible. It makes no difference to him: the sun and the moon, the way they come and go each day. And they don't have to answer to anyone.

***

Lizzie pulls up a chair to George's shiny chrome-plated wheelchair. She leans her head against his shoulder and cries, tears darkening his shirt. Her breath flings itself into his chest and he lets her sob. George thinks how the past crushes us and the future is defined as what there is to apprehend, the possibilities, what can happen. Time being its own propaganda. What about time as a healer? He feels his weight in his chair and is aware that he can't leave it. Lizzie is trying to stop crying, pulling a handkerchief across the bruised landscape of her features.

"It's okay," he says patting her back.

"No, it's not. I don't know what to do. Jay's not home much anymore. I think he's been going to the King Card Room to win money. He says he needs money for the restaurant. I'm doing the best I can. And now he's sleeping in another room and he comes in at crazy hours." She is starting to cry again. She thinks of George's weak muscles, atrophied under his clothes, dust she could blow on and it would scatter. His shirt is soaking against her cheeks. It is as if rain had burst in the windows and doors and embraced them.

"I guess this means we won't be seeing you at poker for a while," George says as Lizzie wipes away tears. He pats Lizzie's shoulder with his hand that can barely retrieve or hold inanimate objects.

***

Lizzie feels a green leaf's impending transparency, stippled veins rooting, spreading their lopsided fingers to the sharp corners, expanding, before fall arrives. She can almost see the coming snow chuckling through the empty branches, guffawing with the wind into piles that remind her neighbor, a taxidermist, of his unused supply of sawdust. The threadbare hills that convivially preserve the past, geography, or a wild animal's short life. "The leaves are getting thinner."

Jay looks up from his paperback, for a moment unaware that he is in their backyard until the trees become palpable, a slight cool breeze insulting his neck. "I'm going to ask your mother for money for the restaurant. She has some extra money and she could help out."

"I don't think I would do that if I were you." Lizzie doesn't know what more to tell him. The warning. A cruelly bad idea. Lizzie has never asked her for money. What would she do? She's almost curious.

"Put me on the phone the next time she calls." He has decided. He has asked everyone else.

That evening the phone rattles with sound and Lizzie wants to pretend she is a dog barking at intervals to disguise the phone's fierce repertoire, to end it. The sky at the window is spangled with stars and the pockmarked, drifting moon. "Hello." She turns to the curved kitchen tabletop stretching away from her toward the landscape, toward weather, patient at the sliding glass doors like someone waiting for a quick religious conversion. "Now Jay has something he wants to ask you and feel free to tell him no." Her stomach falls, a parody of a heavy ball dropped from a great height. Her breath is fissured. She wants to beg Jay not to do this and yet she doesn't want to

get in between them. A nonexistent, invisible ghost. She
cannot chose sides, each one as dubious as the other. She
cannot listen to Jay describing the picturesque restaurant
just needing a little more "capital." The phone wrestles
with their words. Then he hangs up. "What did she say?"
"She's not sure."
"Oh." Lizzie doesn't understand what that means.
She wipes the yellow formica kitchen table speckled with
white triangles comparing her own version of Mother's
possible reactions to Jay's interpretation. Truth has its
own discourse, its own reality. Sometimes it's so separate
from her own. And unimaginable.
The phone screams out its question again. Who's
there? Jay holds it to his ear while Lizzie holds the striped
towel distractedly like a referee busy at a boxing match.
"Yes." "No." "Of course not." Jay doesn't say much. He
hangs up the phone, his chin rests on his plaid shirt, his
eyes dance on the burnt orange carpet on the floor. Lack-
ing enough furniture for his dark eyes to rest on they waltz
over Lizzie's face like two small boats trying to escape
shallow waters.
"Who was it?"
"My mother."
"Well what did she say?" Jay's mother rarely calls.
"Your mother called mine to tell her that I had
asked her for money and that she certainly couldn't afford
it. She's on a limited income. She implied that my mother
raised a son that isn't capable of standing on his own two
feet."
Lizzie wonders how Mother found the number.

***

Silence muscles the house. Lizzie has learned the various

sizes of silence: the kind that fits into a drawer, or a purse, or a spoon, between the pages of a book, or even a house. She recognizes its different versions, uses, one that paralyzes or calms, one that erases someone or makes her want to scream. Silence is leaning against her, breathing down her neck, getting too friendly and comfortable. It is past midnight and Jay isn't home. She heard a plane fly by two hours ago, listening closely to its receding insect hum, disappearing into a darkness shared with deer, elk, bear and eagles.

She telephones the King Card Room, "Is Steve Glaze there?" The name sticks in her mouth as though she is asking for some stranger.

"Hold on," the man's voice says on the other end. A few minutes later, "Yeah, he's here. Do you want me to get him?"

"No." Lizzie returns the receiver into the cradle of the phone. Where there's smoke there's fire. The lies blister her. They make her tired, angry. They peel her skin down to a rawness she can't accept. Their familiarity. Jay is hanging from her fingers over a cliff and she can't let go and watch him become an unrecognizable dot in the distance, disappearing into water. She needs to go see him. See what he is doing, how he initiated this situation. How he lies to her, avoids her. How he might extricate himself. She has to see the results for herself with her own eyes.

She gets in her car and drives to the King. It is an old remodeled bar with two decrepit card rooms in the back. The rooms are wood-paneled and there are lots of people there in the middle of the night. There are large round tables with scattered red, blue and white chips. Cigarette smoke somersaults in the air and circles a tableau of partially filled drinks. All kinds of people are at the tables, young, old, bums, the well-dressed, a few women,

men, cowboy hats, the turquoise-and-silver set, Native Americans. All hold their cards close to their chests, professionally, as though someone could snatch their cards away. It is so different from George's house where friends can wave their cards around and everyone laughs. Here everyone is serious, careful, glum. The bar and card rooms are both busy with people spilling drinks across the sawdust floors. Shadows glide over the floor and the ceiling. Lizzie spots the waist-length dark hair of the woman who had been in the restaurant. She is dealing fast and furiously at the table where Jay or "Steve" sits. Her fingernails flash pink as she releases the cards with their all important numbers or pictures of royalty. "Possible straight, two of a kind, possible flush, nothing there," she is chanting.

Jay is sitting at her table with a small heap of different colored chips against his chest. Lizzie goes to the railing near the table. Someone asks if she wants a drink and she says no. She stares at him. A part of her can't believe he's actually here, desperate, imploring money, using a phony name. She is flattened, a page in someone else's book struggling to be more, fighting to get up and relinquish the volume. The pain of both her mother and father. She watches him blatantly ignore her, not caring. There he sits, Jay or Steve or whatever his name is. He stands up and goes to Lizzie with his dark hair rumpled into a dying flower and his shirt sleeves rolled up. "You're humiliating me," he hisses at Lizzie. He swerves back toward the table, sits down, and plays cards.

Lizzie turns around and walks out the door wondering what she could have possibly done to him.

***

Mountains improvise animal shapes with clouds. Lakes

are scattered below like pages from an open book. Birds flicker, resilient punctuation, and Lizzie consults her interior landscape, a dialogue about faith, abandonment, failure. She remembers that life is about change and how much she hates it with its incoherent dictionary.

***

The restaurant slides toward bankruptcy. Jay tells Lizzie not to mention it to the five people working there. She glances at them like a domestic animal sauntering by their yard, stopping a moment to see what's there and then trotting on quickly into the lush, fugitive forest. Jay stays out later and later. Sometimes in the middle of the night Lizzie suspects he is growling at the white walls in his separate bedroom. His failure becoming tangible into a subdued howl. Then she knows he has lost at cards another time.

It is winter again with ice creeping up the windows and snow hurling itself at the house unceremoniously, making mounds or layering into contours. Some days bare tree branches crack and fall to the ground, becoming lost in the surrounding snow. Lizzie has learned to invent a world vivid with colors against this backdrop of blankness. If she were a painter, she would use spring colors as her palate, thinking of all the things she could do outside soon. It is hard to stay warm. Men call the house at all hours, saying through the crisp, cold air, "You owe us" and "We intend to collect."

Jay and Lizzie's life together spirals smaller and smaller, almost becoming invisible. Jay needs tranquilizers all the time and can't sleep. He lays awake in his room staring at the white ceiling, denoting meaning and significance to every incident that has occurred, until he can rise and go to the restaurant. For each event foretells his uncertain future. One day he calls Burlington Northern to complain that their trains made him wait fifteen minutes at a crossing. "And don't do it again," he screams, slamming down the phone.

Then the toilet overflows at home, soaking the maroon bathroom carpet. Lizzie is afraid to tell him and his door is closed. The toilet keeps overflowing with its own mysterious inner workings and Lizzie doesn't know how to stop it. The phone rings and she hears a man threaten, "Pay us soon." Jay comes out of his room and is immediately angry when his feet sink into the soggy carpet. He yells at Lizzie, "Are you retarded or what?" and slams the bathroom door so hard the knob punches a hole in the wall.

There is the stain of him all over the house, in shadows, in holes, dents, things broken. Lizzie can hear his voice when he isn't there, criticizing or saying, "If you walk out that door you won't see me again," and her feet are frozen and she doesn't know why. The threats are part of the noise of the world. Lizzie thinks he probably would not follow through. But there is his furious mouth working him into a frenzy as though he knows it is difficult to be understood, almost impossible to be loved. A struggle that remembers everything, the good and the bad, a hint of color under snow, the collapse of trees under unusual weight. And Lizzie loved the person he used to be, the one that didn't neglect her, who had dreams, who didn't seem to hate himself so much. Someone who had been aware of which bird would wake them into the light of a new morning or someone who laughed at blowing darkness away with one large breath. It is all history, she realizes as she lets him go into the outside world where he spreads himself thin. She emerges with herself, conspicuously without any more dreams about men. She expected love to be difficult but the disappointment is a little metal piece lodged behind her breast. She can feel it sitting, bending, that small vibrating, a tuning fork, a trembling when she breathes. She walks out the front door with her belongings stuffed into two small suitcases. She had the recurring nightmare with Jay as the vampire on the throne instead of Mother. No more. She unrolls the car window to allow the scent of pine to enter, the slightly crushed needles with their unwieldy cones. Minor damage is the reason for the aroma, so magnified, distinct. The pungent smell maneuvers over her suitcases to rest dissonantly between her flesh and the plastic seat. She will take it with her as far as she can.

She sends Mother a holiday card with a picture of evergreens and snow. Printed inside it says, "Best wishes for the holidays and happiness throughout the New Year," and at the bottom she writes "P.S. I just got divorced."

She knows Mother would say, "Do whatever it takes to get rid of the hurt."

And Lizzie would answer, "It's too late."

Somebody Cares, Claire, 1977

Claire finds a man she loves at a bar. It is a college bar and his red hair lights the ceiling, the mirrors, and his green eyes effervesce with his beer.

"So these guys, a group, a family are like all dressed up," he runs his hands through strands of his thick red hair, "with black suits and white shirts. They've got these heavy black bibles under their arms. It was like a whole family with women and children and shit. And they're going door to door. Jehovah's Witnesses or somethin'. And I just got up out of bed. I'd had a big night out on the town the night before and I'm just looking at my pants and shirt and thinkin' about them." He wipes his nose with his finger. "So I'm like buck naked and the doorbell rings. So whaddaya think I do? I opened that fucking door real wide. And then all of them Jehovah's Witnesses witnessed something real. And whaddaya think they do? They go like screaming down the hallway and out the door. Whaddaya think of that?"

Claire smiles into the sheer mathematics of his hair and eyes. They are with a group of students, drinking. It is April Fool's Day. Claire is nursing a beer for show, sipping it periodically. She has held that beer for hours.

"You look familiar," she says to the apostrophe of his hair. Thinking it sounds like a line but she has seen him in the sea of students at school. It's hard to forget his hair, the grass color of his eyes. She swallows bubbles and the dense, bitter taste of beer and a little foam fill her mouth again.

He focuses on Claire, noticing her curly dark hair, the swirling blue shirt, her small quick gestures like a bird, the sadness emanating from her pale skin. "Yeah, I've seen you before." He takes a gulp of beer. "Yeah."

"I know," she says, "I've seen you in my philosophy class." She has experienced a few boyfriends at school but they didn't work well together. She is still recovering from a lover who turned from her body to another woman's body, telling her only after someone else already told her. She doesn't want to have to excavate lies or misrepresentations like blood coursing under the skin, always moving just out of reach, deep in the body. She just wants to be loved as simply as pulling on a clean, plain dress, comfortable with the contours of her full figure. But she acknowledges that most relationships aren't so easy.

"Hey. Life, Death and Eternity." He is laughing, observing how round her clothes are, filled with broad lines. Her silhouette balloons when she turns to the side.

"Yeah. That's the class, Life, Death and Eternity," she chuckles, putting down the heavy glass half filled with beer.

"Hey. Let's go outside so we can talk some more." He pulls her from the crowd, a misruly thread drifting from a garment, and they make their way, stitching haltingly across the floor.

"Okay." But she is already moving.

They shuffle outside. She can feel his hand in the small of her back, directing her, resting, already almost possessive. They wade through smiling, talking, standing, sitting students, one who, laughing, sprays his drink onto the back of a chair, imitating a heavy rain or garden hose. They sit on some stone steps watching the moon shellacked to the night sky. Trees sway, composing and then delivering their familiar sentences. Claire hears their rustling, the near words. She has a sense of a river nearby as though she could taste or smell the water dense in the air.

She places her palms against the grass, gently cognizant of a tickling sensation. She is hopeful about this handsome man.

"Hey, what's your name?" His hand ripples through the top of his head.

"Claire. What's yours?" She feels a slight chill in the air and shivers.

"Charlie." He puts his beer down on a step with a clank. He feels light pulsing inside the building, hears stereo music, talk and music vibrating the stone like his heartbeat. He can feel the bass through his pant legs. "So philosophy huh? It seems like we have a lot in common."

"I'm a philosophy major," she says, thinking how she drifts into decisions. She is pulled by the eddy of life and wants to see where she washes up. It is a form of philosophy, after all. She is used to agreeing, saying okay, to other people. She is used to subsuming her wishes, not even knowing what they are. And other people's desires seem so strong, so all-important.

"I'm graduating in three weeks," he says standing, unable to sit any longer, restless.

"Then what will you do?"

"I dunno. Get a job probably." He runs his palm through his red hair and then extends it. "Would you like to dance?"

"Out here?" She giggles.

"Sure, why not?"

She stands up brushing her skirt and he enfolds her in his arms. The trees are engaged in a full discussion and the dancers' feet step across stone squares among the grass. She is warmer, fitted against his strong body. She can feel his tight muscles through his clothes and she melts into him, his strength, his desire, his need. He is jumping with her wildly from stone to stone and laughing into the air. She is just attempting to keep up with him. By pleasing him she pleases herself.

He feels the palpitations, the warmth of her body against his and he stops a minute to kiss her. A long kiss. Then they dance again. She wants more kissing but he is already part of the night, the music, the impatient exertion of his body. He is gone into the dancing. Then he is back again discontentedly in her arms, trying to figure out where to go next.

"I want to tattoo you," he whispers into the dark brush of her hair.

She retreats a minute and then laughs at this unpredictable man, resting in his excitement, swept into his angular face, his need to take her, the shock of his red hair.

"Okay."

***

Claire eats food without tasting it, coconuts, pineapple, mango trying for an exotic flavor. She doesn't enjoy anything. So this must be love. Its definition eludes her. Charlie is one ghost from all the people she has known, haunting her disproportionately, enthusiastically. He is just out of her reach, wavering, fading in the sunlight, one person rolling out with his red hair from her memories. She thinks about him constantly. Even more when he's not with her.

Even in the throes of Charlie she is immanently practical, sleeping regularly, concentrating on school, scheming how to keep Mother and Charlie apart just as Lizzie has done with her relationships. She tries to analyze love on television but doesn't understand the sleeplessness, the total disregard for food, the way feelings spread rapidly like some disease. It is a quick fire. While she feels as if something is caught in her heart. More of a slow smoldering. Still she misses the varied flavors of food, convincing herself of Charlie's incredible importance. For love is an accommodation. It is the food's blandness she learns to love. Claire combs her dark hair and, becoming distracted by her thoughts, forgets the comb. She walks to classes with the black plastic ridges decorating the back of her head until someone interrupts and informs her, "Hey, there's a comb stuck in your hair." Then she's absolutely sure she's in love.

***

Time with its imprecision implores Claire to forget everything. Its flimsy premise, its impolite discontent reminds her of a distant, visiting relative. She wakes up two years later with bed sheets and a blanket twisted and uncovering her feet. She thinks of the metal that hugged her legs, the twist of her thighs as a child. She awakens to light sneaking into the room from the blinds and darting into the corners so as not to be seen. It's eight-thirty a.m. on a Sunday. She loves this house in the middle of a New York suburb where she and Charlie moved to be close to his family. Even though they are surrounded by young families with small children who are always screaming "Come on, leftovers again tonight" through their screen doors. Neither she nor Charlie want little hands crawling up the length of their bodies, the crying, the diapers. She likes Charlie's arms encompassing her in bed at night, his iron biceps, the rippling surface of him is like a hard, ransacking river from working construction jobs all day. She smells the slightly sour sheen of him, thinking of an ocean creature abandoned on the beach for hours by the waves. She places her will within his driven will, satisfied that he is making the choices. She is happy within her home, cleaning it to excess, easy within her own territory, furniture arranged the way she likes it and she can contentedly relinquish the world. She likes rain knocking at the windows, trees brushing the roof, the way the path from the house to the main street slips into the mud of their lawn some days. She can sense their new dog, a Lab, straining at the screens enclosing the porch, looking at a squirrel or a cat and shivering with desire to have it in her mouth. She assumes this is a domestic dream.

The telephone rings and she hesitates because she figures Charlie is already working on something in the house with all his energy. He'll get the phone. But the phone is insistent like a language that asks for what it wants over and over.

"Hello?" She pulls the receiver to her cheek creased from sleep.

"Hi. Were you asleep?" Mother's voice.

"No." Claire knows it doesn't matter whether she says yes or no because Mother will continue on anyway. So she usually says no whether she is asleep or not.

"Well, guess what? I'm getting married again."

"Who is it?"

"A man."

"I know it's a man. What's he like?" Claire realizes she doesn't live far enough away from New York City, like Lizzie out in the wilds of Montana.

"He's retiring from a newspaper and he has a house in Connecticut and he's good looking...." She giggles a little.

Claire hears the front door close softly in another room. Charlie tiptoes in and running his hand through his hair he smells of stale cigarettes, beer. He hears Claire on the phone and thinks: oh no, I'm coming in too late. He is irritated by his ball and chain, at the keeper of his time. He likes independence in women, likes the type of woman who enjoys being a part of the world, who first says "yes" to everything and then later says "no." He slips into the bathroom, into the shower, the water running over his body is a bridge between two lives, washing away one of them.

"...and you should come to our wedding in a month." Mother wishes Claire and Charlie would get married but after the surprise of Lizzie she won't recommend it, won't commit herself to that piece of advice.

"Okay." Claire wants to get off the phone to see Charlie but Mother won't stop talking, her words falling, impaled by gravity, littering the lines. Claire doesn't care about a new stepfather. She doesn't have to since she doesn't live at home anymore. Claire is too old. She doesn't have to be a part of Mother's life anymore. Mother is a show tune she hums without being aware she is doing it sometimes.

When Mother's chattering stops Claire hangs up the phone and goes into the bathroom, wild with water. She starts wiping up puddles around the blue toilet, the sink, underneath the cascade of towels. She is talking to Charlie who is in the shower.

"That was my mother. She's getting married again."

"How many times has it been?" The words come through the pounding water. "Isn't this one the charm?" The water's conversation sudsing them, coercing them into this lugubrious interchange.

"This is her third time. And I can make fun of her because she's my mother but you aren't allowed to. By the way, where were you? At your parents?" Claire thinks of his Irish father, Italian mother at their house door with all seven children lined up in a descending row by age.

He is rubbing his underarm with soap. "Yeah. I just had to stop by and see a motor my father wanted to show me." He is comfortable speaking to the sheet of glass, the shower door is between them with mist crawling up his side. He is so full of a desolate want he doesn't know where to begin. An immaculate emptiness burns through him. A part of him needs to say: Let me explain everything. A larger part of him doesn't. He washes himself off.

Claire exhales and her shoulders relax. "She wants me to go to the wedding." Charlie steps out of the shower and she can see the almost invisible remnant of his birthmark, a fading red trellis up his spine. It disappears a little more each year into his skin, blending.

"Why not, babe?" He quickly adds, "I'm not going though." He shakes his head and wraps his towel around Claire's back, pulling her to his naked body.

She holds the sides of the towel and curls her hands over his shoulders. She feels his taunt muscles, the rustle of his breath. "Oh, you know how she can be."

"How about in the bathroom, babe?" He turns her around, slowly collecting her nightgown crumpled in his fists. He has already decided. She is facing the blue sink, the mirror where all that is reflected is her hair rhythmically covering her eyes, her collarbone extended toward the wall. She knows something should be said right now, but she has no idea what it could be. She closes her eyes to her hair.

He thinks that every woman wants to be needed.

***

Claire and Charlie are sitting on a grassy hill. Against the elbow of the obsequious landscape is a sprinkling of wildflowers, red, blue, purple on stems the color of

Charlie's eyes. Trees are pleated, in folds renouncing the various greens on the hillside. A small white exhalation of cloud, a filmy occlusion, moves through the bright, blue sky. Their picnic is spread out over the dog-print pattern on the blanket. Plastic forks and knives, paper plates curl at the edges around their center of uneaten food, the open straw basket, the ice case of beer. They can see the tiny, brown dot of their dog nosing the weeds in a pasture, an ocean valiantly delivering one of its boats. Claire is cleaning, trying to put the utensils, the food, neatly into the basket in the same way she would like to order her life: her job goes here, family into this compartment, love with its complications and contingencies can be deposited into several pockets. Charlie pulls off his shirt. The sun is alive on the curves of his construction-work muscles, his sunglasses swerve to the fence with its large DO NOT ENTER — PRIVATE PROPERTY sign and he knows that is where he wants to go.

"Hey. I think I see something over there." His head is tilted toward the fenced land.

Claire sees the fence skeleton in the glare of his sunglasses. He can't survive without excitement. He is an adventurer in modern times. And she is interested in the ride, likes the wildness vicariously. "Oh yeah, and what do you see?" She catches the passing storm of a bird traveling across his sunglasses. She turns to the sky to view the real bird, a small outburst, flapping against the azure sky.

"Well, like, I think there's something metal. Look, look right there." He is pointing toward the base of a tree.

Claire squints to see a long, thin glare, a sliver of moon, a pencil of light. "Maybe. What do you think it is?" She already knows what he thinks and doesn't really have to ask.

"Uh, well, like it could be a UFO." He is a little embarrassed.

"Why do you think that?"

"Well, look at the metal. I just can't tell from here." He starts to stand up.

"You know there's a no trespassing sign. Why would you go over there?" She is curious about his motivation, already certain he has to go over the fence.

"I have to check it out. If it's a real UFO and I find it, I'll like be famous. It would be something important I did with my life."

And nothing else is? Including her? "Good luck," she says to his departing back. She knows his needs often better than her own, believing people project their desires onto abstractions or, in this case, into abstract shapes. The same way history is various perspectives to different people, a warning, an example, the future, a description of who people are.

Their brown Lab comes back to Claire to nervously nose the basket of leftover food, the namesake blanket, the palm of her hand as if to say "Pet me now." The dog's back legs shake with her breath, with her tongue hanging from her mouth, her eyes fixed on Claire, half of her world. Claire pulls the wiry fur toward her lap, petting her head, speaking in low tones to the brown dog. She feels a spine and ribs buried beneath the earth-colored coat. Her paws are powerful, expressive and a funny, almost triangular shape. "Good girl, Mer." Short for Meryl Streep who was in a movie they both liked. Claire loves how dogs give themselves completely to whatever they are doing, digging a hole, licking, chasing an animal. Charlie is rummaging around the tree. Claire can't tell much from the distance but her heart quickens as she thinks of the owner from the house she can barely see greeting Charlie with a loaded gun. He doesn't think about safety or consequences, just action, a dervish held in a snapshot. Perhaps he does these things to thrill her. Doubtful. Sometimes she thinks he can't feel much unless he's breaking the rules. Like a child expectant for the attention from a spanking. But she sees his face triumphant, then fallen. He won't be famous.

Light coalesces into new wildflowers sprouting on the dog blanket, on the tips of Claire's toes. She wiggles them still retaining the warm touch of the sunlight's petals. Mer chases them, immersed in their darting, in the minuscule hunt, an ineffable prayer that can be transfixed by her teeth, subservient, jawed in her mouth. Unlike people Mer doesn't worship the inscrutable but the tangible, a favorite ball, a bone, grass crushed into another home, a squeaky toy. And cicadas begin and stop their cacophony, their religious hymn dedicated to air, the way it flows through their bodies, somewhere between humming and a song.

Charlie clamors over the fence, catching his sunglasses as they spring from his nose toward the ground, a grasping gesture as though he needed to snatch them back from a fist of wind. She doesn't notice anything else of importance in his hands. Shadows romance Claire. Fabricated tattoos.

He sits on the blanket, playing hide and seek with his fingers with Mer as though he has something precious or interesting for her. Mer barks a little, jumping from side to side on the dog design blanket. This labyrinth of games is her pleasure.

"Well?"

He tightens his knuckles behind his back, shifting from right to left and back again so Mer is racing after the inclination of his body. She is chasing his shadow. He halts and the dog halts also and they stare at each other. Mer barks loudly lifting her voice up to the sky, the subliminal clouds. He brings his right fist forward and turns it palm up, open for inspection. Both Mer and Claire gaze at a shiny, worn gum wrapper. This is what all the fuss is about, Claire thinks, what a disappointment. Mer lies on the blanket, her paws crossed over one another, her chin resting on top of them, her head and neck stretched like a flower without water, draped against earth in its last little piece of time. She moves her head to the side, a crescent moon descending into an animal horizon, closing her eyes with their dog eyelashes.

"Big deal. Huh?" He crushes the gum wrapper into a ball and tosses it into the far wildflowers, grass, weeds. "I'm getting tired of construction. All the shitty bosses. Man..." He shakes his head, saying no. "Maybe I should think about heating and refrigeration school." He thinks for a moment. "I hear the money's pretty good."

"I always think of the three bears. One too hot. One too cold. And finally one just right." Is there such a thing as perfect happiness? She'd certainly settle for contentment, peace, perfect temperature.

"No, really, waddaya think?" One hand is running over the dog's fur, persevering. Mer is dreaming, unfashioning the contours on fire hydrants, birds interrogating the sky with their wings, straddling benevolent shoes. Her eyes motion under her closed lids, a slight movement in her paws, snorting. Perhaps she is running or chasing in her sleep. It is a small afternoon nestled among many years together.

Claire wonders what Mer is hunting or escaping from. Time hurries in various directions. But she can't speak and Claire doesn't want to interrupt her in the middle of a dream. Claire would like to tell her to name the shape she wants. "I believe you can do whatever you want to do. I know you can do it if you want to." What would this mean to their relationship? Having lived together now for four years. "Would we have to move?"

"Hey, yeah. Let's try Florida. I hear air condition- ing is booming there." Mer is awake and licking her paws sedately with her pink tongue, saliva is around the edges of her mouth. The afternoon extends itself with changes, assuages itself with sky. "So we'll get married here in June and then, like, leave."

"You don't mind leaving your parents?"

"Naw. They're getting pretty old anyway. It'll be fun."

"Okay." She's excited now. Contemplating a wed- ding, astonished that loving someone is having passion with no other place to go. "Right, Mer," she whispers in allegiance into the paper thin dog ear, seeing its smooth, shell-like convolutions, intricate, fissured with attention. Coiled, flesh-colored she can get lost in there.

"Waddidya say?" He asks gazing past the fence, toward the fragment of the house streaked with obdurate sunlight like a candle carved eventually toward extin- guishment, night.

"Nothing." She is attracted to his determination, how reluctant problems vanish for him.

***

Claire remembers the plane to Florida where the depart- ing landscape was Braille she wanted to reach out and understand and read. What was it trying to tell her? One message: Don't stop here, keep on going. Another mes- sage: Don't leave what you know, are so familiar with. The hills and valleys below resembled a cousin's combed, green, well-known hair.

And Florida, Tampa, is bright, sunny, new. The white walls of buildings hypnotize the blue sky, sunlight enters every space, even climbing into Claire's dark, low cabinets. Palm trees, banyan trees slip roots deep into the cooler soil so they can push up their leaves as offerings to the unrelenting sun. Light overpowers most plants, driving them mad, brown, dried and curled into themselves. Only certain types of grass survive. Claire grows accustomed to sun crawling up her skin, through every crevice, sweat creating another body from hers, the shape of a puddle, a wet shadow. Insects complain about the food and demand more. Large ants and fleas drown themselves in sodas, in beers enticed by the taste, the delicious cool. Claire becomes attached to ice cubes, cold glasses, liquids, air conditioning. Summers she feels the terrible heat fling itself against their new house, determined to enter, to hug her, hold her until she sleeps. It is a lifestyle where everyone is on vacation, the shorts, flower printed shirts, bathing suit tops, straw hats for the tourists. The new malls are strung together for miles, all look the same. And underneath it all is decay. The humid, hot swamps with thick, watery air where everything dissolves. The rot, where things disassemble and are rearranged as something else. It's a place where former lives dissipate and people start new ones.

"Hi. Mother's divorced again." It is Lizzie calling from Montana.

"So what else is new?" Claire is watching water like insects drip down her glass of water onto her fingers.

"Three strikes you're out."

"Not her. She's a TV wind-up toy. She keeps going and going and going."

"Guess what she did now?" Lizzie and Claire spend much of their phone conversations discussing Mother and her antics.

Claire wipes a drop from her glass, balancing it on her finger. "What?"

"She got all dressed up. Even called me to ask me what she should wear. Just like the old days. So she goes over to her new ex's house all dressed up and tells him she has a present for him. That she wants to talk about getting back together. When he lets her in she goes right for his favorite painting, the Degas, with a knife from her pocketbook. And she's in a black sequin evening gown." Lizzie laughs at the image. "I told her just to forget about him. They're divorced. But no. She just has to make trouble."

"Did he call the police?"

"No. He grabbed the knife before she could do anything."

"Was she drunk?" Claire is determining the whiteness of her white walls. An ant stains a wall, lurching slowly across it. Claire wants to crush the insect, to remove it.

"Probably. She's still taking sleeping pills too. A different kind. But I know the combination is bad." Lizzie sees a tree sway out her window, grass flattening at an angle. "I've stopped drinking. I just decided to after Jay and his pot-smoking. It's time for something new."

"Good." There is some silence.

"How's Charlie, the good old boy?"

"Please don't say anything mean about him. He's my husband."

Lizzie tries to respect her wishes, although it is hard. Once when Claire and Charlie and Lizzie were all in New York visiting Mother Charlie draped himself outside the window of their car hurtling downtown to a restaurant screaming names at passersby. "Stupid," "Ugly looking," "Nigger." Lizzie assumed it made him feel superior although she was embarrassed and hoped they would get caught by a streetlight so someone would pluck Charlie from the car and teach him about "stupid" fists. Mother and Claire didn't utter a word. There is a bandage for every wound. The innate way they find each other. "He makes you cry." "That's the way I am. I cry easily." She wipes the glass tear on her pants leg. She notices a line of sweat beading in the air, running from her underarm down to her waist. "I'm a follower."

Lizzie imagines Claire tied and tucked into her Doctor Dentons. Lizzie doesn't flinch as Claire's forehead dances against the headboard, bone against wood. Childish games. Flesh and blood twitching, chattering about heredity. Lizzie wants to protect her. From whom? Herself? She wants to keep the varieties of darkness at bay for Claire. Stop her at the threshold of inhuman disguises. To hug her, encircling her navigable heart. Knowing, like a tourist gazing on the immense, jagged, geometric New York landscape, that there is nothing she can do. That the shadows are proportionally wrong and unrecognizable. "I've been hurting myself in my sleep lately. Twisting into funny positions so I wake up in pain. Jay said I used to moan sometimes or mumble but I didn't notice it (of course, I was asleep). I wonder if there's anything I can do."

"I don't have any trouble sleeping."

"No, you lucky thing. You never did. But you did get migraines."

"Those were my 'mother migraines' and I don't get them anymore. Thank God."

"So what do you want to bet that she gets married again. Let's say within three years. I'd bet ten dollars on that." Lizzie is smiling slightly at the thought.

"Oh, you'll win. I'm not much of a bettor."

"I think it was the times that made her crazy. The conventions of the fifties — marriage, children, all the prescribed methods of living." Lizzie knows she is explaining, reaching, adapting.

"Dream on."

"What do you think?"

"I spend a lot of time trying to forget my childhood." Claire waves her palm at her chin hoping for a slight breeze.

"I don't know if that works." Lizzie thinks memory is a slight gesture, how a scene or dialogue emerges from the past because a shirt falls on a shoulder a certain way or a nose tilts just so.

"Sometimes I think you are much stronger than I am."

"I just have more complex ways to hide my vulnerability. It was my role. I admire your vulnerability. The way you can feel your emotions. At least you can cry. I haven't done that in years. It's as if I won't give anyone, including me, the satisfaction." She shivers watching the cool Montana wind bend tree branches, ruffling the bushes and then hesitating before starting all over again.

"I certainly don't think of that as a gift." Claire acknowledges the weight of the heat, feeling it press in on her.

"Well, I love you and miss you and hope to see you soon." She wants to say: Don't let Charlie exhaust you into submission. Don't let him make you dizzy, turning you around and around until you don't know where you are. Like childhood. But she can't foist her own definitions and she promised not to badmouth Charlie.

"I love you too." Claire hangs up the phone and goes into the pure white bathroom. Mer follows, wanting to be petted, wanting to go outside for a walk again. Claire turns this way and that in front of the mirror. She contemplates the reality of her reflection, gathering the flesh around her hips, touching the mottling at her neck, the tired branch of her nose. She is jailed in her body. The helpless surface, a student of gravity, rinsed by the collusion of darkness, light, and glass. Her features slur into obliqueness, possibilities, as she swirls buoyant as a ship against the constant gaze. Fluid for an instant. Her limbs jewel together, commit to stillness, are heavy in their attachment, their claim. She wants her body disciplined, obedient, malleable to her ideal (and society's), a belief in faith and perfection. She moves sideways, drawing in her breath, looking at the straightness of her stomach lines, knowing they won't last.

***

"Hey, babe. I smell dinner." Charlie washes his red hair through his fingers. His own wet odor, a heavy, second skin, embraces him, pauses, wafts with the breeze. He walks toward Claire with her back toward him, her hands busy over the stove.

"Hi. It's Italian again. How was work?"

"Fine. I'm going to shower." He pauses and looks at her. He goes to the bathroom and his dark silhouette wavers behind the altered shower glass door throwing shadows across the white tile floor.

Claire hears the rhythmic spray of water in the background. Dinner is almost ready. The shower stops. Charlie shakes his wet hair around the room, like Mer, flinging droplets toward the ceiling, showering the furniture and floor around him.

She meets his eyes for a moment, annoyed. "Come

and eat meatballs and spaghetti." They both know she will
be limply on her hands and knees in a few minutes with a
dishcloth lifting water from the couch, the carpet, the arm
of a chair, feeling its lightness as though it were music
halting in the air, descending later. He sits down to eat at
the glass table displaying the white lawn of carpet underneath. She reaches for the dishcloth and as she kneels there
is anger in her breath. She acknowledges the small trickle
of it and buries it, a mine, deep below the pit of her
stomach where forgotten insults, ancient hurts, sharp irri-
tations, and old judgments lie. He lifts the fork twisted
with noodles, drenched with sauce to his mouth repeat-
edly, leaving a trace of red splattered around his lips. His
fresh smell of soap fills half the room. He is in nice, clean
clothes.

"How is it?" She asks starting to stand up.

"Okay. Next time more meatballs, babe." He wipes
his mouth on the flowers permanently imprinted on his
napkin. She has made dinner for him for ten years now.

"Stop right there." He is speaking to her crouched back.

"What?" She is frozen, uncertain. Perhaps it's a
spider.

"Like I can't believe your hips. Turn around." He
pushes the wiped plate away, into the middle of the table.
The dog's leg peeks at him from the glass corner. Claire
rotates to face him. "No, wait, stop there." She is sideways,
cowered. "Shit, like, look at your stomach." Her hands
flutter over her jeans zipper. "You have to do something
about that body. My mom always said that you marry
them and they go to shit."

She is humiliated, turning toward the shape in the
mirror that she wants to disown. She is quiet, wanting to
camouflage herself in the house, draw the furniture close
around her, pull the mica ceiling over her head like a

blanket. The walls could contain her, rock her. Yes, she has a rounded stomach, more hips. But nobody's perfect. She gulps half words down her throat, a wave of hurt flooding her face. She goes to Mer, smoothing the bare part of her stomach as Mer lifts her front legs, ignoring him.

He stands up, pushing the chair out from his knees. "I gotta go." He is searching for his thin, denim jacket.

"Where are you going?" She is under the corner of the glass table, one hand on Mer, the hurt veined with anger. Her dinner sits untouched, a red pile slightly steaming, fogging a circle on the glass.

"Out, meeting the boys. You know."

"A drink? At a bar?"

"Yeah, like always." He is smug.

"Why don't you just leave me?" She had to say it.

"Whaddaya mean?" He stops ambling for a minute. His constant restlessness halted.

"I mean why don't you go and not come back." She hesitates. "If you're so unhappy, I'd be happy to set you free." Free from my ugly body she thinks. She won't be his obstacle. His excuse. A whistle to call him back, a warning.

"No." He looks disgusted. "I don't mean that." Although he has thought about walking out that door and not coming back. But he's too unsure. "Just get it together more. You know what I mean." His voice trails out the door.

She hears the car motor screaming in the garage. Like me, she thinks, when his hands are on me. She doesn't know when he will be back. Drinking with his friends again, the smell of liquor and cigarettes makes a path to the bathroom at night. In the morning he has showered, brushed his teeth. So there are no traces of the person who came in the night before. "Daddy's going, going, gone," she whispers to Mer. She can hear her words resonate, echoing under Mer's fur, in the hollow parts of Mer's body. Now she cries. Because she can. The tears are translucent lurching down her cheeks, reeled into the creases. She cries for a long time, for herself, for her imperfect figure, for all the amassed wrongs. She holds a tissue to her eyes until it is a soaked ball disintegrating between her knuckle bones. Through the blur she notices the photo of Charlie with his arm around her, grinning. She places it face down as though she wouldn't allow him to see how he makes her suffer, resembling an animal distressed by her own skin, fighting to remove it. That would be all that's needed, is another divorce in this family. Her failure exemplified in this man whom she has spent half her life with. He is her whole life. This man who isn't here. Who is in some godforsaken bar. She will do better, exercise, adjust as she always does. She is sobbing, wiping stray tears with the back of her hands. The wetness streaks her hair making it darker, soggy, threatening her face. She puts her arms around Mer, kissing her, tumbling into her fur body, tipping her problems toward Mer's eager attention. Mer comforts, her paws lined up, ready for a chance to please. Like Claire. Waiting for endearment. Even if it takes a long time. The phone rings. She pulls stray fur from her lips. She dries her eyes, clears her throat. It is Mother talking. About her third ex husband she says, "I have cured him of marriage."

***

Sunlight interrogates the stubby, Florida grass. The years with Charlie accumulate under Claire's fingernails, where her jawbone meets her ear like dirt, or desiccated into sand running plentifully under her toes. She sighs, sits back into the routine of married life. She is thread sewn into the

garment of their relationship, patiently stapling it together. She is dusting their photographs, quiet squares
freezing moments from wilder days, hot air ballooning or
skiing with smiles down oceans of forgotten snow. So
much like life, but even more dependable and consistently
available. His wide shoulders, resembling a muscular
puzzle, set against the unfettered sky. She can lift the
photographs, unfold a happier time, remind herself of the
real thing, caught, expendable, something she can ask the
world for again and again. She picks up Charlie's picture
and moves him to the forefront, her hands slow to release
the frame. It all comes down to relativity. A neighbor's
darkening windows she can only guess at. Or a woman's
wobbly legs at the grocery store. She makes assumptions
about appearances just like everyone else. Deciding what
makes the woman's legs so unsteady that day. It is omi-
nous, portentous, the window shutting her neighbor inside with its impenetrable blinds. People's quiet suffering.
The doorbell rings and she carefully answers it, recognizing a married friend of Charlie's.

"Hi," she says opening the door wide to his dark,
handsome head surrounded by the blue chiffon sky. "What
are you doing here?"

"Is Charlie here?" His hair rakes his ears boyishly.
He steps into the white living room.

"No, why?"

"I just wanted to drop off this cable for him." His
eyes search the tall room sparse with patterned furniture
and a small glass table near the kitchen. He focuses on the
patio listing toward some older palm trees as though
Charlie could suddenly materialize there. His eyes settle
on Claire. He drops the cable onto the floor and inches
closer to her. Mer's ears are pricked, alert to unusual
sounds, to the new aroma of Old Spice although her body

lies inert, floating near sleep. Claire's hands knit themselves behind her back, her legs in shorts feel stripped and
stark like light bulbs on a shadeless lamp. Each word he
enunciates is raw against her bare knees. "I know this
sounds weird but I've wanted to tell you how truly beautiful you are for some time now." He looks at his sneakers,
at the cable resting against the couch like an oblivious
animal.

Claire is flattered and something quivers in her,
discards some heavy object, gathers, fluttering above her
stomach. Someone inside her, another person says "Yes,"
"Yes," "Oh yes." And where is Charlie anyway? Gone. The
other person churns, longing to stroke the handsome, dark
friend and exhale "finally." He could burn off the clouds
on an overcast day. His sunny face imprints her flesh,
leaving his image. "How's your wife?" She finally speaks,
looking into his dark eyes. She is determined not to become Mother. Her beliefs and principles swim through
her, surfacing, directing her. She can close her eyes and
breath without thinking, progress through murky water
and arrive at some destination without guilt, sacrifice,
confusion. It is a straight shot. No water left dripping
slowly. No hesitations. Nothing leaking from her. She
wants to be better than that. And she's seen the results,
being one herself.

"Fine. We don't get along all that well. But that's
not the point." He rests his fingertip on her shoulder. "You
are," and he kisses her unmoving mouth lightly.

Claire is stony, absent, having closed herself off to
him, encased herself in something hard and shiny, she has
decided. She is elsewhere. Unavailable. Sure. The refrigerator sputters and Mer rises on stiff legs, walks in half of
a circle and collapses again onto her bed, a lumpy pillow.
She looks at them as if asking "What are you doing?"

Nothing, Claire replies without speaking. Claire is glassy eyed, far away as though hypnotized by the brazen sunlight, stunned into warmth, heat, and motioning him out the door. "Good-bye. I'll tell Charlie that you stopped by," she pauses, "and nothing else." She is posed by the open door, her heart unmoored, drifting secretly past uncharted currents, pounding in waves. Her fingers, glued near the keyhole, are shaking as though she is cold. She is distracted as if Mer is mutely calling her back inside.

"If you ever change your mind..." and his voice grows fainter.

***

The television talks to Claire. But she doesn't understand the words, the unending parade of words, sentences breaking against her in waves, because she is half listening. A snarl of clouds emerge and disappear, caught and framed in the square set. Change the channel and a woman is talking to her jewelry. There is scribbling at the bottom of the screen, phone numbers, dollar amounts resting on the hair of her arms like insects. On another channel there is a face that would be familiar to her in its stardom if she could notice and not think about Charlie. Where is he? He should have been home hours ago. Her mind distracts her from the entertainment, the company. The television light tries to hold her expression, her countenance, and cannot. He could be in a ditch, dead, hurt. She searches through her hands as though they could have the answer and tell her. Mer sighs and sits at her feet with her fur head on her paws.

She has done this before, this dance of anxiety, her veins pressing against her pale forehead, her unsettled feet and arms like birds to be held in a mouth until they stop shaking. Sometimes she will turn off the sound to the television and watch people move and speak without meaning, resembling ghosts. Or abstract paintings. She doesn't know what is happening on the screen and doesn't care except for the companionship. Then she will turn the sound on again just to discover what events are occurring, what time it is becoming. It is a connection to the world outside herself. She turns the knob off. Charlie said he was going to a friend's house from work. It is two in the morning. There was no answer when she called the phone number. She goes into the bedroom and lies on the quarrel of sheets and blankets on the bed, uncharacteristically messy. Her body slips easily into the same spaces she created an hour ago. The bedspread climbs over her and she stares at the mica ceiling thinking of bombs, earthquakes, gunfire, all the disasters out of control, thinking about the pain that flickered across Charlie's features yesterday as he drank too many beers. The image scuttles into her mind like a small, hard pebble underfoot. She wants to sleep. But she keeps remembering how he closed himself off from her that day as if he wanted to slip out of his own skin, his chosen life. Instead he drank until he was dizzy and lay down on this bruised bed. She grips the sheets in her pale fists and acknowledges the ceiling again. It is a backdrop to her thoughts, a blank page in her story. The ceiling is whatever she makes it. And silence is another person in the room. It is the room itself. Claire feels its noticeable presence and thinks again of the television. She listens past the silence for the hint of a car, a footstep nearby. Mer is lying at the foot of the bed, the brown wreckage of a dog.

She ascends into the living room again and adjusts the spill of television light, the voices. A different ceiling, looking very much the same. Sleep isn't her usual friend tonight. Mer follows with her brown tail down. Seconds tick by. She feels them in the sentences covering her, rolling off her, repeating themselves from the television. Time. She can't imagine being without him, the way he directs their lives, throwing himself into decisions, right or wrong. Her limbs are tense, muscles clenching and unclenching to the rhythm of time like flowers opening and closing. She can hear her own breath. The gestures of people on television appear normal and she wants to imitate them, the casual placement of an elbow, legs crossing, a relaxed leaning into speech. She wishes her marriage could resemble some of the ones on television, the kisses, embraces, dovetailing into one another easily, the lyricism. But after nine years of marriage she knows better. She is more familiar with the angry silences, sulking, fights, moodiness. Although there were times: out on a boat staining a lake, pulling in fish with water pirouetting around them, taking their breath away; or they were laughing so hard at a restaurant once that she spit her food into Charlie's plate, spraying the table; or she watched him dare to cross a barricade and enter a waterfall where his body became dim, foggy, a cloud in the rain of water. She still hasn't lost him.

It is seven in the morning. Mer is curled into sleep, on her side with her stomach towards the mica ceiling. The television programs now have a perky, too cheerful quality that irritates her. Claire yawns in her sleepiness and feels the world is distant, removed from her as though each movement is executed in a dream. She finally hears the car engine in the garage and relief floods her.

"How's my lady?" Charlie tries to say cheerfully with pain edging his face as he comes into the house.

Claire throws herself onto Charlie, checking him for any cuts or misuse. He has a sour, pungent smell under the alcohol and cigarette odor. He seems intact and Claire is happy. "Are you okay? Where were you?" She is eager to know.

"I'm fine." He unwraps her arms, placing her shoulders an arm's length away, his expression frozen in midair. His bloodshot eyes are entwined with hurt, his forehead wrinkled, his red hair tufted, his teeth grinding, his jaws stiff, unyielding.

"Where were you?" Relief blankets her and now she has questions, her heart beating loudly. She feels scraped up from the kitchen table, tired, used, left over.

"What's the worst thing you can think of? What's your worst nightmare?" He looks as though someone has hit him but hasn't left any marks. His face is cringing.

"That you slept with another woman."

"Your nightmare has come true."

She stares at his wavering face, bending in the heat. It is misplaced. Silence. Then, "How long? How long has this been going on?" She wants to know. Her voice is incipient, mumbling.

"Three weeks," he says to the kitchen, subdued.

She recalls his ridiculously long bicycle rides, excessive time spent in front of a mirror, the abrupt phone calls when she entered the room. The morning is amorphous and she cannot breathe. It is ebbing, draining from her. It has all been right there, right in front of her, accreting and futile like snow. Of course, people betray themselves in insignificant details, a head turning, a phrase, too many showers. They want to. She should have known. "I'd be willing to try and save this marriage. We could go to a counselor and work on it. But you'd have to stop the affair." Someone else is speaking from the empty shell of her body, imitating the necessary motions. She's not sure she is still alive.

"I can't."

It feels like a punch. "You can't or don't want to?"

"I want the both of you." He runs his unsettled fingers through the jumble of his hair. He shakes his head and looks at her almost appreciatively. "I could keep seeing the both of you."

She is unfeeling, the morning is kneeling before the afternoon implicitly. "What? Until you decide?"

"Yeah." He is unapologetic, familiar with her mind, the way she thinks. He is intimate with her thoughts, her buttons. How she is a bystander, waiting. Waiting for his decision.

She thinks of the infidelities sprinkling her childhood, her cheeks shriveling into paper burnt in a fire. Her nose is bruised, worming its way toward her eyes. Her face feels blasted, collapsing under his proposition, under his artifice, his deceptions. He is unrepentant. Her needs percolate like warm water under ice. They are melting an unaccustomed path to her indiscreet features. She requires trust, allegiance. She wants someone with her, on her side. Her mouth is stippled with light, twisted so she won't weep. She could blossom, relax with a companion, someone she was comfortable with. And he is disassembling her world, the house, the marriage. It is in little pieces with nothing to hold onto. She splays her body across the door and her wooden legs are suspended over the threshold.

"I'm going out for a walk." The minute she is past their house she exhales and is hysterical, crying as she is shuffling down the street. Sunlight writes paragraphs across her arms and legs but she cannot read them, aware of only her damaged heart. She is crying onto the cement sidewalks, staining their fractures and watering the weeds with their suspended arms waving at her. She is a cloud

186

hovering over a lake, expectant of her circumstances, impaired by the sky, and attempting to run from harm's way. Pain. She glimpses a neighbor at his window and doesn't care, still crying. She passes lawns, bushes, flowers, palm trees asking to be left alone and people walking their dogs, suspicious, who cross to the other side of the street. She notices a rock across an avenue, large, decorative, gray among professionally landscaped bushes with a glass and steel building flying up behind it. As she gets closer she identifies black etchings. It is initials of the loved or lovelorn and she sobs louder at the little carved hearts. Windows of cars and buildings seem to rush by her like wasted love. Tears brush her shirt, wash her hands. She grows heavier, soaked, rain sustained by the ground, levitated, walking. She can barely breathe but there is something in her fighting for air even as she swallows her own mucus. She wants to become a puddle but cannot. She stops. She admires a worn, wooden bench's attachment to the earth that doesn't want it, doesn't care about it. She is somewhere on a street in Tampa.

Sunlight falls against her shirt on its journey somewhere else and warms her. Her blouse peels from her ribs and shivers, tries to join a breeze, tries to extricate itself from her, tumbling, disappointed against her chest and stomach. A failure. What does this woman have that she doesn't have? Besides her husband. She is taking her life away and Claire would kill her if she could. She wonders if he has done this before but it just didn't work out for him. Like when they relocated to Florida. Her body is becoming the bus bench, the surfaces resemble one another. She glances at the street with its script of cars and white lines, curbs and wires. Victor flickers at the edge of her thoughts. She can almost see him, with his half smile, leaning against a hydrant, arms crossed, wiry gray hair severing his face. He whispers, "You'll get over this too," and fades. A palm tree momentarily pauses from trembling in the wind. Fading light conveys some heat, warming her knees, her chest, her neck and she cannot hold onto it or command it. She doesn't complain or relegate the responsibility for decisions. It is time for something different, something new. Time to follow their own separate, intended roads, destiny which she believes in. Otherwise the relationship will go on forever like the elderly man across the street, proceeding in circles with his walker, forgetting that he just turned around. Doing it over and over because of habit. Habit, that comfortable ritual. She looks at her hands and understands again that they are her own. She watches the elderly man orbit emptiness unwittingly. His deep green clothes are the color of old institution walls or the hue of being permanently alone. She doesn't want to return home and see Charlie's carrot-topped face, his loosened body worried about his future as well as her own. That stupid male body that betrayed her. She would like to hit him, punch him as long as she could feel how her own body is connected to her, the blow. As long as it is her own fist sinking into the flesh of his stomach. It would be a hollow pleasure. She really doesn't want to see him, the darkness filling up between them, their hopscotch of useless words. The deeds are done.

There is movement. Footsteps. Lights begin to unbutton the night. A door opens and closes. A man's familiar, grimacing face floats toward her without a body.

"I have decided," that is already a lot for Claire to say, "to divorce you." A surprised look from him. "Please get out right away."

"Hey, babe. Like where am I going to go?"

"How about your girlfriend's?"

"It's not that kind of relationship yet."

"How about a hotel?" She's not interested in arguing with him about details. She doesn't want contact with him at all.

Fuck you, he thinks, getting angry. He's unprepared for this. Getting thrown out. He thought she would let him decide in his own time. "This is a surprise," he says giving her a drop-dead look. "Like this is my house too."

This isn't a surprise for her? Claire blinks, visualizing her father crowbaring their apartment door in fast-forward motion. It is a frenzy. The hole grows wider and wider in the midst of all the clanging. Suddenly Charlie's features fill up the hole, his aquamarine eyes seem to look right through her. Then there is a flower there with a green stem and crimson blossom. She wants to pick it but is afraid to touch it.

"Okay." She is disappointed with herself. "You can stay here for two weeks." And then she turns to look at him. "Then you have to get the fuck out."

Flying, Isabelle, 1989

"Let me tell you about having sex with a woman."

"Why, Mother?" Lizzie gets that exasperated sound in her voice. "Are you giving me a hint?"

"No. Be that way." Mother is annoyed.

"What way do you mean?"

"You know."

"All right. Tell me."

"Clara and I did it in her living room while Frank watched." She wants to tell her, share. She needs to.

"Who's Frank?"

"A handsome friend of ours. He really enjoyed himself."

"I bet he did. Anyway, now that I'm divorced I'm sorry to say that no one will think I'm a lesbian. Huh, Mother?"

"Well anyway. I was calling you because I'm getting married again."

"Great. Congratulations. Is it to Sherman?"

"Yes, of course."

"Well it could be someone else." Lizzie likes to tease her.

"Who?"

"How about someone you found on the street who said they would marry you. Or maybe Frank."

"Very funny, Lizzie. Anyway did you hear that Claire is signed up at about three different singles agencies?"

"No, she just got divorced. She should take a rest and think about things."

"I think she's got a lot of guts to just get right out

there again. It's like riding a horse. When you get thrown you're just supposed to get right back in the saddle again."

"Charlie was like a horse all right. A horse's ass. No one ever liked him except Claire. But I'm not supposed to say anything bad since I promised her I wouldn't."

"So both you girls can come to my wedding. It should be fun. Small because he hates to waste money and he doesn't like parties much. That's probably how he saved all that money."

"He doesn't sound like the right man for you." Uh oh, Lizzie thinks, here we go again.

"Besides, you should come because Carl is dying."

"Again?"

"I heard it from my dentist. And he was your favorite father. You have to come to New York before he dies. He likes you the best."

"He almost died a year and a half ago too. Remember, I came to New York. And he was still kicking. He was just fine." But Lizzie knows that when Mother calls she'll come. "How old am I supposed to be?" The old, repetitive question. She hates it, hates lying, but is afraid she will undo Mother's relationship. She is reticent, complicitious about this folklore. She scissors her feet, her adult red toenails seesaw effortlessly like scarlet birds breaking into flight. The boneless stars squirm just beyond her window, resembling exhausted artillery, their light is opalescent, bursting, considering how immersed they are in the obliterating night.

***

Night and Isabelle mulls Sherman's fence of bones hanging from his gnarled spine, his ropy arms, hair laminating his ears, his torn and dirty underwear when she touches him. Her fourth husband. And counting. Lots of movie stars have had more husbands. He goes to sleep early and unceremoniously awakens early. She goes to sleep late and rises late. Cradled by the bed covers, she dreams of his body slithering against hers, beseeching her, adhesive under the sleeveless stars. They dribble their light insinuating its way into their labyrinthine New York apartment, acquainting themselves with the poverty of his youth, his diligent cheapness. He won't buy anything unless it is on sale or has a coupon. They rarely go out to eat. He exclusively uses the subway. His money remains unchallenged, lonesome, a useless keepsake. Just like him. She has thought about trying to kill him, simple salmonella poisoning from food left out too long and he eats anything. But he is in his eighties, set in his ways with the world, unchangeable, flourishing, and indestructible. The confetti of sunlight has followed him for hours, corseted to him, already this morning. He is in his bathroom-sized office giving instructions about television programs over the phone. There is one window like a poster pasted behind his head. Music from boom boxes, the clatter of a nearby stable's horses' hooves, cars, and loud theories shouted from the street find his good ear. A bouffant of early light huddles on the wall, oscillating like Isabelle too early in the morning or right after a delightful, late-night party. He finds her less remarkable the longer the marriage endures. He wished for breasts he could swim in, her face mullioned with interest, a good cook, someone to listen to the radio of his voice, his ideas. The brilliant rotunda of him and his work. Now he enjoys the incumbent morning greeting him while Isabelle is still tossing and turning in the bed they once couldn't wait to share.

Isabelle wakes up, realizes she is in the sprawling apartment on the West side of New York and frowns. The visceral, dark wood floors in the apartment eclipse her, autopsying the space. Prominent cobwebs climb the walls along with Impressionist paintings. She shivers. She remembers their argument last night, furious against these walls, echoing down the hall, glaring at them and over nothing, a small jealousy or a man's offhand remark. Vowels ransacked their closets, loud with clothes. Even her bangles shook in her jewelry box. She lists her complaints against him in her head as well as over the phone constantly. Egotistical, cheap, inflexible, self-concerned, and no fun. She can't discern any possibilities in him. She dislikes his Jewishness and in doing so dislikes that part of herself. She strives to be his opposite. She cultivates contrary qualities hoping she can recreate her husband, coerce him to become someone new. The way she recognizes her favorite shirt on a stranger in the subway and then dismisses it as ordinary. Its estimation plummets. So she wears its opposite. And they know how to drive one another crazy. It is too easy. The accumulated resentments, big and little. The frivolous renditions of former fights. It is a circus in the apartment with its share of acrobats, clowns and tightrope walkers. Even Lizzie says so.

This morning is another birthday for Isabelle, a mere invention of time, another precipice. One version of her age. A hollow day. An unpleasant invention unlike television, VCRs or the telephone. She turns on the television, her steady companion, avuncular. She counts the sleeping pills in the bottles tucked behind the mirrored bathroom cabinet like cohorts. There are enough for a month or two. She told Lizzie that she is certainly old enough to get her own doctor and prescription instead of borrowing hers sometimes. She sits in front of the enlarging mirror, her face filling its emptiness, her eyes dislodging refracted light. The eyes follow her everywhere. Tubes, bottles, small cases and pencils encompass her, awaiting a request. Their colors in loose disorder like flower petals gliding through a courtyard. She banishes wrinkles, discolorations, imperfections from her skin. Flesh-colored powder sprinkles her lips, rests papery against her cheekbones. Darkness learns to shade her eyes, a blush returns to her cheeks, her red lips kiss themselves against the mirror. It can take hours. Her straw-colored hair coils around her long neck.

There is a small white box with a green ribbon sitting on her dresser when she emerges ready to meet a girlfriend for lunch. She hurriedly opens the box and finds tufted in cotton a pair of antique earrings, gold with pearls. Cheap, she thinks, disgusted. These are from his vault, were on the ears of his dead wife. He had asked Isabelle to wear one of his dead wife's dresses for their wedding. A nightmare reliving itself, a circus. Sherman is a mercenary monument to the past, cocooned in a time with outdated conventions, paintings depicting another era. She is interested in the present, the future and what can be acquired and retrained. A fortune teller down the street shuffled her tarot cards with their pictorial summaries and confessions. She told Isabelle that Sherman is an unfortunate man. He would die in his sleep soon and that Isabelle could expect love and money shortly afterwards.

She returns to the bathroom with its curious, consensual light, its metal and tile constituents. Opening a drawer she removes several tampax, scatters them around her make-up like memories. He believes she is much younger. She doesn't want to suffer his touch, the shudder of his old man's body. His snoring that reaches out for the moon. She will curl into herself, the soothing voice of television, the movie stars, perhaps sleep, drifting under

194

the screen's fish light like waves returning to themselves. After all it is her birthday.

***

Heart to heart. Each night Isabelle relaxes by drinking tea, plotting, taking a bath. Tonight, Isabelle allows the warm water to wash her limbs. A white smear from her foaming oil appears. It resembles a white skirt or clouds ripped by the jagged arm of wind from the days she used to fly an airplane. She was twenty years old and would talk to the sky but never received an answer. "I'm coming," she would say to its indifference. Or "Watch out," as she turned a dial, shifted a gear, looked straight through the sky to glimpse trees or houses in Pennsylvania. She thought the dwarfed towns looked like children's toys she wanted to examine, rearrange. She enjoyed the excitement, the belief that she was departing on an adventure, that she would go someplace better. Yet she wasn't accustomed to reaching out for small objects and not grasping them, possessing them. And she realized that the sky wasn't hers, that all she could do was to pass through it. Even though the tiny houses weren't hers it was as if she could pinch them between her fingers for a second, make them even smaller and hers temporarily. She wasn't familiar with traversing somewhere without changing, disrupting, transforming a placid surface. "Paris for lunch?" she would rhetorically ask Jordan, an old boyfriend, or whomever accompanied her. She gazes at the bath water pimpled with bubbles, allows the streaked water to clothe her, a tributary tracing the length of her arm. She is consumed with contempt for her husband two rooms away.

***

Within each one of Isabelle's gestures lies another gesture, snaked, embryonic, waiting to be released. The punch contained in crossed hands. Within shaking hands is a tight finger of anger or the open palm, a question of acceptance. Within a kiss is a greeting, jealousy or perhaps the possibility of love. In New York society Isabelle tries to interpret gestures to understand their true meaning. To understand someone. To have passionate affairs of the heart.

A sparrow sits in an occasional New York tree and Isabelle greets a lover in the park. He left a string of messages on her private phone that when played from her answering machine all sounded like "I am drowning. I need to breathe you." His voice is grieved, time is heavy as a stone dropped through water. She sees his expression is an apology for transgressions he didn't even realize he made. But he does want to know what he's done to make her cool, distant. And she's just bored with him.

"You're being childish." She acknowledges that he has other women right now. They have described their lives apart to one another like a blink of an eye, a blindness, before being able to see again. That was when she liked sleeping with him. When it was exciting. "And besides I'm married and my husband might find out."

"I don't care." He is younger, less experienced, and entranced by her mystery. With the lack of conveyance about her he can make her into whomever he desires.

"He'll kill you," or me, she thinks. She will let this lover know exactly what she won't do, who she won't be.

"He can't if he doesn't find me."

He is becoming difficult to loosen, an insect still stuck to her skin, an eternal bite. She wants to go home, even with her husband there. "But I can find you."

"I want you to." He is thinking of the mole on her

thigh, the easy way she slips into his bed.

"If I can find you then so can my husband, moron." She slaps him. For insistence, punctuation, for his stupidity. To end it. A leaf falls between them in the deserted portion of the park. Trees quiver, subside into the sky.

He looks at her, an older woman in a cream Dior suit, with his palm to his cheek. He pushes her hard against a tree where she crumples into the roots, hitting her back. "You're such a bitch," he mumbles.

Just the way you like me, she thinks. "Get out of here before I call the police." She is standing, brushing herself off, earth and leaves tumble to the ground like a list of injuries. "For assault by a stranger in the park." He's become a liability.

His head moves toward her but she won't look at him. He's not ashamed of what he's done. He will think of her at night when the darkness is half finished, spread out against his unmade bed. This woman, troublesome, the mother of two children, the wife of a wealthy, older man. There are lots more fish in the sea, as they say. He leaves her for now.

His head of blond hair, the back of his jacket, his jeans fade through the bushes, the latticed, ordered garden, the relentless green trees, the ghostly iris nuzzling the air. She is relieved, the pain in her back is insignificant considering the possibilities. She is the kind of woman who can turn the other cheek. She is glad to watch him leave.

On the way home she stops at a department store. She is undone by the bargains, silk blouses, imported shoes, aisles stitched with merchandise under the sharp, unforgiving light. She has run her fingers with joy or sorrow or boredom over the conflagration of clothes, jewelry, and accessories. She has bought things just to appease herself, an offering. The kind of present she would give a guest visiting her home too long when she wants to get rid of them. A gift to go. She knows Lizzie and Claire are afraid she will break. They want to protect her. From whom? The world? Herself? Is there a sign? You break it, you pay for it. She finds a moss green silk blouse muscled with fringe that she likes in a bin.

Her high heels click down the street puzzled with trees and people. Traffic is insistent. The smell of frying food, gasoline, the heat of motion from the sidewalks. Litter flings itself around her feet. She is slightly unsettled, a bruise ripening up the length of her back. Her shopping bag rustles outside the apartment door as she finds her keys. She breaks a fingernail. The door opens into the musty, dark rooms of the apartment reminding her of thrift store suitcases and her need to get out, go somewhere else, escape. Sherman is sitting in the living room near the legs of the piano, a book is open on his lap. He is always sitting there. He rarely goes out anymore.

His colorless face turns toward her. "Where have you been?"

"Out shopping and for lunch." There is a throb along her spine. "Ouch, I broke a nail and it hurts." She lifts her finger up, inspecting it. "Why? Do you want to see my new shirt?"

"No, not really. I was just wondering."

She pivots and moves down the hallway, relieved but yet ready for a fight at the same time. She picks up a hanger and her new blouse immerses itself in the closet bursting with clothes. At the mirror in the bathroom she turns each way trying to discern any marks from the break up, the bruises from a lover's attention, the remnants of his supposed love. She is suddenly impatient. She walks to the apartment door again.

"Now where are you going?" he asks.

"Just downstairs to give the doorman something a friend's going to pick up."

"What?"

"What are you? The apartment police?" She exits the door. She descends the marble steps with iron balustrades until she reaches the storage units for the various apartments. She has rented one of her own. No one else has a key. She rearranges two valuable first-edition books, several small bronze statues, letter openers studded with gold and stones, miniature clocks, pencil holders, silver pens, watches, etched flasks, gilded picture frames, ornate candlesticks, even one world globe until she reaches a platinum bowl and gold bookmark. She holds these two items toward the dimly lit ceiling. These are what she stole from this lover and they are only a fraction of what she deserves.

***

"Women are jealous of me," Mother explains to the beige telephone receiver. Its flesh-colored curve around her jaw is reminiscent of a flower stem bending with its own gravity toward the earth. "They want what I already have." And she lists her assets to Lizzie. The acquisitions she collects in a glass curio display case, a husband, money, jewelry, social connections. She constantly rearranges them. Often it is as if she is talking to herself, regurgitating her day to decipher the hidden meaning, the importance merely in the telling, in having someone listen. She'll talk loudly over Lizzie's words when she's interrupted. She's not finished yet. "That's why Sally is so bitchy with her remarks." She can't remember whether she is speaking to Lizzie or Claire sometimes, calling one by the other's name until they remind her which one she is talking to. And then she continues, costuming her time with incidents, interesting, wild tidbits about what she did, thought about doing, or what people did to her. The wrong-number caller she tried to meet or a friend asking her to pretend she's his girlfriend. The depilatory smell of hair remover reaches her nostrils from the thin, pink mud on her legs. "And why shouldn't they be jealous of me? I have everything." She observes light vivisecting her pink ankles, stopping on her shins, considering her calves. She feels encased in the chemical smell, the extra layer tight and heavy on her legs, making them slick. She is aware of a tingling. The cream is working noticeably while she is still talking on the phone. The conversation meanders toward Lizzie so she swerves it back toward herself, opening the day's events like a book and reading every last detail. For herself, about herself, often repeating herself. Because she feels so unalterably alone.

***

Sherman and Isabelle are going out to eat at a nearby restaurant. The last, deafening rush hour traffic with headlights throws their pacing shadows in makeshift shapes against the city walls. Sherman walks head down as if listening for uninvited laughter, crushing concrete under his feet, irritable at spending money. Isabelle's eyes are caught and held in picture windows filled with clothes, jewelry, and household items. The sidewalk before her is cut like an apple into matching pieces of window light. She believes light is eccentric like Sherman, easily disrupted by a switch, falling into unpredictable places in its various escapades. She likes those qualities, the unending gymnastics of illumination, the unlimited consumer goods visibly for sale in the windows. Passersby brush a sleeve, a skirt, one pant leg with their different languages, pieces of dialogue captured by an ear. And the smell of food on the street can traverse the distance of up to a block. Dirt mixes into the odor of Chinese, Italian, Mexican, German, deli, even Hungarian, African.

"When can we have sex, it's been such a long time?" Sherman is visibly anxious.

"We did!" she exclaims. "We had sex last night. Don't you remember?" She's beginning to wonder about his memory. He is in his eighties but to forget what they did just the night before is surprising.

"We did not. You're such a liar." He stops in the middle of the street glaring at her, daring her.

"We did," she emphasizes, getting frustrated with him.

"We did not."

"We did too," and she slaps him, annoyed at his obduracy, his ridiculous, stupid face. She wishes he would wake up and come to life in a positive, not an irritable way. The sidewalk is frescoed with their gesticulating shadows admonishing each other. People walk by not noticing or not interested in their discord. Their argument fades into the general din, the slap fades into tires against the pavement, the tapping of shoes against cement, doors and windows flagrantly open and close, the syntax of conversations. They are two people in a city of millions.

"You slapped me." His palm is covering his cheek, the sensation is a splash of water, a physical request, a flower petal reminded by the wind about the world around it. His eyes grow wide. He untethers his hand and raises it, stepping toward her. He stops, restaurant lights transfixing him, looking at all the people eddying by them as though he is lost in the cadence of their steps. He pushes her slightly with the tips of his fingers. It is almost a deferential gesture. He knows she is stronger than he is.

She advances toward him and hits him again but he jumps to the side, brushing a man's striped shirt. She feels his upper arm, dense, stapling her fingertips. "There. I hit you again." She is defiant.

He turns around to go home, disgusted. He looks back once to be certain she won't be behind him suddenly. Then he disappears into the crowd, the bobbing heads, bouncing limbs, colors on the West side. She wonders if he was just arguing so he wouldn't have to go out to dinner and pay for it. Or whether he really forgot. Such a deteriorating memory. Or what an incredible insult. He is a hard man. Cheap. He drives her to it, the slapping, the abutment of wills. She picks difficult men like arpeggios, challenges, finds them, pursues them, marries them. At this rate he will forget they had an argument, forget where he is in the middle of the street. What is there for her?

She enters a tall, stone building. The brick frontispiece is etched with a woman's name, Christie's. She goes through the perpetually circling glass doors, walking until she is in a large room with people filling row upon row of chairs. The chairs are arranged in boxes. The man at the podium, speaking quickly, reciting numbers, holds antiques up into the assembled light. The audience waves placards over their heads. Isabelle sits down, judging what time has done to chairs, tables, paintings, mirrors. People are bidding on the ruins of furniture, certain that the passing of centuries gives objects value, makes them rare, precious, confers worth, importance on them as long as they are in fairly good condition. Unlike women growing older in this society. She notices an animated stranger, a woman in formal white gloves, blue ribbons fluttering from the edge of her hat. Does Isabelle know her? She looks familiar. The woman is bidding for roomfuls of furniture, her placard waving in the noisy air. Probably a divorce or a complete redecoration. No, she doesn't think she knows her but she could, passing one another on the upper East side, exchanging tidbits of their lives, gossiping about movie stars or acquaintances. It's recognition, of the familiar sort. The man at the podium reaches for something small, a piece of jewelry. Isabelle sees it glittering, sidereal, fracturing the overhead light like a constellation stirring in the dark water of night along the horizon. From his stage of ornaments, bric-a-brac, the man lifts a diamond ring. Antique, big, beautiful, Isabelle thinks. She gasps. The bidding begins.

"Bidding begins at thirty thousand dollars. Do I hear thirty-five thousand dollars? Do I hear thirty-two thousand dollars?"

The woman's placard goes up.

"Do I hear thirty-five thousand dollars? Thirty-four thousand dollars?"

Isabelle's placard levitates. Sherman would have to pay for the ring. He didn't get her a nice one initially but this would certainly make amends for it. And after all, he's her husband.

"Do I hear thirty-six thousand dollars?"

The woman's placard ascends.

"Thirty-seven thousand dollars" Isabelle screams, assenting with her card.

"Do I hear thirty-eight thousand dollars? No? Going, going, gone to number sixty-three over on the right."

Isabelle sits down assuredly, content, places the card next to her change purse in her black shoulder bag. She shifts her lipstick, her compact case and thinks: I do it because I can. He should have taken me around the world already.

All the King's Horses, Stan, 1991

Isabelle is completing her fourth divorce, polishing another man into emotional oblivion. Did he ask for it? As much as any man does, probably, considering the arc of her arms, the way she concentrates on lifting a forkful of food to her red lips, as though there was nothing more important in the world. There have been so many women since her and still the residual memory of her remains. Stan has tried to make women happy. But they are insects alighting a short time on his forearm, holding his skin to their touch, crawling because of their curiosity or weariness and then departing for the sheet of clouds and sky, for another wrist. Sometimes he wanted to inch after them, sometimes he waved to them as they left.

He lives in Florida, a short distance from Claire, a shorter distance from his own mother in a nursing home whom he hasn't seen in more than twenty years. He likes the sun on his face, inscribing, glazing, intimate as the kind of burn a passing, casual glance can leave. A digressing kiss. He enjoys the way the sun grips him and isn't afraid to announce its presence, making him perspire. It has been twenty years since Lizzie spoke to him, trying to avoid him at a favorite uncle's funeral. The dark outline of his uncle in a box pushing away the available light. Everything in that funeral parlor quiet, frozen, his uncle's lively eyes closed, aimed toward the empty ceiling. He hoped his uncle would get up suddenly singing "Yes, Sir, That's My Baby," his favorite song. Making it all a mistake. He was so young, in his fifties. Cancer, beginning in his stomach, invading the rest of his body. And Lizzie ran to another funeral car requesting to join them, not saying a word to him. He wanted to slap her, make her come to her senses like the store salesgirl. How he broke down and cried in the middle of a mall thinking about it all just last year. All the sadness, all the harm. Right there he was sobbing like a baby, people passing by him with packages, asking if he was all right. Yes, he blurted. He sat on a bench, his hands drawn across his watery eyes while bright sunlight danced from window to window, disappearing down the length of the arcade. What has he done? What has been done to him? He wept more, comfortable in the anonymity of the place, somewhere he wouldn't be recognized or pitied, an old man crying about his life. Another man who is lost, adrift. Someone who let his family go. That was the same year he had a triple bypass, wondering about his mortality, feeling the crispy fat consumed from meat, the Mallomars, the cigarette smoke attempting to drift through his clogged heart. He still smokes, unable to give up the bitter taste, that tap against his chest like rain, the cigarette cloud that trespasses, staining his whole body. He tries to smoke less, a few a day. He does eat better, trying to avoid the knuckle of fat in meat, opting for lighter foods, salads and fish. Because somewhere he realizes his life is at stake. But he thought more about Lizzie that year, seeing her back, his fingers reaching out for her, the way she walked past him, not seeing him as though he was already a ghost.

He speaks to Claire, calling her dutifully once every two weeks. He is concerned about her life, involved now in a fatherly manner he couldn't be before. She is cold, distant, sometimes defensive.

"Hi. How are you?" He has still retained his New York accent. He is fingering the white river of his scar curving down his chest beneath the miniature, opaque buttons on his shirt.

"Fine," Claire says tersely, vaguely wondering what he wants now.

"How's work?"

"It's fine. I've got a new supervisor and I think she's going to be really hard to work with."

"Why?" His voice is upbeat, a salesman's voice.

She wonders why he asks. Why would he care? Why now? "Because she already told us she'll be watching the clock to make sure we're in on time and don't take any longer than half an hour for lunch. She said we have to take a minimum of ten calls every half hour. We call her 'The Nazi' behind her back." There, she thinks, are you satisfied?

"Wow, that sounds pretty bad. Is there anything you can do?"

"No," she replies in a monotone.

"How about transferring?" He is trying to be helpful.

"Nope. I'm not allowed to for one year." Okay, she thinks, I'm a big girl now.

"Well, maybe there's something you can do."

"We'll see." She knows events sweep you along in their current, swallowed, descending, spiraling, until you conclude on a bank somewhere and then perhaps you might try to understand what happened.

"So, what else is new?"

"Everything's fine."

"How's your boyfriend?"

"Fine." She scans the white walls of her house as if looking for a clue towards his whereabouts.

"Are you going to see him this weekend?"

"Actually Lizzie is coming for a visit. And I was thinking that maybe the two of you could get together."

She doesn't know what's going through her mind, a recon-

206

ciliation, a lessening of the burden. It just fell out, a coin dropping at the bottom of an empty, porcelain piggy bank. "If Lizzie thinks it's okay. I have to ask her."

He hesitates a minute. "Yes, I'd love to see her. Let me know. Bye. I love you." He always says that. Always at the end of the conversation like an afterthought.

***

"Hi, Lizzie." Claire twines the telephone cord around her fingernails, looks at Mer with her big, dark eyes. A twig seems entangled, protruding, flaring from her smooth fur until she rakes her back with her teeth.

"Hi. I just talked to Mother a few minutes ago. It was her third phone call so far this week. But she seems happier without Sherman. She has her own apartment, money, and she's dating some. I told her to give it a rest. But you know her. I was telling her that sex is about hope and possibilities, not how you give yourself away and to whom and for how much. It's not about who wants you but about what you want. Do you know what I mean?"

"Yeah. For me it's about how you feel." Claire dislikes analyzing, the probing into furtive crevices. Sunlight brightens the house, slips over her like a veil she doesn't want to be forced to see through.

"I don't know about getting married ever again. What's the point? You can grow and have hope and sex without getting married six times like Mother. I felt trusting and all those dreams were shot to hell. And everyone feels like a failure. Sometimes I think it's more about what's not said than what is said. Anyway, sorry, I'm rambling on. What's up?"

"You're still coming to visit this weekend, right?" Mer's head follows the noise of an airplane transpiring through the ebulliently blue sky. Claire balances over her disheveled bed.

"Of course." She is thinking about the secrets and habits of sex and marriage.

"How about seeing Stan?" No answer. Sunlight is scrawling on her white walls, blending in. "He'd really like to see you after all these years."

"I'm sure he would. Let me think about how I would feel." This is a surprise. She lays her left hand down like a present in her lap. She holds the receiver closer. "Where?"

"At the restaurant. I see him once a month like clockwork. I'd come too."

"Let me think about this a minute. Didn't he ask you for money a little while ago?"

"Yeah. But I told him no and quickly hung up the phone. He said he was a little stuck. He hasn't asked again and he definitely won't ask you." Silence.

"All right. But let him know I could be angry and I want to be able to ask him any questions I want." And she realizes her anger is her vulnerability and her strength.

***

Stan sputters around the boxy rooms of his apartment, a puzzle with square pieces. He is trying to visualize how the pieces fit together, trying to prepare for talking to Lizzie. There isn't much furniture hurling itself against him, in the hollow recesses of the bachelor apartment. He walks into a corner, and stands there looking at the blank wall as though there is a silent dialogue occurring there. He doesn't actually discern his furniture but views it as different shapes to avoid, to walk around, not quite recognizing or acknowledging tables, lamps, a stereo. Cigarette

208

smoke follows him as quickly as it can, trailing behind him in fading wisps, tangling in his ears and hair when he stops moving. Eventually in stasis, and it vanishes. He is also playing with a coin in his pants pocket, running it through his fingers as he thinks of possible questions Lizzie might have, thinks she could make an ugly scene at the restaurant like her mother. Claire will be there too tomorrow, a referee. He chuckles at the coincidental wall. He is weary, feeling the late hour tug at the circles under his eyes, his head is bulbous, heavy. This is the first time he has had trouble sleeping in a long time.

***

Lizzie wakes up in Florida. She tossed and turned and capsized much of the night. She loiters on Claire's patio, closes her eyes after being in the sunlight and watches wonderful red, green, yellow, sometimes black and white forms resembling abstract paintings against her shut eyelids. They have darker and lighter patterns that seem to change. Afterimages. But more than a reaction to the stimulation of light, they are full images, complete paintings she would like to try and recreate someday. She notices them at night sometimes just before she goes to sleep. If she tries perhaps she can capture them. A product of her imagination? Or just an afterimage? Is her whole life an afterimage, a reaction to a childhood that happened so long ago? She hopes not, although she knows she has been altered by the past. She contemplates making something beautiful from their history the same way her eyes translate the sudden lack of light.

A knot of sun ties the sky as Claire and Lizzie drive to meet Stan at a nearby, famous Cuban restaurant. Stan is sitting outside on a bench, Spanish tiles and cigarette smoke halo his hair. He is perpetually early. As they drive by Lizzie rolls down her window, yells, "Hey, are you my father?" He is the only person waiting there. It's been twenty years since she's seen him. The ornate tiles, the warm Florida air embrace him. He stands up, crushes his lit cigarette under his heel, expectantly. As they are seated in the restaurant Lizzie notices his New York accent, his bifocals, his lumpy face, his hair dyed to a honey color. He resembles her father but with another facade, as though he embezzled this body and used it too much. He has aged so much — is nearly seventy years old.

"You haven't changed much," he declares to Lizzie's older countenance, her hair shorter, layered. He thinks of the Navy for some reason, where he was tossed on a ship in a storm, losing his kneecap to a metal one in a war. This couldn't be any worse than that.

"Thanks." Lizzie has learned to withhold her feelings, her true self in the same way her parents did to her, though unintentionally. Lizzie is aware of what she can deprive them of, if they cared. She removes her shoes under the table, letting them balance on her toes sheathed in argyle socks. She swings her feet back and forth in the air filled with the smell of food, Cuban food with its plaintains, rice, black beans, and rich spices.

"Do you have any questions? Claire said you did."

"Tell me about Mother and her family."

"Her father was charming, dominant. It was a long, long time ago." He is uncertain of the direction she will go.

"Did he spoil her materially, but stay distant emotionally?"

"Yes, he probably did. But I can't really remember." Next door, in another dining room, they hear the clicking of castanets, the stamping of heels as dancers hit the floor in a flamenco. There aren't any such distractions in the dining room they are eating in.

"I'm still really angry at you. For leaving the way you did. For leaving Claire crying, waiting for you, scared. For the way you treated both of us." She drops a shoe on the floor and picks it up again with her toe.

"I'm sorry. I'm so sorry. I left New York state to avoid the child support for you girls. And I know it was wrong. I know I was cold to you girls, didn't listen to you, didn't ever hug you." He seems genuine. As Claire would say, "He *is* an insurance salesman."

Lizzie complains, "We hated being pawns in your divorce and having to take sides."

"And I was really angry at you girls because I got you tickets for a concert and I made dinner reservations and Mother had taken you out of the state and you didn't come back."

Lizzie is silenced, mulling over some forgotten concert tickets. She is startled at the pettiness of his grievance but it obviously meant something to Stan, perhaps representing something bigger.

"We were children and had no control," Claire pipes in. An odd palm tree in a planter rustles, waiters ripple past in waves, carrying plates and utensils. Lizzie realizes she is right, they couldn't pick up and go where they wanted to at that time. They were children.

He hands Lizzie the butter. She sees his contorted features in her unused knife. "I'm still angry at my mother. Her coldness, her headaches when we would confront her. And I wish I could have gone to your wedding. Either of your weddings."

"You didn't miss much." Lizzie laughs a little.

"Would you have gone if Mother was there?" Claire asks, already anticipating the answer.

"No." Succinct and quick.

"I'd like to see photographs of the family if you have any." Lizzie requests.

"Sure. I'll send you some. Do you have any more questions?" He is internally sighing.

"No, not right now." Lizzie wonders if anger is contagious.

***

It is another hot day in Florida. The humidity is uncomplicated, comprehensible like work ballooning to fill up the mysteries, the complexities nagging each day. Stan steps outside for a moment, surveying the white plastic lawn chair, barely used, the oceans of green grass at the apartment complex. He is searching for a nest of doves, still unborn today, still squeezed, gathered underneath their thin shells. He is waiting for them to click, to sputter into this world although what they will do after that he is just beginning to consider. To fly, he thinks, that must be the answer. To learn how to fly. But he is never patient enough, always returning to his ribbons of paperwork, the phone calls embracing him even in his sleep. He misses the Navy, where there were no revelations, no denials, only plain and simple work. Where you were propelled into it immediately after rising, eating, with no time for garbled thoughts or desperate, passionate acts unfolding as promptly as a play you never paid to see. Participation, not a word for him. He gathers old family photographs to mail to Lizzie. Lizzie is riddled with too much thought and Claire, his Claire, with too much expression, too much boiling at her center and she doesn't even realize it. There isn't enough time for regret, he thinks. One hand rests on the sliding glass door that lets almost everything in, and one hand searches for a cigarette whose smoke makes everything vanish.

***

The following year Stan notices the stubborn clouds fixed like coconuts in the shifting blue sky. Day is just beginning to cross the street when he gets into his car to visit a potential client. The car radio whispers unconnected sentences as he twists the dial and then turns it off. He whistles a show tune instead, the litany of a sale assails him. He wants one, repeating its attainability in his mind. He can do it. He likes this work, this convincing, this gentle nudging toward the insurance that can protect lives. It is a public benefit. The woman he has the appointment with has a young child. He already knows the cheapest, best type of health insurance he will present to her, cajole her with nuances, persuade her slowly into acceptance like a monotonous rain. He loves the moment of a sale, at that one instant he can do almost anything. The sheer power of it. His 1990 Buick shines maroon in the sun, a motif of palm trees sweeps by. His windshield catches the empty sun-drenched streets, the black tar highway with its directional white stripe. The stationary white houses wave him by. He likes moving, driving with the landscape propped up like a photograph for him to view at his leisure. He can outdistance it and find another that is perhaps even more interesting. It is early and he is tired. His bifocals are fogged with cigarette smoke. The car ashtray hangs open like an animal's tongue coated with dirt. Some of the gray ash scatters, showering the carpet below the foot pedals. He sees his hand gnarled with blue veins, sprinkled with brown spots. He is getting older like the rest of the world, his heart slowly giving up on him. He knows where he is going. He could close his eyes and drive to the address in Orlando by pure memory, familiarity. He considers doing it because he is sleepy. The streets are deserted, only the stoplights with their signals changing for no one. He releases his burning cigarette into the car ashtray. Smoke coils to the roof where it rests in a hazy thickness that even the Florida sunshine can't penetrate. He dozes a little, shocking himself awake periodically to peer at the road, acknowledging that he is going to the correct destination, is on the right road. He leaves the window open so the air will slap him to attention. But he feels the heavy tap of the morning sun warming his shoulders, a spot on his cheek, making him drowsy. Smoke snakes from the ashtray, twining through the lens of his glasses, drawing curved lines across the windshield, disappearing overhead. He can feel its light touch patting his nose, his newly colored hair, his necktie like a relative consoling him, saying "It's okay, don't worry." He is sleepy, fading away and then he is back again like the traffic lights. Underneath everything he does is a permanent sadness, frustration. He feels his heart spasm. Stan thinks briefly of the girls, all of them. He detects the cigarette stub with its last glow, the encompassing, insipid hug of heat, the rancid smell of smoke permeating the car seats and his clothes just before the impending white wall casts up its blank face.

***

When no one was looking Stan died. A stone is thrown into a pond but the ripples reverberate, affecting the shore, fish, even the variegated clouds. The policeman who first came said, "It could have been a heart attack or maybe he fell asleep at the wheel." He thinks to himself that it could have been a suicide. "But anyway, he died instantly. He probably didn't suffer."

At the funeral Lizzie stops and starts, her feet across the old, creaking wooden floor sound like bones breaking. The Florida sunlight streams in lines across the boards but there is still the cracking and shifting of the ligaments of the older house. Facing the closed box are pews bolted to the floor resembling children standing straight, upright. A few people fill the rows, a man with jowls and yellow hair nesting on his head like the murmur of bees. A woman crying with rouge staining her initialed handkerchief in smudges and a child climbing the stiff pews in a shirt splattered with flowers the colors of the rainbow. Lizzie doesn't recognize anyone and neither does Claire with her dark hair wet with hairspray and sweat, describing the shape of her head. Mother couldn't come, with the parties and social obligations in New York. Besides, Lizzie thinks, you can't force someone to love you. You can try but it usually doesn't work. She runs her eyes over the box that compresses what's left of her father within it. There are the survivors of love or attempted love, wounded, ruined for others as if after a shipwreck. Lonely, searching, sifting through the pieces of other people for clues about their past, how to make themselves whole. Like Stan who ends up as a piece of a man in a box. Kaddish hums against the walls. Claire sighs in unison with her shoes pressed to the floor. She looks at the charm bracelet unfolding against her wrist and pulls at the silver dog Stan once gave her as a present. She is tipping toward sentimentality watching the tiny, dark shadow of the dog galloping across the room. And there is much of her that doesn't care, the imperceptible way you can grow used to your own ugly elbow over time and sometimes even mistake those imperfections for love. She can't say she will miss Stan but she'll notice his absence, the lack of his punctual phone call once every two weeks.

"We should have hired mourners," Lizzie whispers into Claire's ear. In old books about other cultures, people were paid to cry wildly, flail themselves across a coffin, carry on as if the world might end. It would liven up the funeral, make it appear well attended. She thinks of a stranger's countenance she glanced briefly once as he sped away on a train. His dark, handsome face seemed surprised and yet in the throws of pleasure, half smiling with his jaw forward. An overhead light caressed his cheekbones, grabbed him by his lapels. Lizzie considers loving that man, perhaps just one alluring, fleeting moment is all we are granted. And she will remember him, imagining him in other situations. She thinks of the tributaries of the bypass scar reaching up toward Stan's chin even in death.

Outside, air is tethered to the earth by heat. Otherwise it would rise, rush away towards the clouds resembling waiting sheep. Leaving them to breath nothing. Men lower the box into the ground with death inside, knocking against its container. Kaddish fills their voices, suddenly singing, the chant of time. Undulations of light. A woman with a child comes to Lizzie. Her face is stuffed with sawdust, her clothes are shades of red, the matching choreography of hair. She holds the boy hard, gripping him. She looks at the ground, at Lizzie's black shoes, the keyhole of her mouth rimmed with lipstick says, "I'm so sorry. He was coming to see me." Her red shoe sweeps the grass. "I was going to buy insurance from him, for me and little Mickey here." She pauses a minute, tucking her vermilion belt. She gazes at little Mickey who is scrutinizing a tree in the distance, intently squinting. "Do you

know where else I could get good, cheap health insurance?"

Lizzie wonders what the handsome stranger on the
train would reply.

Hearts and Minds, Lizzie, 1992

Lizzie doesn't want to make another mistake. She wants a quiet life, an unobtrusive cloth threaded with silent, indiscernible stitches. She has lived in Montana long enough to be considered a Montanan, ten years, and now is restless for culture, argument, even tall buildings. She knows almost all of the available men in town. She can describe the layout of her favorite restaurants and movie theaters. There are few surprises. Her girlfriend, Julie, wants to discover Seattle, inquire about jobs, about places to live. Lizzie will go with her. The water there. In the morning hours fog is embedded in the movements of people waking up from a vivid sleep. A big city. So they heard.

In Julie's flesh-colored car scabrous with peeling paint they take turns driving the simple white line of the highway. The sun is indisputably in their eyes until they are out of Spokane. Insects accumulate on the windshield blending into the top, dark spaces of the leafy trees they pass. The car windows groan as they unroll them for the breeze unfurling from the hinges of evergreens. Their seats sigh with the profundity between air and plastic, between landscape and sky. They eat sandwiches wrapped in cellophane and cheese doodles out of a bag. They discuss what they would do if they won a lottery as trees fight tooth and nail with air, wind pummeling them along with the grass. Until they give way to more bodies of water, ponds accompanying the car a short distance, lakes offering their reflection for a little while longer. At rest stops they drink coffee, watch families file in and out of their cars, laughing at their resemblances to friends or cartoons on television.

218

In Seattle they stay with a friend and go their separate ways. Lizzie to bookstores, schools, sightseeing the rough shapes of buildings visible from the downtown skyline, on a ferry crossing the gray expanse of water with rain tiptoeing around her. Julie goes to job interviews dressed as a school teacher waiting for the wrong answer, in long, severe skirts and jackets with buttons it would take her hours to completely fasten. For fun she looks at apartments, imagining herself in the blindness of their walls, fixing dinner on the uncaring stove, sleeping just so in the indifferent bed, warming her hands over the irrefutable fireplace. At the end of a week they climb back into Julie's car to return to Montana. They are silent through Washington state's venerable landscape, hardly noticing the disappearing trees, the chagrined grass. The radio is low, playing a hum of songs that fly by them while they are intently peering out the windows noticing their own thoughts. The names of the towns come and go, the mileage between them and Missoula grows smaller. Lizzie thinks about Seattle with its choices, the arts, the varying degrees of gray in the horizon, the touch of rain like a membrane, the jobs, a perimeter of theaters edging the city, the pinwheel streets rotating around pedestrians. Music spills from downtown streets at night. People of different hues are dancing. Birds, gulls and sparrows, tap at the high rise windows to be fed. There are whole neighborhoods where people in houses are acquainted with one another, fending off strangers arriving in the wrong area, bringing coffee or sugar to a house if it is needed. The mountains visit periodically with their worshipful, white peaks thrust into the overcast sky.

They are in Montana, will soon be back in Missoula. Julie and Lizzie discuss their childhoods like bad weather. Here today, perhaps gone tomorrow. Julie's father drinking until the floor embraced him and her mother always trying to die, thinking about death in a kitchen knife, pills, even an innocuous plastic bag or bathtub. Her family was afraid to leave her mother alone. Lizzie believes that everyone has story, comes from somewhere. Trying to do the best they can to enjoy what they are given. Julie turns the wheel to avoid the carcass of a dog, a brown lump melding into the pavement, a few bones protruding. Lizzie feels the clench of sadness in her stomach. What is she returning to? The staleness of a social service job she's had for several years, a recent divorce, the knowledge of the town she has lived in for almost a decade. When sunlight questions her window she answers by raising her hand, inspecting her fingernails for dirt. She turns to Julie, "I want to move to Seattle."

***

In Seattle Lizzie rents a house handcuffed to a hill. It squints down tentatively at other houses, dawdling immeasurably on a steep road. She lives with a friend from the writing program in Montana. Electric wires and television antennas laminate the gray sky, crisscrossing stammering, green trees. Julie agonizes in Lizzie's bedroom until she can find a place to live, her sleeping bag and clothes hibernating like large, bulky animals in a corner during the day, seem to scavenge at night. Julie splays her hair in the mirror each morning from its rack of curlers, a bumpy halo circling her head full of ideas about men. "You should meet some."

"First I need a job. But I wouldn't mind just dating as long as it's not serious." Our family history, she thinks, is wanting to be wanted, no matter who it is and I want to stop it here and now. "I'm not ready for anything serious."

The moon outside the window is pleading without heart to remain in the viscous, morning air, fading like spilt milk into pale carpet. Stars are cinched behind clouds.

The exclamations of Julie's eyebrows go up. "How can you not be serious about dating?" She laughs as though her mouth is full of food.

"How can you not be serious about finding a place to live?" Lizzie can imitate being Mother successfully. Noise from a radio slips through some rooms, wandering through the rest of the house. Lizzie's new cat is finding different places to sleep. She'll notice a paw stretching from an angle in Julie's maroon sleeping bag, a tail swishing from a lump of pants.

After several weeks Julie discovers a "satisfactory" apartment to rent and in moving out delivers a man's name and phone number to Lizzie. "For a technical writing job. A friend of a friend," she explains, grinning.

Lizzie finds herself calling up strangers and trying to sell herself. "I think I'd be really good at underwriting (what is it?) or taming wild birds (do they bite or just peck?) or catering (oh God, would I have to cook?)." But she can't give herself away. "Almost free," she wants to say but doesn't mean it. At night the cat cries to go outside or wrestles with a spine of starlight across the worn carpet, confusing the real with the imaginary. She crouches, waiting for movement, the slow drinking of the moon by night.

Lizzie is impatient. Not the continual impatience of Stan or even Charlie but one that is temporary, easily erasable. She stops finishing her sentences saying "and this friend. Oh, never mind." She cups the door knob to one of the boxy rooms in the sprawling house as she walks while reading a book. She plays with the cat while on the phone discussing a job. She uncrumples her balled fist, walking it across her bedspread floating with purple fish until the paw catches her fingers, tasting them in her small cat's mouth. "Yes, I am a team player, self-starter who is detail oriented." She knows the lingo, the right words. She wants her life to begin again.

She calls the friend of Julie's friend, Mark. "Come over and have some carrot cake. We can talk about technical writing." She wonders just how technical it is. She suspected other motives when Julie provided the phone number.

Mark arrives on her doorstep the next night. He is younger, wearing black, heavy-soled shoes, the whisper of fine hair around his ears, over his head, a mole dropped like a stray chocolate spot below his left eye. A mustache webs his upper lip, moving as he speaks. He is carrying an armful of books.

"Come upstairs to my balcony and sit down for a while."

It is an envelope on the edge of the house. Mark opens the books, lecturing, teaching Lizzie their importance one by one. The cat meanders around his legs, changing direction like an imperious river, trying to dissipate his tall stone legs into pebbles by rubbing them. She lies across the black bones of his shoes, a spider, holding them against her stomach. He seems uncomfortable. "Do you want me to put the cat downstairs? Is she bothering you?"

"No. It's fine." He was told how much she likes her cat.

"Thanks for the books. Are you able to hire people?"

"No."

She loses interest in this man, unsuitable to employ her, not her type as a boyfriend. Too straight, she thinks, judging the suspenders, his brisk gestures, the cautious shoes. Too young, she focuses on his eagerness, the prominent ears, his faint smell of pudding. They compare the movies they've viewed, sharing moments from foreign films, all glamour, intensity, and the explosion of recognition. Aguirre on a raft surrounded by wild monkeys or two men in love with the same woman and one of them driving with her off a cliff. And all through images and subtitles.

"I'm going upstairs to sleep." She touches the door, turning her back to him as though to a piece of dust, he thinks. Her red shirt revolves near the kitchen, her blue jeans clasp her legs.

"Can I call you?" He is back on the threshold, wondering how badly he did, wanting to brush the thick onset of her dark hair with a hairbrush just as he did to his old girlfriend. Hoping to see her soon but not wanting her to recognize it.

"Maybe." He contemplates the red hush of her back again.

***

"I had the strangest dream last night. It was one of those real ones that affects the rest of the day. I dreamt that I was in bed and talking to God on the telephone. I don't remember anything that was said but I can remember the feel of the plastic in my palm and close to my lips. It was so strange and real." Lizzie's fingers are deep in fur. Her cat's purr is paper rustling. She questions how the dream will affect the remainder of her day.

"It's too bad you can't remember anything. It could have been important too." Julie half teases her. "So what did you think of him? Not God. Mark." She essays an air of nonchalance that isn't convincing.

"He's all right. Not for me. He can't hire. He wants

to go to a movie." He's not what Lizzie is looking for, an older man with perhaps one child. He's another potential mistake. The cat leaves with her tail pointed toward the ceiling.

"If you think he's all right, go to a movie with him. For God's sake give him a chance. No pun intended."

"A chance for what? If you like him so much why don't you go out with him?" Light spills over her knees like a cat.

"Aw go to the movie." Julie rummages through her hair for a sliding bobby pin. She studies the avocado walls in her new apartment, bleary with dust. She needs furniture and she needs Lizzie to accept her advice.

"I'll tell you what. You come to the movie with us and I'll go." She's intrigued just a tiny bit by the pudding smell. She rakes her leg where it is warmed by the whimsical sun.

"Like a chaperone?"

"Yes."

"You've got yourself a deal."

***

On their third date alone a man is cavorting at a bus stop, singing loudly to himself, his earphones are buried in his pink and green hair. He dances wildly, unabashedly at intervals, lifting his legs, offering them to traffic. They are walking to Mark's house. Lizzie enjoys the varieties of ruin they pass. A house attempting to hoist its frame from the earth holding it close. Businesses closed and scattered like false promises amid the neon signs where customers' lit faces shine in assessment. Vegetation leaning its wet forehead against a door frame. She likes the dark undertones, the truth in what collapses, failure so overt. Every house is a book, she thinks, to be opened and read, each one different, divining the owner's personality. She imagines what it would be like to live in every one of them. "So let's be friends for a while," she says.

His features fall. He doesn't hear the "for a while." He believed she was growing more comfortable with him. On the first date he posted a notice on his front door: "This is the right house." So she would know, being new to Seattle. On the second date she galloped through his house, a caged bird, almost overturning a chair in her nervousness. He shivers at her hardness, the way she equates him with her past. Her feelings are fugues, drawn out at will. And he wasn't even in her past. He had his own romantic problems, Midwestern women not liking him because he is Jewish or women who didn't appreciate his staining their dinner plates with ketchup until they said "Stop." He didn't understand why they wanted to pour it themselves.

But Lizzie is different. The sudden distance like a sneer. She picks up and leaves because of small things. Once he elevated her eyeglasses at a movie theater, rotating them against the screen to educate her about her prescription and she didn't speak to him for a week. He traces her happiness, uncovering the fossil of it as a present. He gives her books. For broader understanding. She says, "I know the love and hate of relationships, their push and pull." Believing within everything is its opposite. Within every smile she is anticipating a frown and within each broken object is the memory of its wholeness. He listens to her heart with his second-hand stethoscope. Sometimes she is reluctant to see she still has one. He can hear its pizzazz with the steel button snaking over her thin shirt.

She's not like other women he's dated. He never seemed enough for them. They were looking for a man with a better job or more hair or a bigger house or someone more romantic. He felt like smoke the way they walked through him and onto someone else, cicadas wheezing in the background. At his house, grudgingly overlooking the white scalp of the street, he says "Are you comfortable?" And he brushes the insistence of her brown hair with a stiff hairbrush. Jazz records turn in the record player, their black shine around a paper label resembles a monstrous mouth or Lizzie's hair, but blacker and combed with bristles and light. Dark strands fan out with electricity over his wrists as he brushes intently, a faint smell of strawberry shampoo. He can feel the fog outside, stretching around the house, across the roof, embracing them, peering in. The home grows undetectable, fading into invisibility, oblivion. She turns and touches his mustache with her forefinger. He stops brushing her hair, it is enough.

"I have a twin brother." He is friendly, slightly formal. He understands he cannot push her.

"You do? Does he look exactly like you?" Her untangled hair flies, bumping her cheek. He selects a photograph from the impinging clutter and offers it to Lizzie. It is a thinner Mark without a mustache. Lizzie scans the picture. "Are you identical twins?"

"They didn't know if there was one or two placentas at birth. They didn't do a dye diffusion test. So we're not sure if we are identical or fraternal." He enjoys the technical, especially technical explanations. He illustrates the dye diffusion test in immense detail, animating his hands which swallow air and are often more content with machines, the accomplishment, the immediate reward in creating or fixing objects. He comprehends love with repairs or edges.

Lizzie still has no idea what a dye diffusion test is, not listening carefully to his explanation, but imagines parts of the body, the placenta, turning different colors.

There are all the possibilities of twins: switching places at school; two people doing one job, taking turns; filling in for one another at events; deceiving women in bed. "Did you two ever fool people, trade places?"

"No, we wouldn't do something like that."

This is a man that doesn't even own a television, who reveres big band jazz and its style of dress. Also, he doesn't lie. Unlike the twins from her high school, broken pieces of one another, making a puzzle whole. "Are you two close?"

"Yes, I miss him. He lives in Indiana, so far away." He slips the pale comma of his arm around her shoulders, his face moving toward her.

She demurs, goes to his bathroom. In the mirror is her hair, a dark cloud, and underneath her skin stretches, porous, sandy like a desert. She likes her familiarity in the mirror. She fingers a slight bruise at her temple, a small sting of recognition. Every attempt has to be hers, her own choosing, her own features, all in her own time. She won't compromise herself to anyone's wishes again. Any mistakes she makes again have to be her own.

"Hi, how are you?" His profile is subdued, the mustached Jack on a playing card.

She falls into his arms at her own pace, the mustache tickling, his palms sweeping. She mistrusts his lips under their umbrella of hair, their softness nudging her into the sofa's crooked spine. She thinks inappropriately about doing dishes, the foam, the soapy wetness, water dripping onto a floor, pushing her hands into the warm, opaque sink and discovering one more dirty dish that nicks her finger.

"Let's go upstairs," she decides.

***

Months later, in Mark's study there is no room for Lizzie to walk. Books are everywhere. In high piles, stacked buildings about to topple over. Scattered in between but mostly on top are sheafs of paper, pens, a few staplers, wires without beginnings or ends, discarded tobacco pipes, eyeglass cases, some open, some closed like never ending seashells, complete within themselves. Paperbacks, hardbound books, spirals, all different shapes and colors lie against one another. Some are leaning on the windowsills with a view of the back yard. A musty, damp odor reaches Lizzie. At the threshold of the study Lizzie sees Mark at his old, wooden, teacher's desk with his back toward her. If he stays much longer he will be buried, she thinks. By books climbing the table, ones reaching up his legs from the floor. He is peering at a stray wire under the bright, metal desk lamp. Lizzie waves at him but he cannot see her. "Hi," she says.

Mark turns slightly in his chair with wheels. His striped shirt twisting in the light. But he cannot turn and face Lizzie. There are too many piles of books in his way. "Hi," he says partially turned.

"I think I'd like to get married." Mark had not mentioned it as much lately, in the last six months. "I think I'm ready if you are."

"Okay." And Mark turns back to his wire, long, blue, shiny, two types of metal twisted and glinting inside the insulation, under the fierce, round light. He is smiling.

**

The ringing telephone punctures the air, rattling the furniture, shaking the bones deep in the house.

"I love him," Lizzie admits to the speckled receiver. She no longer fights it, acknowledging her feelings.

She usually wants to be alluring, desperately and passionately wanted. Oh, she thinks, this love is a Band-Aid, or something adhesive, sticky, that coheres to an old wound and no matter how much she tries to fling it off her skin it stays. It holds its place.

At the other end Mother chews her lower lip and says, "I'm coming right out." Lizzie can faintly hear traffic appraising the street in New York and receding.

***

Mother walks slowly up the stone stairs of Mark's house which is leering over neighborhood cars. She is dressed in a black leather skirt reaching to the middle of her thighs, fishnet black stockings, black patent-leather high-heel shoes. At the window frame Mark whispers to Lizzie, "She's not very motherly, is she?"

Lizzie shakes her head, laughing to herself. An understatement. She watches Mark pump her hand at the doorstep.

Jazz thrums around the three people, Mother taps her feet like rain breaking through the roof, thudding in syncopated time.

"Mark, what else do you like?" Mother appraises the house, the furniture, the car. Lizzie imagines her purring those words to a man in bed.

"Hats." Mark tosses a fedora onto his head. "And electronics." He points to the restored Ampex recorder sharing the living room. "Books, watches, music. I have unlimited interests, right Lizzie?"

Yes, she mimes with her head.

Later Mark is in the bathroom. Lizzie and Mother are surrounded by old amps and electronic equipment, books peer down at them from shelves. Shadows from his furniture enclose them.

"You'll have to do something about all this stuff," Mother says, calculating.

"I was pushed kicking and screaming into this relationship by a friend," Lizzie confesses, relinquishing him so easily.

"He'll make a good, solid husband."

How would you know? Then she acknowledges Mother's vast experience. "I love him." She addresses the objects in the room. She tells herself, sometimes within the disorder lies organization, caring, a place to rest. She is glad Mother approves, even with the barrier she's erected between them saying, "I won't be like you," in an unwritten language. When Mark returns he sees two women complacent, smiling. He relaxes, sinking into the jumble of machines, the open arms of marriage finally offered like comfortable couches and chairs. He has known since the beginning that he wants to marry Lizzie. She is the one at the periphery, afraid to come to the center, nervous to take what she wants, unsure what she really wants, opening a book but uneasy, anxious, unable to read the actual, written words.

***

A week before the wedding Mark and Lizzie are driving on a thin muscle of road stretching from a beach, bordering on the Sound, to their house. Waves blare their constant complaints, which recede in the expanse behind them. Tall trees appear in their windshield suddenly and leave. His shoulders are two levers of bone lifting and lowering over the steering wheel. Lizzie wants to grab them in her hands to stop their carousel movement, the up and down.

"I think you were right. You're too old for me."
That was the argument Lizzie used not to get married. His
eyebrows are surprised, his skin taut over his chin, he is
trying to watch the roadway.

"Are you saying that you don't want to get married
now? Because I'm four years older than you?" Trees shake
their leaves at her through the side window.

"Maybe it's just cold feet but I think perhaps you
were right." He looks at Lizzie, her heart sinking to the
floor, her eyes filmy. He was always the one who had
desired to get married.

She cries loudly, disassembled. She is nothing. She
is within herself, the hurt is a turning away without repair,
a pain that is deeper than the measured world. It is about
what is spoiled at the center of everything, the unworthi-
ness. The distance between need and care dwindling again
to insignificance. She almost never cries and rarely will
again so wholeheartedly. She is sobbing as the nervous
trees, the other cars rush by.

"I really didn't mean it," he says, feeling guilty,
planning on having bad dreams the next few nights.

"Are you sure?" She is calmer, stuffing her pain
like an awkward potato in her pocket. Lizzie thinks of her
cat slipping into her arms soon, burying her nose in fur.

"Yes." His eyes are on the white line leading them
home.

***

Lizzie sits at her social service job where she listens to
people's problems. She wants to scream. She wants to
exclaim, "I'm not like you!" But she is. The relentless,
incantatory voices are suffused with unhappiness, complaints, injustices, serrated by inescapable occurrences

like spines askew, aggrieved by their own crooked vertebrae. Car accidents, divorces, fights, new babies, the usual.
Some days they become one large drone. Yet Lizzie wants
to help, has conspired to help even when poetry is more
important to her.

"What's the legal age for rape if it involves a
minor?"

She doesn't want to know why someone is asking.
Some days a caller will request the time of day as though
she has nothing better to do. The people she works with
wanted to give her a wedding shower. "I'm not absolutely
sure," she told them. "He might back out." And she still
received a wooden salad fork and spoon, a carnival glass
bowl from them. She bites her nails, unsure what necessity
eludes her. She disintegrates into each day before the
wedding, paper dissolving in water.

***

The day before the small wedding the separate families
arrived. Lizzie's shoulders lie in her wedding dress, saying they are bigger. She tries to embezzle Mother's beauty
for this event, trying the gown on to show Claire and
Mother. White fingerprints of clouds sit in the gray air
watching. It is August. The sky is overcast, unsettled,
envisioning its own special circumstances, making up its
own mind, deciding whether to rain or not. It is Seattle.
Where weather is the stuff of dreams, hazy, vague, formless as if you could pull anything at all from the stone-
colored soup.

"Let's go on the ferry to Bainbridge Island. There
are shops and it's a short forty-five minute ride." Lizzie is
trying to be entertaining.

"Great." Claire is eager to sightsee Seattle.

232

The ferry is water-slicked and big; it insinuates itself into the Sound's neck, tossing water, making way, filled with unassuming light. A man with black ash on his forehead orders french fries. An older man with white hair stares over the rail, transfixed, a scarf of wind against his tweed jacket, birds sew the air, trying to keep up with the boat, their wings adhere to the breeze. Hills curve against the horizon, retreating.

"My daughter's getting married tomorrow," Mother says to the distinguished-looking man. "And she's barely out of high school."

Lizzie rolls her eyes and takes Claire to the front of the boat.

"And there she goes...." Lizzie doesn't want to hear anymore.

Mother is animatedly talking to the white-haired man while Claire and Lizzie sit on the plastic seats shaped like two cupped hands side by side. The faster the ferry, the colder it grows outside. Lizzie notices the surfaces of the water, of people, of the boat, of Mother, wondering what is beneath them. What is it that connects any one thing to another? What makes a relationship?

"There she goes again." Claire could be discussing a whale.

"At least she keeps trying and trying and trying."

"That's a polite way of putting it. And you're getting married tomorrow. Are you getting nervous?"

"Sure. But I guess I'll just close my eyes and jump. I'm afraid of mistakes. Of making more than my share."

"It's a family curse."

"Ha, ha." Lizzie twists her head toward the back of the boat and points. "Out there you can see the Seattle skyline. It's pretty with all the buildings downtown." The man with the bellybutton-sized ash on his forehead walks by, swallowed by an enormous jacket. Bainbridge Island, dotted with houses and stores, looms up.

***

Mother, Claire, and Lizzie return to the ferry quickly after strolling a few streets in downtown Winslow on the island. It is lightly raining, undoing their hair, polishing their skin and clothes. Mother is quiet, unable to find anything interesting to purchase. Back on the ferry the waves applaud. The homes on the island become freckles as the ferry slips back toward Seattle. Clouds stripe the ship and all the people.

"I want to be filthy rich," Mother declares.

"Well, you're working on it." Claire focuses on Mother's few wrinkles embedded around her eyes, at the corners of her downturned mouth. She thinks the body is an anchor weighing our emotions down.

"So how's your sex life, Lizzie? You too, Claire, although you're not getting married tomorrow." Her profile is juxtaposed against the food counter.

"The usual question." Lizzie shrugs it off.

"No, I mean it. In New York I was getting my nails done for a date and ran into this other guy and invited them both to a party last Thursday night..." Mother launches into a monologue about herself. Lizzie used to put the phone down when Mother called and do a few chores, come back, and say "yes" and resume the conversation. Mother didn't seem to notice. There is no give and take with her. Lizzie wonders who Mother thinks Lizzie is. Her daughter who listens. But does she have any idea what kind of person Lizzie is? She could be a thief and Mother wouldn't know the difference. Sometimes she thinks she is a thief, stealing time or beauty or secondhand

234

clothes.

Lizzie partially listens. The two men almost meet. A plane over the Sound trails a banner Lizzie tries to decipher. It is biting the wind. She can read it after a few moments, "Doris, will you marry me?"

"Isn't that cute." Lizzie points out the glass, interrupting Mother while she is talking and rummaging through her handbag at the same time. The Seattle skyline blooms, growing into suddenly wider and taller geometric buildings. Lizzie can perceive cars, people, a woman wearing a red hat. The edifices resemble the teeth of a lower jaw. They are almost back.

"I'm having a heart attack," Mother suddenly says, reaching dramatically for an arm rest.

Lizzie giggles as Mother mauls her chest.

"No, I'm serious. I'm having a heart attack." She is pacing, her features stricken.

Lizzie looks at Claire, suggesting, "Maybe it's indigestion. You did eat and drink an awful lot last night."

"My chest is palpitating." She spits her words at them.

"Do you want me to call an ambulance?"

"No." Mother is wincing in pain, sits down, riveted to the ferry which has already docked in Seattle.

Lizzie decides Mother will deal with the consequences of her actions. She finds a woman ferry worker, "My mother is having a heart attack." She leads the woman to Mother doubled up on a plastic seat. The outline of a drizzled mountain lassoed by clouds is in the background. Fog soils the sky.

The woman wears an official blue ferry apron out of which she extracts a walkie talkie. Behind her the ferry is empty except for knickknacks repeating themselves, brochures worrying table tops and seats, the smell of food against Lizzie's collarbone. She presses a button, speaks, "Send an ambulance to the ferry dock." Lizzie has visions of helicopters, doctors, hospitals.

"No," Mother sounds as if she is swallowing. She pushes herself to stand, level with clouds juggling birds outside the window. "I'm all right," she states to the woman. "You girls will help me get to my hotel room, right?"

They nod yes.

The woman presses the button again. "Cancel," she says. "Are you sure you're all right?"

Mother nods yes and propels herself stiffly off of the ferry. She walks haltingly, precariously down the street, stopping every few feet, placing her palms against her chest, praying for her own heart. Lizzie turns to Claire, "You can go sightsee more if you want. I'll take her back to the hotel room."

"Okay," and Claire eagerly twists and ambles down the street.

Mother's face is crumpled, wincing as Lizzie helps her into the pale sheets in the dark hotel room. "It's fine if I die now because I've had a very full life."

"You're not going to die. It's probably indigestion."

"I've traveled a lot, Europe, South America, Russia, Egypt. And I've had lots of men. I've been everywhere and done everything. I can go now." She lifts Lizzie's hand, confining it like an apology against the blanket and sheets. Lizzie flinches a moment at her unaccustomed touch.

Grow up, she wants to say. Instead she catalogues, "Think of all the places you still want to go, Africa, India, and all the men you can still meet."

"That Claire left me having a heart attack. I'll remember that." Her face is a moon, eclipsed, disapproving in the blackness.

"I told her to go." Because this isn't that important. She endures Mother's hand limply, shuffling it across the flowered bedspread until she hears her steady breathing, her weight resting against the solicitous sheets. Then Lizzie departs.

***

The next day Mother is dazzling in a polka dot silk suit at the small wedding. The families gathered are bouquets, picked, arranged in various hues, plucked and convincing in their colors, apricot, peach, plum. Like fruit on display at Mark's house after the glass is crushed, broken into agitated light, and the chuppa disassembled into arms and sticks and white sheets. Lizzie likes the brush of lace, cobwebs against her limbs, a rumor of shadows patterns the skin around her neck. All the smiling is arduous, the unending photographs near the bushes. The jokes laugh at themselves.

"I like being married already," Mark tells the rabbi, whom he knows from childhood, dissolved into his past like stone crushed by water. They are pale imitations of the people they were, a rambunctious twin child and a leader from an Illinois community. Changing with time, overgrown by the world.

There is the gibberish of trees in light outside. The music. Hors d'oeuvres circling around love. To Lizzie it had been an illusion, a delusion, an impostor dressed as an idea or romance with a large, flowing, complicated hat with a veil, a flower and ribbons perched precariously on a head. Claire, lovely Claire, in a blue dress with ruffles spinning around her shoulders eats, stands quietly by a bush. No more Lillitoes staining her life. Lizzie is not done with love, just beginning to see how it taints everything it touches, in its simple way. She thinks now how she ran past the ruined rooms in childhood.

Mark is not submission or struggle but a continuous conversation that contains all emotions. Being loved is different than Lizzie expected, it is a space she can occupy or not, growing like a tree branch into the suspended air. There is more freedom than she thought there would be. Anger, disappointment, discontent are all included. And her love for Mark is strong, subterranean, lasting. After her own initial hesitancy she likes the comfort of being known and the derangement and unpredictability, the commitment to the human heart and its foibles.

Lizzie looks at herself, sees how others view her: bony, weary, happy, all in white. A thin, walking lace tablecloth. She laughs for herself, then for the camera. Lizzie understands Mother's attempt to be herself, unbound by children or husbands but what she concluded with is half a lie, an unknown. There is familial and romantic love and everything in between. And each one affects the other. Lizzie thinks: I am another bride. Not the same one as before. She wants complete erasure, starting all over again, not this perpetuation of beliefs and survival passed down from generation to generation like a spoon Lizzie sees her own reflection in, distorted, white, angular and just as unreal as the next spoon and the next, all lined up for future use. She thinks love is a muscle that grows flabby with disuse. She notices Claire eating cake, an encyclopedia of emotions, wanting to hold her, loving her, sharing their history, the past. She sees Mother fixing an ankle strap while talking to Mark's parents. It is slightly flirtatious, a river flowing that she just can't stop.

As Stan once said, "You girls were never battered,"

but there is still damage, odd fault lines that are not overtly perceived. Claire's desire for doors, the easy way they open and close. Lizzie forgets herself inside clothes that are too large, she swims in them without any make-up. Her insistence on truth, the lack of trust. She seeks proof, needs to see what is happening in front of her face in order to feel it, in order to know its reality. Abstract scars. A slow, smoldering fire that results in ashes.

Lizzie was told once that the response to her past is either anger or forgiveness. She knows someday she will choose one. When Lizzie has a daughter two years later she has a Lowenstein dragonfly nose poised on her boiled face, above her changing grimaces and sudden frowns, her restless limbs. Lizzie hopes she'll know what to do with her.

Mother's polka dots collide in the sunlight, under her slick, tea-colored hair. Her heart thumps its own song buried deep in her body, grass cascades under her high heels.

"How are you feeling?" Lizzie inquires.

"Perfectly fine," Mother replies as though nothing happened.

Lizzie knew it. The collection of aches dissipated at will, dialogue loosened, champagne, the larger gestures, their shadows bruising the house, how sunlight tentatively enters the rooms. This is a makeshift celebration to Mother. It is how she makes up her mind.

Her Mind, Isabelle, 1949

They aren't generous to each other. My mother and father, that is. He withholds things from her, presenting them to me, a beautiful, long mink coat, jewelry, even an adorable little sports car. Both my sister and my mother are jealous, surreptitiously watching me go to school from a window in our Philadelphia row house. I see their faces ricochet from window to window like two women prisoners as I get into my new two-toned convertible to drive somewhere. Too bad for them. I enjoy my car, chrome burnished by the near summer weather. I've memorized my mother's doughy, round, slattern look and my sister's twisted, fierce features pasted to the glass like old paintings, luminous, rich with details and fading in the smoke of my exhaust. None of us are quite ourselves before afternoon, my mother runs in ellipses to my father with cups of coffee, muffins replete with butter, freshly squeezed orange juice. That handsome, charming man loves the attention and still just ogles me and winks.

Last week my mother wanted to take my new fur coat away from me, insisting that it was too expensive a gift for a young girl. I grabbed it from her, tearing a sleeve, ripping one of her fingernails. She provokes me. Silly old woman. It's mine and I'm not that young. He gave it to me and said I could keep it. It is one of my presents because he loves me more, secretly, than anyone else.

And I am also the apple of Jordan's eye. At school I prance around in my shortie shorts, a parade of one, my feet sunk into the extravagance of green grass and trimmed hedges, the gray college buildings with ivy obscuring any views. I gulp too much sky sometimes, thinking about becoming an architect, seeing Jordan in my art classes, a bribe. He sketches me, preferring lady-like poses, hands and legs crossed, glancing downward with my dark hair shrouding my ears, an aristocratic expression. I'm determined in my shy way to get everything I want. And I lose myself in men, boys, men now. They fall into me, ghosts desiring me. Their eternal reasoning, their heavy fingers, the lure of money, travel, romance, dinner. They can never truly have me. I want to be wanted in this world revolving around men. Sometimes when Jordan throws open a door or borrows my waist with his palm I wish I could bite him hard enough to touch bone. Jordan is busy with colors over his drafts the way bushes or shadows under trees seem to move when you are walking but its really you that's moving. I scramble over the white paper.

Outside the building at a speaker's corner a man is raving about earthly pleasures. He is standing on a box where the fishy sky lets a cloud swim toward the deciduous trees, becoming nebulous in the light. There is a flinty, dusty feel to the air in Philadelphia. The man spits, "The price of sin...," as I stroll by hoping the cost is very high and worth it. Society places a value on everything. So do I. My boring, sensible shoes resound on the cement path winding through campus. Ones my mother bought me. Jordan blatantly tries to take my hand and I push him away.

"That's why I want to move to New York."

"Why's that?" His books are in one arm, provisionally at an angle.

"It's the kind of place where you can breath without dust filling your lungs. Where there's diamonds, caviar, parties, famous people on a street corner. Where neon lights up the streets at night with such glamour."

"So you wouldn't settle for plain, old, gray Philadelphia?" He shifts his books from arm to arm.

"Why would I want to stay here?"

"The history, for one good reason."

I hear the long tones in his voice, the Phillie accent.

"The big stupid bell?"

"More. And there's me. I'm here."

I hope I'm destined for more than this cow town but Jordan is awfully cute with his reassuring blond crew cut, his contrived lake blue eyes. "I've got to run home now."

"Will I get to see you later?" A tumult of water from sprinklers seesaws across his pants legs, painting shadows on his knees.

"Maybe," from the red stain of my lipstick, my eyes blinking under sunlight. I am flirting.

***

I like guilt. It has so many uses. If you break something I get a new one. If you believe you are essentially good I will ask you to prove it. Mistakes intrude tentatively from the mirror until you can make them vanish. I can tell you how. Punishment is as simple as the sputter of jewelry across my neck or the flutter of money with its green portraits describing presidents. The money is a substitute for something even better. Punishment is its own perfume embellishing the available air.

Our townhouse is a brick rectangle with white columns. Sometimes greenery extends its wrists to enfold the house. Windows don't tell the truth about light. They are often covered with tumbleweed-colored curtains ambushing the morning sun, disregarded in the afternoons. The tables, chairs, couches shine with mahogany, carefully cleaned by a maid. My sister stands at a triptych of open windows, her dark hair ablaze, her features chiseled into the tiny binoculars that she is adjusting against her eyes. The curtains billow toward tea that has been left sitting and cooling in its cup.

"There's a flasher in the neighborhood," she says to the sound of my horrible shoes behind her.

"And I thought you were spying on me." I see her short cropped hair, her eyes we nicknamed "stars" as in "keep your stars to yourself." She poked one once with a dress pin by accident as she clamored into a formal evening dress. But she is wearing tights, galoshes under her skirt and it is almost summer. I want to sigh. "Or you're looking for a rich husband again. You're the older sister so you better hurry up." I glance at my mundane shoes, at least they are better than her crazy ones.

"Mom, she's bothering me again" she shouts and then she takes her place back at the window. "Get out, get out of here" she addresses me.

I remember the proprietary crook of her arm against my neck in the middle of the night when we were children. She whispered "Daddy loves you more but Mommy likes me better," a nursery rhyme she repeated over and over, tightening her grip. Until she forgot where she was and went back to sleep. I've slept warily ever since, watching for her stars flashing, adhering to night.

Mother ignores us as always. Packing for another trip, perhaps California or Mexico, she caresses father's clothes with her fingers, lingering on his striped tie, a tongue trying to speak from the open luggage. His starched, white shirts tossed on the top like painted boats above waves. She does too much for him. Buttering his toast, his corn, packing for him, catering to his every whim. I think of the bare flesh above his ear before his wheat hair begins its fall to his nape. His dark, family eyes follow me everywhere. Mother just gets in the way with her toothy smile, her wide Polish face, her nose gripping her cheeks. She laughs too much. Her silly grin confuses her face, a rendezvous of lips and daydreaming eyes crested with dangerously arched eyebrows. We don't like each other. She advises me, "Never turn your husband away, when you have one."

I walk into the room filled with clocks, father's hobby. Just sitting in a chair is so noisy I can feel time beating against my heart, the nervous knocking, the measured moments with their relentless ticking. It is under my skin. There are cuckoo clocks, grandfather clocks, an elephant extending a clock disguised as a globe, a dog who wags its tail telling time. It's a room where I never feel alone or lonely. It's where father can spend hours fixing the delicate mechanism of seconds, minutes, days, nights, his hands plunged into the metal cogs, sprockets, rakes and springs. His eye grows enormous under the round magnifier, a cyclops picking through the iron teeth, combs, ratchets, a scavenger unswervingly finding treasure. I am afraid he'll turn his eye on me, this man who owns coat factories in New Jersey, who has a chauffeured limousine pick him up every morning for work. But I like this room that is him, that is like talking to him only mechanically, impersonally through instruments somehow. I can hear voices in the next room even through the constant ticking like many resounding heartbeats.

The woman: There are so few family members left. It is so soon after the war.

The man: I have let them do what they wanted. But they are Jews and need to know it. The older one is just a little too strange right now. But he is from a good family. Jewish, not like that other one she likes. We will introduce them. I know his family, knew his father before he died,

244

good stores, good people. We'll see what happens.
What about her happiness?
We'll just see what happens.
I sit in a corner facing a wall covered with cuckoo clocks, all brown, tinged with green, sprinkled with red and their birds periodically chiming, reaching out for me like a dunce learning a lesson. It is about power. These quiet, hushed noises, unobtrusive from an adjoining room, a conversation with clocks. The grandfathers, the pendulum timepieces all swing through empty air, fighting time. And I am the main course of a dinner passed from plate to plate, each person helping himself, appraising the difficulty, the skill of the cook. A forkful smoldering in their mouths. Do I love Jordan? How can I know? Light bouncing from the moving parts chases other light. I think of my father's scarf wrapped around his neck in the wind and how it has a life of its own, struggling against his chest, flying into winter, dancing in meter. It is sacrificed, discarded so easily. Is love a lack of fear or Jordan's paper face burning, his blue eyes blindfolded with moonlight? I don't know how much he understands about me. Father wants a Jewish marriage and children to replace those lost in the Holocaust. Not me. But Father usually gets what he wants. I cross my feet on an olive chair among the wallpaper of clocks pronouncing their repeating words, an intruder kissed softly by their faces, engaged in an ongoing dialogue.

***

It's a different language. We leave each other notes on the refrigerator door, not signing them, understanding one another's handwriting or thinking we do. They are translations and I sometimes need to read between the lines. My sister's are the most difficult: "Every one of my bones is broken" (I want milk); or "Instructions to objects to move to...."(I want to go to...); or "The portrait of syllables is breaking down" (I need to talk). Her notes are like fortune cookies, predictions. They have evolved over the years becoming more complicated in her needs, more quizzical. Now it's as if she has a fever and no one responds. Father's, in contrast, are absolutely direct. "Get me bread," "More ketchup," or even just plain "Butter," a bark. It was the "I need to see you now" that my sister and I cherished and feared the most. Mother's notes are singsong reminders: "Don't forget so and so." Mine are full of unseen cruelty although I can't deny father anything. "Nice, new hairdo" for my sister. "Dressed as a man?" for my mother. There are only so many things I can care about: the architecture of beauty; the blunt future; marriage. So much is an act. A headline. The past was the war, a depression, a scar on my knee since childhood that is fading. History seems comprised of repetitious events. Lots of people have reinvented themselves since the war. It's only fair.

I take a large breath, feeling the ribs around my heart expand like an adjusting embrace. The note for me against the gleaming, white refrigerator door reads, "We'd like you to meet someone tonight at 7 p.m." My grimace pours into light, air.

***

I go to the bathroom, ornate with gold admonishing pale porcelain and tile. I sit on the toilet, my knees rawboned without pants or stockings, my right leg rebuffed by a wooden vanity table. I light matches, and wait for them to flare out one by one. I am nervous, acquiescent. The sharp, comforting, sulfurous odor enters my nostrils in profusion, a burn, a quick punch. The tart aroma lingers between the striking matches, becoming a ponderous, smoky smell, a subterfuge for thinking, for going to the bathroom. I need the distraction of fire to pee. My thoughts adhere to the flames just long enough for me to make water. Sleep and bowel movements are more elusive. Always just beyond my reach. Shadows from trees furrow, sway against the frosted glass. My lips are contorted, fraying. I think of the matches burning, burning. I don't want to think about tonight, my body enunciating itself. I pull up my shorts, flush, open the door, letting the feeble breeze loosen my disguised smell at its own volition. The sour beneath the acrid, an animal's breath. I am quiet, embarrassed.

***

I think about sex, the beginning, the thought of it reaching down along my spine. Good girls don't do anything more than kissing. I am alone on my bed, the blond wood box designed for escorting my body toward dreams, light swing dances across the ceiling. There is wonderful jazz in New York right now. Every night. The new fashion magazines and movies show yellow, peroxide hair, in the styles of Betty Grable, Veronica Lake. I pick up the heavy black telephone and dial. "About tonight," I say, "I can't."

"Why?" as though he could learn how to understand me.

"My parents have set up an obligation for me." I look at the red moons of my toenails against the turquoise, chenille bedspread. Jordan is a small, gray bird hopping in its cage, wanting my attention.

"Oh. You mean dinner with a lot of old people, family friends?" He feels this tentative love for her with-

out understanding, a fragile moth filtering down toward a
mottled light.
    "No, I don't think so." I like the lie he offered
better. But there isn't anything I can do. It's either elope-
ment or suffering his anger because he can't get what he
wants. "They want me to meet someone, a man."
    "And you have to?" She is receding, becoming
formless, nameless, an object he once loved but dropped,
rolling out of reach under a mohair sofa.
    "Yes."
    "You are unfinished still." Jordan is transient, al-
ready changing himself. Hurt but young enough to think
of the years uncoiling, leading him somewhere else.
    "Then why did you want me?"
    "To complete you."

                              ***

I elevate my face in the hand-held mirror, my translated
nose, the door of my forehead, my penciled-in eyebrows,
the coifed, smooth, dark hair. I add what I can, lipstick
knowing all about the color in red roses, powder dissolving in the still light, mascara outlining the reticent eyelashes. Parts of a whole. Bound by form. The way a painting or a building becomes a familiar thought inside my
head, a visual recognition. And what holds it together is
my father, the muscle, the flesh in this family. I remember
in childhood I was his landscape. There was no horizon
between us, he could rest in me, my arm was his and his
leg mine. I called him "Curly" because he was almost bald.
This tall, handsome man with etiolated eyes. He called me
"Slim." Now there are no more pet names. He can't touch
me the way he used to, an elbow hurled over my shoulder,
his fingers sliding through the weight of my hair. Now I'm

older and he must give me away. No more games or presents. I apply perfume to my wrists, my neck, sitting in my silk underwear. The world beckons with movie stars, with its implication of movement, lights, and how I can unfold there, marveling, baffled by uproarious music, my proclivity toward defiant colors. The mahogany furniture moves away, against the white walls, against the one window with its sparse, subsiding light. I will miss my father, perhaps Jordan also, in this completed blueprint of my life, discovering what I am capable of, what I can intentionally do. I smell my skin and the perfume. My face is done. I need to describe my body, make it visible through clothes. But what to wear? How to manufacture beauty. With its certainty, startling colors, unforgettable features, the way it assumes ownership, possession of everything in the vicinity. There aren't any questions. There are only easy answers. I think I hear my sister at the keyhole, drowning in her vision of me, her fist clenched at her stomach. I casually fix a black dress spreading like water against my collarbones and hips. A mannequin. A model for her gaze. A silver sequined sheath and I turn our centers toward her. I finally decide on the herringbone beige dress, unlacing it, stepping into it as I would into an inheritance, smashing the excess cloth around my knees, crinkling it, lifting it onto my shoulders. By the time I open the door she is gone.

Father is there. "I like the suggestion of red in your necklace and earrings. Your lipstick. You look lovely." He takes my hand gently, a kiss spills from his mouth against my knuckles.

With my other hand I adjust my earring with a red fingernail. "Thank you," I say to the top of his bald head.

He takes my arm in his, an interlocking puzzle, two triangles. We walk down the blue carpeted hall into the living room where my mother is talking to a young man, dark, handsome with a complicated nose. I can grow into my own version of the truth, the way I can go to New York and become anyone, a wife, a mother, a diplomat, an architect, an artist, a criminal. I feel my necklace around my neck, scraping as I move.

"Hello," he says standing up, dazzled by this long-bodied, herringbone, dark-haired beauty.

I take my dreams seriously. "Hello," and we look at one another as though we could make each other happy.

Laurie Blauner's first novel, *Somebody*, won a King County Arts Commission Award for Publication. She has also received a National Endowment for the Arts grant, several Seattle Arts Commission grants, and an Artist Trust grant for her fiction. She is the author of four books of poetry. She received an MFA from the University of Montana. Her poetry and fiction have appeared in *The New Republic, The Nation, The Georgia Review, Seattle Review, New Orleans Review, American Poetry Review, Poetry,* and other journals and magazines. She lives in Seattle, Washington.